CURRENTS

IZZY MATTHEWS

A Riverbend Romance

Digital ISBN: 978-1-7350526-0-1
Print ISBN: 978-1-7350526-1-8

Author's note

Dear readers,

This book is dedicated to a good, loving man, who's supported me in every endeavor. I'm sure he's smiling down on me saying, "Well it's about damn time!" And it is. **Deep Currents** is the launch of my Riverbend series, stories that have been spinning in my head and heart for quite a while.

So, let's go for a lazy sail down the river, where at the end you'll find true love, and maybe even a little magic.

Contents

Chapter One

Marcus Mackenzie took a pull from his Heineken. The malty taste, the familiar aroma of burgers, and the innate, earthy smell of river at the Black Horse Bar & Grill worked as well as popping a Valium to end a mind-numbing week. And without the side effects. He grinned.

Perched along the Delaware River, The Horse was once a stagecoach stop, but was now a popular watering hole in Riverbend, PA. Marcus and his team had finished the Lehigh College proposal and came in under budget. And to top it off, an administrator at the college had sent him a confidential text that Mackenzie Construction and Engineering was the top pick to build the new dorms.

A relief. But he frowned when he thought about the unexplained vandalism on their last three projects. It had put them badly behind schedule, and if the vandals weren't caught soon, it could ruin their stellar reputation in the industry.

"Hey, man, after we eat, let's find a couple of pretty gals." Bret Hammond, an old army buddy of his now working for his firm as an engineer, provided a welcome break in his thoughts. "I need to get laid to make up for pulling double shifts all week. You up for it, Mac?"

Taking another pull from his beer, Marcus put the bottle on the bar and ran his hand through his hair. Christ, he was fried. But hyped up at the same time. If he wanted to sleep tonight, he either had to get drunk or get laid—the perfect cures for insomnia. But forty-three was too old to get drunk. And somehow he hadn't had a woman in six months. Six long months. No, it was more like eight months. Or...nine? Shit.

Nine months without getting laid. A record. Can you get carpal tunnel from jerking off? What a clusterfuck. Jacking off night after night to the mental image of the lovely Cassandra Bennett, imagining the things he'd like to do to her someday—if he could get her into his bed. When he found out that she was moving back to Riverbend, it erased all desire for any other woman. A jolt of arousal hit his dick with just the thought of her. As if it knew that it wanted only her.

Bret elbowed him. "Are you in? Sharon Miller is playing pool in the back. Why don't I hit her up, see if she's with a friend?" Bret adjusted his cock. "Come on. I'm so horny, I'll go off if a chick with a big rack just smiles at me."

"You're a man-whore, Bret. Or so I've heard," Marcus chuckled.

Bret punched Marcus's shoulder. "Only following the Master."

Marcus picked up his beer, mindlessly running a finger over the spout. Yeah, he was a master, alright. Of one night stands and empty pussy. Sharon was a hot fuck. He'd had her last year, but the thought of her didn't register even a glimmer of interest from his dick.

It was sick, not taking an easy woman for a hard ride, all because of Cassandra...a woman he'd never

2

even met. But he knew her well enough through Pete and Shirl Hoffman, the best people he knew, who had saved his angry, hopeless, sixteen-year-old self from destruction, all those years ago. From the first time he'd stepped into their farmhouse, photos of Cassandra were scattered everywhere, and over the years, he'd seen her grow into the beautiful woman whose smile lit up every picture she was in.

But it was that one photo of Cassandra he'd seen at Pete's nine months ago that had shaken him. Framed in silver, it showed her sitting at a table in an outdoor cafe between two teen girls, unmistakably her daughters. They'd pushed their chairs close together, their arms around each other, the three of them laughing with such open abandon that Marcus could feel the joy radiating out of the picture.

He'd never in his life had a reaction to a woman like he'd had that day, and it was only a damn photo. And though it made him uncomfortable in a way he couldn't define, he'd wondered what it would be like to be the focus of her happiness.

From that moment, her picture had haunted him.

He'd picked up the frame when Pete left the room. "Lovely," he'd whispered to nobody. He ran a finger around her face, wishing she were right there with him so he could feel her skin under his hand. Was it as smooth as he imagined? Then Pete was there, and he'd grabbed the photo with a possessiveness that surprised Marcus. "She's something isn't she? A beauty, and sweet, but smart as a whip, too. Marcus, you've heard it before, that she's the daughter I never had. Sad as I am that Ron died, she's making this old man happy coming home where she belongs. And I'll see to her."

Maybe I'll see to her, too, he'd almost said out loud, infatuated with her for years, but not realizing it until that moment. And lucky he'd caught himself, because Pete looked him dead in the eye and warned, "Don't go there, Mac. She's a good girl, and you're an operator. I mean it."

Cassandra had a wholesome beauty that shone through even in a photo. And Pete was right, he was a player, with tainted DNA to boot. He knew he didn't deserve her. But that photo made him want to sink his cock into beauty and goodness for the first time in his life.

"Mac, come back to earth," Bret slapped Marcus on the back of his head. "Buddy, where've you been?"

Obsessing about a woman. Marcus rubbed the scruff on his jaw. He needed to think, and Bret was in his way. "Give me a sec, okay?"

"You take all the time you need, I'm going to scope out the place," and he took off.

Signaling the bartender for another beer, he considered his next move regarding Cassandra. She'd stayed in the cottage on Pete's farm for the past week and was briefly flying back to California, tomorrow. But in three weeks, she was moving back to Riverbend for good. If he hadn't been working around the clock, he'd have been able to meet her and see for himself what that captivating photo of her only hinted at, despite Pete's warning.

Yet his infatuation was troubling. He controlled every hookup. If a woman wanted more, he made sure that his message was brutally clear—once and done. Now he wanted to pursue a woman for the first time in his life, and she was ruling his mind. Maybe it was fate that he'd had to work around the clock instead of dreaming about Cassandra. But shouldn't he break this hold she had on him before she moved back?

Picking up the bottle, he drank, put it back on the bar, and fell back into thoughtful reflection.

Cassandra had snuck into Marcus's consciousness before Pete told him she was coming back to Riverbend. He played with the paper label on the bottle. It really began when he moved back to Riverbend himself four years ago, after being away from the area for twenty-four years—first in the army, then college, then working for engineering firms, from coast to coast. Even though she'd been married, whenever Pete mentioned her, he wanted to know everything about her. Her writing career, her children—any information that Pete would part with.

But even then, he couldn't explain why she intruded into his thoughts from time to time. Maybe it was that they were both close to Pete, though he didn't think she even knew that he existed. But when her husband died—over two years ago, now—yes, he nodded to himself, that's when his interest turned into fascination and, finally, into intense need.

If he went after Cassandra, likely he would lose Pete, who'd been like a father to him, and that would be a mortal wound. But there was something about her that was strangely compelling for him to be willing to risk that profound loss. It would never be a permanent relationship, because it couldn't last between them, and in the end, she might not be interested in him at all—but he craved her.

Those scenarios bothered him, and he was damn tired of obsessing about Ms. Bennett—it was driving him crazy. He'd been leaning against the bar, but he stood up straight. There was only one way to get his life back on track—he had to find a Cassandra Bennett cure. And he had three weeks to do it. Tapping his finger on the spout of his beer, he thought long and hard.

He snapped his fingers—yes, that's it. He'd have to force the issue, because he had no desire for another woman. First, he'd find Sharon, offer to fuck her. No, have her suck him off. Yeah. His dick wouldn't be able to ignore a blow job. Would it? And if he got off, then he'd be free of this strange hold Cassandra had on him. Then tomorrow, he'd tap some other woman's ass and fuck her brains out. And finally, he'd be back to being—being what? *Self-absorbed? Empty?*

Masterfully, Marcus evaded the truth. No woman was going to control him ever again. The malicious bitch of a mother who'd raised him taught him that lesson. But instead of a sense of relief, the plan left a gaping hole in his gut. *What's going on, Mackenzie?* He signaled the bartender for another beer. Was he already on his third? What the hell, he needed it, tonight. Picking it up, Marcus turned to face the room, leaning back on the bar.

Suddenly, every cell in his body went on alert, every thought wiped clean, when Marcus spotted the luscious redhead with long wavy hair who'd just walked into the Horse. Slowly, he perused her alluring body from head to toe. This was not a rail thin twenty-something, but a tall, curvy woman, who filled out the thin sweater that accentuated her lovely breasts. He thanked the heavens when she turned around to talk to someone behind her, revealing a magnificent ass, striking in her dark jeans.

She stood in profile to him, but the contours of her face from this angle were striking. Full on, she'd be stunning. But what had him pumped was that this woman's presence had started a slow burn of sexual need in his groin, and had obliterated every thought of Cassandra Bennett from his mind. He broke into a smile. He'd found his cure.

After this beauty was seated, he'd scope out the situation, then make his approach. If he got lucky tonight, she'd be under him, her long wavy hair spread over his pillow as he thrust into her.

He sipped his beer, noticing that she was with another woman who took off into the crowd. When a waitress motioned her to follow, he savored how she moved with confidence and grace, her hips swaying slightly—hips that a man could grip while he fucked her from behind—it was sexy as hell. He watched her closely, imagining exploring a body that screamed sex—hopefully with him. He laughed softly. Cassandra's power was gone.

Suddenly, she stopped, turned to the bar and stared right at him. Marcus froze in sudden recognition. The noise and smells of the Horse melted away. His mouth went desert dry and gaped open.

None of the photos had done her justice. Cassandra Bennett was more captivating than he'd ever imagined, and in that moment, she was the only woman on earth.

He lifted the corner of his mouth and slowly studied every dip and curve of her body, from top to bottom. Her face flushed pink, and her lips parted ever so slightly. *Very nice.* He'd embarrassed her, but her inviting parted lips looked like she'd felt that spark between them, too. She quickly averted her eyes and followed the waitress to a booth that was situated directly across from where he was. Even better.

He shook his head at the irony of the situation. She was in his sights now, and he was in full pursuit. Without even knowing it, Cassandra had cast her spell, entangling him again.

****

"The Horse is hopping tonight." Madeline Harper, Cassandra Bennett's younger sister, had to raise her voice to be heard over Patsy Cline's *I Fall to Pieces* and the packed room. *Perfect song choice*, Cassie mused, hoping it wasn't an omen of her decision to move back home to Riverbend.

"Let's wait for a booth," said Cassandra. Maddy nodded and held up two fingers at a harried waitress who mouthed *one sec,* then took off carrying a tray loaded with beers.

"Sis," Maddy's arm circled Cassie's waist, "I've missed coming here with you, and I can't believe that in a few weeks you'll be back to stay. I hate that we've lived apart for so long."

Maddy leaned in for a hug and squeezed tight. Cassie squeezed back, and Maddy gazed up lovingly. She was a petite five-three to Cassie's five-nine, and sporting a stylish pixie cut, her raven black hair layered with lavender. And though Maddy was the wild child of the two sisters, her face was stunning and angelic. Cassie remembered how often Maddy used her sweet looks to get herself out of trouble.

"I missed you too, baby sis, but we're together now."

Maddy nodded, and fought back tears.

I ran away from Riverbend as soon as I could and left Maddy behind. Guilt pulled at Cassie like a swift eddy on the river, but she shut down the emotion. She loved her sister, but she'd worried that moving back to Riverbend wasn't a great decision—it was filled with emotional landmines that she'd eventually have to face. But not tonight. Tonight was sister time.

"Hey Maddy," someone yelled. Steph, a friend of Maddy's, waved her over. Cassie waved her sister on, "Go talk to her, I'll wait for the booth." A quick peck on Cassie's cheek and Maddy was swallowed up by the crowd.

Then she felt it. A startling tingle slowly stroked down her spine.

Cassie shivered at the feeling of being watched. Quickly scanning the room, she didn't notice anyone looking at her. Moving to the side as people continued to enter, heading to the bar or the back room for pool or darts, she shook off the feeling. *I'm just edgy tonight because of the huge changes I'm making.* She bit her bottom lip.

After Ron died, she'd attended a bereavement group back in California, and the facilitator had talked about moving on, and eventually finding a new path in life. Since there was nothing left for her out west, her twin daughters, Eva and Abigail, both first years at New York University, joined Maddy in urging her to leave California and move back to Riverbend.

With great trepidation, and despite bitter memories, she'd agreed to move into her family home, left vacant since her mother's fatal heart attack fifteen months ago. Oddly, she rarely thought about her mother. *Something else to figure out.*

But coming back also meant she could reconnect with Maddy, and Danny and Jason, the nine-year-old twin nephews she barely knew. And since New York City was only a ninety-minute drive from Riverbend, she could easily see her girls.

And then there was Pete, whom she loved dearly. He was like a father to her, and Shirl, his deceased wife, was the mother she'd longed for when Bill and Debbie Harper couldn't fill those roles for her or Maddy. She was temporarily living in the cottage on Pete's farm, her favorite place on earth, while she updated the kitchen and bath in her home that sat along the banks of the Delaware.

No, she shook her head. Being unsettled wasn't new. It was a frequent state of mind that went even beyond Ron's death, leaving her a widow at thirty-eight years old.

Suddenly bumped from behind, Cassie turned and saw that a man had been pushed into her by the surge of people entering the bar. He quickly apologized. Cassie nodded that she was okay. A sharp bite of grief hit when he put his arm around the waist of the woman he was with, tucking her into her side to protect her from the crowd.

God, how she missed the feeling of being physically surrounded and protected by a man. She tried to shake it off, but the incident started her mind racing with the very thoughts that kept her tossing and turning all night long—for many months now. Her insomnia wasn't only caused by the move or other life worries—lately, it was also about sex. Raw, dirty sex.

She longed for a man's touch exploring every inch of her skin, setting her nerves on fire. Guilt hit because Ron's image was not part of her fantasy. It never had been. She always imagined a faceless man who could fulfill her sexual fantasies in the ways that Ron couldn't. She leaned against a wall, imagining the strength and weight of this dream man as he pressed her into the mattress, spread her wide, and rode her hard.

Cassie sighed. She was sexually frustrated, but those yearnings told her that she was healing from grief, not just numbly trying to get through the day like in that first year after Ron's death. She was coming alive. She wanted sex again. And if the fates aligned, someday in the distant future, she hoped to love again.

"A booth opened, miss," the waitress interrupted. Catching Maddy's attention with a wave, Cassie pointed to the waitress who was heading for a booth. Maddy nodded and mouthed *just a minute.*

Nearing the booth, it happened again. But this time the sensation was down-right physical—like bold fingers caressing her spine. She shivered. Someone was staring at her—hard. Looking around, she turned toward the bar.

Oh. There he was. Big, and rough looking, radiating a primal masculinity that stole her breath.

When their eyes met, his mouth dropped open in shock. Then his expression turned hard and dark, pinning her to the spot. A corner of his mouth tipped up. *Oh boy.* Lazily, he stroked her from head to toe and back again with a heated look that scorched her body, as if it might leave behind scar tissue.

Stunned by his intensity, her libido roared to life, and a delicious warmth settled in her belly. Cassie blushed, averted her eyes, and walked to the booth with a pounding heart and shaking legs. No man had ever looked at her like that—like something hunting in silence, its next meal already doomed.

The booth was directly across from where he was standing at the bar, and she could feel his fierce gaze still on her. *Do not look at him.* With a mask of calm, she ordered a beer and pointedly began to study the menu.

Only moments ago, she'd been thinking about her faceless fantasy man, and here he was in the small town of Riverbend, standing ten feet away and making it blatantly clear that he liked what he saw. His hungry, almost possessive gaze had set her nerves roiling. She had no idea how to handle this kind of animal.

Ron was intelligent and sweet, a kind man who made gentle love to her. Their sexual connection was good, but she had craved more aggressive sex and often wanted to...experiment. Nothing too wild, just adding some toys into the mix, maybe even some light spanking. But even that made Ron uncomfortable. She could tell it was causing a rift between them, so Cassie convinced herself that her needs were wants, and those wants were put away.

But without knowing one thing about this man except how boldly he'd looked her over, Cassie had no doubt that he would take control in bed, demanding she please him and demanding that she be pleased. The image of being sexually dominated by this imposing stranger had forced every other thought out of her mind.

"Here's your beer, are you ready to order now?" the waitress broke in.

"Thanks, not yet, I'm waiting for my sister."

"Okay, give a shout when you're ready," and she bustled off.

Cassie was thrilled. Cassie was terrified. She had to force her hands to stop shaking as she poured her beer into a glass.

"Sis, guess what?" Maddy began talking with her usual exuberance as soon as she slid into the booth. "Steph agreed to watch the boys if you can't do it on Wednesday nights while I'm in school, though I know you want to see them. Only one more semester, and I'm finally a paralegal!" She rattled on, "Did I tell you about that know-it-all guy in my Contracts class who makes me want to..."

It was all white noise, Cassie's mind was occupied solely by *him*. She couldn't help herself—she peeked around the menu. He was still watching her, and when he quirked an eyebrow, her breath caught in her throat. She knew that sign. He was asking if he could approach. She'd have to say something to Maddy, because even if she didn't engage, her gut told her he was going to walk across the bar right to her at any moment .

Her heart was pounding in her chest as the seconds ticked by. Cassie hated feeling insecure and nervous instead of the grown woman she was. She was an accomplished science writer specializing in psychology, she was a mother, a wife...a widow. No. *I am a confident, independent woman who can flirt with an attractive man in a bar. And though it's not really me, I can have sex with that man tonight if I choose. No strings, just mutual satisfaction.*

And if she had a few more drinks, maybe instead of going home to her vibrator she could actually get laid. Well...maybe more than a few.

Serious doubt was creeping in. Cassie had

become pregnant accidentally her senior year of college, and she'd married Ron right after graduation. She hadn't dated or even flirted in a long, long time. She glanced at him.

Casually, he leaned back against the bar, one foot on the bar footrest, the other leg stretched lazily in front of him. But that easy posture was a front. Even from across the room, a visible tension emanated from him as he stared back at Cassie—he was waiting for a sign from her.

Doubt took the upper hand—Cassie suddenly decided that he was too much for her right now, both intensely arousing and scaring the crap out of her. Along with the move and trying to find a new life path...no. She shook her head slightly in the negative at him, but instead of acceptance and a disappointed expression, he nodded *yes*, and a knowing smile tugged at his lips.

Quickly, she turned from him and took a swig of beer, hoping to calm down...

"What's the matter, sis?" Maddy was studying her closely.

"Nothing. Why do you think anything's the matter?" Trying for nonchalance, Cassie picked up the menu, but she couldn't help sneaking a peek at him. *Oh.* Her heart thumped when he winked at her. She snapped back to the menu, "So, should we do burgers or...?"

"You're acting weird, you keep looking over at the bar, and you can't lie for shit."

To Cassie's dismay, Maddy turned toward the bar. "Don't," Cassie hissed.

It was too late. Cassie glanced at him. His eyes left hers for a moment and went to Maddy. He smiled, and then dismay turned to horror when Maddy smiled and raised her hand, calling out, "Hey, Marcus."

He was off the bar like a shot, prowling toward her with intent. She tried to catch her breath as she watched him near. His entire bearing screamed sex and dominance.

"He's something, isn't he, sis," Maddy said. It was not a question.

They both gasped when a young woman came out of nowhere and tried to grab his arm. But without a glance, he shook her off and kept on going.

"Cass, Marcus Mackenzie has you in his sights."

Close to the crease on his inner thigh of his faded jeans, an area was worn to white from accommodating the bulge of a cock he could hardly conceal. Cassie tried to stifle a moan at an unbidden image of herself on her knees, Marcus controlling her head with a fistful of hair, commanding her to pull down the zipper with her teeth. Then she would—

Maddy broke through the haze. "Cassie, where did your mind go? You moaned."

"I did not."

Maddy smirked. "You did. He's smoking hot, but watch out, he's a player."

A player. Of course *he was.*

Then he was there, leaning against the booth in that same languid pose. "Good evening, ladies," the words flowed sensually from his lips while he stared straight at Cassie. She couldn't take her eyes off of him, even knowing that her cheeks were beet red.

"Hey, Marcus, good to see you, too," Maddy replied with a hint of irony. He hadn't even looked in her direction, yet.

15

He lifted his chin at Maddy, said, "Hey," but his eyes cut back to Cassie's when Maddy said, "Marcus, meet my sister, Cassie."

"Hello," she managed to mutter.

"Lovely," he whispered, while his steady gaze roamed over her face. He put out his hand to shake, took hers, and held it, instead of shaking. It was a working man's hand, big and callused. How would those rough fingers feel against her skin...inside her...

When Maddy asked, "Join us?" it jolted Cassie out of her reverie, right into the heated, sly smile on Marcus's face, as if he knew what she was thinking. That caused another blush, that led to his smile softening, and his low, buttery voice replying, "I'd be delighted."

Marcus whistled over the noise of the bar, waving over a handsome man whose light-blonde hair and honey-colored skin gave him the look of a California surfer. Cassie surreptitiously glared at Maddy, but her sister only grinned, then leaned in and whispered, "I know him, you can get laid tonight."

Cassie shot daggers at Maddy, "Sssh."

It was too late to do anything but move over, as Marcus slid into the booth next to her, while his friend sat next to Maddy.

"Hey, Maddy, you're looking great," offered the new addition. She teased back, "Thanks, Bret, but you're not getting lucky tonight. Not with me, at least."

They all laughed, then Marcus introduced her. "Bret Hammond, this is Cassandra, the other gorgeous sister."

Cassie put out her hand to shake. Bret took it and looked at Marcus. "So, Mac, I see why you've been off your..."

Marcus barked, "Shut it, Bret," a bit louder than strictly necessary. Cassie sensed his tension, but he was smiling when he added, "...or your bonus will be missing a couple of zeros."

"You got it, boss," Bret held his hands up in surrender, then turned to chat with Maddy.

Marcus settled in and draped his arm over the back of the booth, his fingers lightly brushing Cassie's shoulder.

Though her heart was pounding, she leaned forward, looked right at him, and raised an eyebrow. He was savvy enough to get the message, though his grin was smug. He moved his hand, but his arm remained over the back of the booth. He leaned close, studying every aspect of her face as if he was memorizing it, and in a low voice said, "Cassandra, you're so lovely, it takes my breath away."

What? They met moments ago, and now he was talking to her like this was a love letter instead of a bar pickup.

When his thigh touched hers, the sexual energy between them exploded with heat, and her body sang with lust. God, she wanted him. Even if she never saw him again, she wanted to know what it would feel like for Marcus Mackenzie to take her body in every way possible. And she wanted it tonight.

Thirty minutes ago, Cassie had decided he was too much for her. But that was fear talking. Fear and how she'd been raised, how she'd conditioned herself to ignore her own needs. Suddenly, Cassie was tired of being the responsible big sister to Maddy's wild child, tired of being a parent to her own mother, tired of suppressing her desires.

She was on a new life path, wasn't she? Why couldn't that include one wild night with a man who looked like a rough version of a Greek sex god?

But her excitement turned to worry when she remembered the young woman—much younger than she—who'd tried to stop Marcus. Cassie was on the downslide to forty, and though in decent shape, she had stretch marks and her breasts sagged after breastfeeding twins. *He's got to be older than me, but that woman looked like she was in her twenties.*

"What are you thinking about so hard, Cassandra?" His hot breath caressed her cheek. When had he moved that close? Then she was caught up in his delicious smell. He wasn't wearing cologne, only a clean, woodsy soap and his unique male scent.

It was too much. She'd be panting at the table if he didn't move back.

"Are you going to answer me, Cassie? Because I think we're on the same wavelength here, and I want to know."

She turned into his steady gaze. This was no pretty boy, but a ruggedly handsome man who looked more like a brawler. His brow was deep, his nose strong and slightly crooked, like he'd broken it. Unruly dark-brown hair that curled in soft waves around his collar had hints of gray, as did the scruff on his face, framing full lips. Lips she'd like to feel against her mouth.

She noticed a thin scar running from his left ear down onto his neck and controlled an unsettling compulsion to trace it with a finger.

Unusual dark-blue eyes rimmed with black lashes reminded her of blue skies covered by storm clouds—

they flashed. "Like what you see, Cassandra? I know I do."

She hadn't realized she'd been holding her breath while she studied him.

"Breathe, Cassie." His mouth twitched when she exhaled with a whoosh.

Mildly dizzy, Cassie knew something had been set in motion that she couldn't stop, even if she wanted to.

Chapter Two

"**I** accepted the date when he asked me out. I mean, I wasn't attracted to Jeff at all. It's not that he wasn't nice, but—"

Marcus sat on a bar stool, legs splayed, a bottle of cola in his hands. Grinning, he listened to another of Cassie's outrageous stories. Once Cassandra had a few drinks and loosened up, she talked about everything— her daughters, freelance writing, growing up in Riverbend. And now she was recounting the one date she'd had last year, in California.

She'd asked him questions about himself, too. He told her that he was long-divorced and had a son, Aiden, a sophomore at Columbia University who he was incredibly proud of. And learning that her daughters were at NYU had him surprisingly thinking about driving her to New York to meet each other's progeny. Where the hell did that come from?

After that uncomfortable thought, he refocused all the conversation toward her. It was a relief because he hated to talk about himself. Anyway, he much preferred the show she was putting on. Cassie's hands were flying around while she told him the tale of the dentist. He tried to listen, but he didn't give a rat's ass

20

about her one date, because Maddy and Bret were long gone and, finally, they were alone.

And of all things, they were waiting for a dart board to open. She'd challenged him to a game. And lucky him, he was her ride home. He wasn't sure how far he was going to go with her tonight. Fucking her wasn't on the menu, but he was going to have himself a taste.

Getting to know a woman in more ways than how good she was with her mouth was a totally new experience. Bret noticed Marcus's play, and when Cassie and Maddy were in the bathroom he'd said, "Never seen you act like this Mac. Cassie's different. You're gone for her, buddy."

Bret had some of it right. He ached for a real woman's body to get off, instead of using his hand like he had for almost a year, but Cassandra Bennett was no one-night stand. She was special. But gone for her? Hardly.

Cassie grabbed a bottle of beer off the bar, interrupting his thoughts. She took a long pull, then continued, "Who accepts a date with a dentist?" She looked at him and giggled. *Cute.*

Smiling at her question, he shook his head. He'd stopped drinking a while ago.

Cassie, on the other hand, had a nice buzz going. "Okay, he's a dentist. Did he stand you up?" He didn't want to hear about the men in her life, but he wasn't threatened. She did say she wasn't attracted to the guy, and anyway, he lived three thousand miles away.

"Stand me up?" She laughed like he'd been doing a stand-up routine in front of her. And though there was nothing funny about what he'd said, her laughing with him was what he'd wished he could have when he'd seen the photo.

"No, but listen to this..." She touched his bicep. She'd been touching him, leaning into him while they talked or while she told him stories, since they'd moved to the bar. He'd touched too—a short caress, a stroke to tame a wayward curl, putting his arm around her waist when something amusing struck both of them.

Their flirting was the best foreplay he'd ever had. Or the only foreplay. He never even kissed women anymore.

But Cassie was going to be well-kissed tonight. She was acting out parts of the date, and when she looked at him, his gaze slowly wandered over her body. Her breasts were a perfect handful, and though she wore a bra, he saw the faint outline of nipples.

He imagined burying his face in the tease of the ample cleavage peeking out of her V-neck sweater, finding out where that delicious smell of coconut on her was the strongest. His gaze moved down her lush hips and long legs in tight jeans, picturing her legs wrapped around his waist as he thrust into her.

She blushed when he looked her over, averted her eyes, and continued, "It might put you off your food, but you have to hear this."

What he wanted to do was pull her into his arms and kiss her until she begged for air. But he was biding his time.

"So, he takes me to a fancy schmancy restaurant,"

He barked a laugh, "Fancy schmancy?" *Adorable.*

"It was, and here's where the *eww* part comes in. He began to describe how to do a root canal as I was digging into my clam chowder."

22

He tuned out because he wasn't waiting anymore. Her generous mouth, her ripe lips made for deep, wet kisses had tantalized him for the last hour. He was hard as a rock.

The game was changing. Right now.

Bending and putting the bottle on the floor, Marcus sat back up and interrupted in a soft tone, "Cassie."

She stopped talking, "Yes?"

He crooked his finger, "Come here."

She started toward him. God, she was stunning—a heart-shaped face with high cheekbones and skin the color of rich cream had him aching for her. And that cute nose wrinkled with puzzlement. All that beauty was framed by long, wavy, dark-red hair that would slide through his fingers like a soft caress.

When he leaned forward, put his hands on her hips, and drew her between his legs, she licked her bottom lip. *Mm.* They were eye to eye, and if he moved just a millimeter, he could kiss her.

"What?" She stared at him out of eyes that were the sinful brown of the finest aged cognac, with shiny flecks of gold. Those beauties, surrounded by thick dark lashes, opened wide.

"Shh," he tightened his hold and stroked her bottom lip with his index finger. He reveled in her tremble. The sexual heat between them was explosive.

Her breath sped up.

Putting his hand back on her hip, he brought her in closer. "We're not playing darts."

Playfully, she tilted her head. "We're not?"

She'd jumped right into the game.

"Uh-uh. Tonight, we're playing a different game."

23

"And the rules of this game?"

A smile played on his lips. "Rule number one, you're going to kiss me back." Placing a hand on her back, her pulled her in until he felt her warm breath on his mouth, holding her jaw with his other hand.

Cassie ran her soft hands up and down his biceps. "I am?" she teased.

He licked along her bottom lip, nipped it, and grinned at the noise she made. "Yeah, you are."

She arched into him. When their lips met, her soft, curvy body molded into his, like matched pieces of a jigsaw puzzle. Hard nipples taunted him when she rubbed her chest on his. Velvety lips pushed for more. His restraint snapped. "Open," he ordered. She gasped, and he swallowed her moan.

He explored her mouth, stroking her tongue like he wanted to stroke her lush body.

Cassie detonated, stroking his tongue in return as their heads tilted back and forth, trying to move deeper into each other. He pulled her in tighter yet and pushed his hips between her thighs. She whimpered, and then he didn't give a damn that they were at the Horse. His dick was screaming at him to bend her over the damn bar, rip her panties off, and ride her.

When her hand snaked under his shirt, reality hit. With an iron will, he pulled back, steadying her. Breathing hard, they stared at each other. Her lips were swollen from his kisses. Her eyes were half-lidded with longing.

He rested his forehead against hers, "Damn, you can kiss."

She murmured, "I've never been kissed like that, ever."

Neither have I.

His dick was throbbing painfully, but he wouldn't deviate from his original plan—take her back to the cottage, tell her he wanted to see her when she returned, kiss her again, and leave.

But he wanted just a bit more tonight. So Marcus made his first mistake with Cassandra Bennett when he asked, "Ride with me tonight?"

After showing her how to mount his Harley and wrapping her arms tightly around his waist they took off like a rocket, heading up into the hills. Over the roar of the pipes Cassie asked, "Where are we going?" Marcus half turned, "Wherever I want."

He rode to the Overlook, a spot carved out of the hills above the river he'd found when he was a teen. It was where he'd first met Pete, and it had become his special, private place, where he went to find peace. He'd never shared the Overlook with anyone before, but for some indefinable reason, that's where he was taking Cassie.

He pulled into the parking area, turned off the engine, and pulled down the stand.

As Cassie lifted her leg to get off, Marcus looked over his shoulder and said, "Stay on the bike."

****

Marcus's bossiness was a maddening turn-on and had her burning with a sexual hunger that she'd never experienced before. If they weren't outside, she'd have ripped her clothes off.

He turned around to face her, said, "Come here," in a low, husky voice, and heat curled in her belly.

25

Yes, that's what she wanted—his control and power. His experience.

When he pulled her tight into his body, the cock so brazenly outlined in his faded jeans pressed onto her clit. The contact shocked her, bringing her to the edge of an orgasm after hours of teasing foreplay.

She whimpered, and Marcus gripped her jaw, burying his face in her hair.

She had to touch him. Her hands glided over smooth skin and rock-hard muscles in his arms and shoulders. They rippled under her touch. But it was his thick, wavy hair that she wanted to play with. She stroked up into it, grabbed a handful, and pulled.

He made a funny noise in his throat—she smiled. Then Marcus took her mouth, hard, and the battle was on. They ate at each other—tongues dueling, teeth clicking, hands exploring. He played with her breasts over her shirt, and her skin flushed hot. He explored her mouth with his tongue, ran kisses along her jaw, alternating with little nips and flicks of his tongue.

She raced her hands over his back to his chest and dipped a finger into the waistband of his jeans, making him buck into her core. Her swollen clit throbbed, and her need built.

Then he used the tip of his tongue to trace a path down her neck where it met her shoulder. "Delicious," he whispered and sucked right on that exquisitely arousing spot. Her neck arched with a long moan.

That bite of pain was explosive. She lost her mind and went wild, grinding into him and writhing on the seat. Anything to get off and stop the throbbing pain between her legs. She had to touch him, play with his magnificent body. Running her hands under his shirt, she caressed his defined abs and thumbed his nipples.

When she stroked his cock over denim, he muttered, "Damn," but pulled her hand away. "No, I'm gonna come in my pants," then ordered, "give me your mouth."

Her lips pressed to his, and he dove in, his taste a potent aphrodisiac. Her hands wrapped around his back, and she scraped her nails up and down, from his shoulders to his tailbone. He moaned, and they ground into each other until he suddenly stopped.

Breathing hard, Marcus pulled back, took her hands out of his shirt, and held them in his.

"No, please," she cried out.

"Not this way. Not with you," Marcus huffed the words, trying to catch his breath. Her heart jack-hammered in her chest. A scream died in her throat when he gently cupped her face and rubbed her nose with his.

Cassie pulled back. "'Not this way?' Are you out of your mind?"

Placing his hands on her shoulders, he pleaded. "Cassandra, listen to me. If we continue, I'll lose control and fuck you on this bike. I'm almost there now. And that's not going to happen."

"Why not? I want it to happen. I want you to fuck me on the bike." She tried to run her hands under his shirt again, but he stopped her.

"No, Cassie. You're not that kind of woman. I'm taking you back to the cottage."

"I'm the kind of woman who wants to get laid tonight. That's what I want."

"And I said it's not happening. Bringing you to the Overlook was a mistake."

27

I'm a mistake? She wanted to curl up and die.

He steadied her, turned around on the bike, and pulled her arms tightly around his waist.

"Hold on tight."

Caught between shame and anger, Cassie couldn't bear touching him, and loosened her hold on him. He started the bike, but before they took off, he tightened her hold on him and warned, "I said hold on tight. You'd better listen."

She tightened her hold, but her humiliation made the ride a living hell.

As if a kind of madness afflicted her, during the ride she decided to try to entice him into the cottage, into her bed. It was a desperate move, but she was beyond caring. She needed to be wanted, desired for her own sake, in the hungry way that Marcus had looked at her at the Horse. Why had he changed his mind? He pulled up to the cottage and helped her off the bike. He took her hand and led her up the porch. Before he could say a word, she put her arms around his neck, "Marcus please come inside, please," she begged.

"No." He took her hands off his neck and held them in his large hands. Hands that she wanted touching every inch of her body. "Not tonight, Cassandra. I want this to be right. Let's wait until you come back. Let's go out, let's..."

"I want you tonight. Even if you never call me again, I don't care if I'm a one-night stand. You do that, don't you?"

His expression turned glacial. "No. I told you, this ride was a mistake."

She jerked her hands out of his hold and whipped around. *I'm a mistake. He's repeating it. Believe him.*

His words scored her heart, and tears welled in her eyes. She'd begged him for sex. Begged. He'd turned her on and off at his will. *He's a player. And he's playing me.*

Furious, she flushed with anger and humiliation. She had to get inside, fumbled with her keys, but she found the right one and slid it into the lock.

"Cassie," he put his hand on her back as she opened the door, "Let's talk about this. I'll call you when you return. We'll..."

But she was finished with Marcus. She couldn't face him, snapped, "Thanks for the ride," stepped into the cottage, and slammed the door in his face. She threw her purse and jacket on the couch, walked into the bedroom, and crawled into bed under a soft quilt.

Her tears flowed that night over two men—one of them gone, the other unattainable.

****

The next morning, Cassie angrily pushed pajamas into the carry-on luggage that lay open on the bed. Her tears had dried up, but not her anger. *What was I thinking last night? Drinking too much, at my age? Flirting and making out with Marcus at the Horse? I was out of my mind.* She moved to the dresser, pulled underwear out of the top drawer, and tossed it on the bed.

She'd taken a risk, played with fire, and been burned. But not in the way she'd craved.

What a fool she'd been. First at the Horse, then on his bike. Cassie cringed at how pathetically desperate she'd been last night. She stuffed underwear into the interior side pockets of the case, moving back to the dresser. She took tank tops and a few shirts out of the drawers, turned to the bed where her the suitcase lay open, and stopped.

The infamous player of Riverbend had rejected her. The memory stung.

Cassie sat on the edge of the bed. The entire night with Marcus had been the most fun, sensual, downright exhilarating time she'd had in years. Maybe ever.

Until it wasn't.

Maddy's ring tone sounded. Cassie picked up her cell and opened the text.

Madwitch2: *There in 15. B ready. U get laid by the hottie?*

There was no way that she was going to tell Maddy the truth, it was too humiliating. She'd say that she'd had too much to drink, so he took her home. It wasn't too far from the truth.

Cbennett: *Meet you outside. Don't ask! :)*

Madwitch2: *Be prepared to spill on the way to the airport.*

Cbennett: *No way.*

The packing finished, Cassie wheeled her carry-on out to the porch. She went back into the cottage. Everything was in order in this cozy little one-bedroom home, filled with comfortably worn furniture, framed antique flower prints, and a rustic kitchen table and chairs built by Pete for the woman he loved. Shirl used it, as she often said, "To get my head together." It was her private place for crafting, baking, and thinking, and it became that for Cassie, too.

Walking to the sofa, Cassie picked up a needlepoint pillow of a silly, black- and white-striped cat with a leaf in its mouth, and suddenly she was back in time.

She was eleven years old when Shirl, Pete's beloved wife, had helped her start sewing that pillow. She'd run to the cottage that day, needing Shirl's love, after a fight with her mother. She'd been bitterly angry because her mother had refused to let her stay late on Wednesdays after school for Mrs. Ravitch's creative writing club.

"But mom, Mrs. Ravitch invited me special because of the stories that I write. It's only for two hours, and she said she'll drive me home after."

"No, Cassie, you know that I need you to take care of your sister," her mother whined from her bed with one of her daily headaches. *"Your father works late every day, and you know how sick I am. Stop complaining, you're making my headache worse."*

Her mother was sick, alright. Major depression was debilitating, but she'd never even attempted to overcome it, to get help so she could be a mother to her daughters.

She placed the pillow back on the sofa next to Shirl's lovely spring flower pillow.

Shirl's presence was everywhere in the cottage, as if she'd just stepped out for a moment. *If only you were here, Shirl. I need your wisdom.* Cassie sighed. Marcus's rejection had led to a wistful morning.

31

Locking the door, Cassie sat on the top step of the porch, her thoughts drifting back to last night. What was his game? He seemed to want her, but why reject her? And why did it hurt so much that he had? They were strangers, yet something about him called to her—besides his sexual prowess. She sighed, remembering the woman at the Horse who'd tried to stop him—but he hadn't stopped, he'd come right to her. *Then why wouldn't he have sex with me?* She stood, dragging her suitcase down the porch steps as Maddy drove up. Maddy popped the trunk, and Cassie hauled her case in. Maybe she'd made a mistake in moving back to Riverbend. But she was trapped now. She'd just opened the passenger door when a text came through. Taking a deep breath, she opened the message. Her breath hitched. She read it again.

> **MMackenzie:** *Good morning Cassandra. I wish you a smooth and safe flight and will be impatiently waiting for your return. The next time we see each other, we will discuss why you refused to hear me out and slammed the door in my face. We're not done yet.*

Grinning, Cassie slid into the passenger seat. Maybe coming back home to Riverbend was a good idea, after all.

Chapter Three

"Un-fucking-livable?" Cassie screeched, disturbing an egret that had been wading at the river's edge. The bird took wing and gracefully flew away over the trees. *Wish I could sprout wings and fly the hell out of Riverbend.*

She thought being rejected by Marcus three weeks ago was a disaster. It was nothing compared to the present catastrophe.

The effing Delaware.

Ten days ago, Maddy called, freaked out. The Delaware had flooded—again. The river had swept through her family with death and destruction numerous times in the past, but it was a greedy bitch and wanted more.

The house was built on the sliver of land that lay between the river and its parallel canal. Cassie stood looking at the house on the small footbridge that spanned the canal and connected to the main road. It was a lovely spot. Too bad the entire area was a flood zone.

A powerful Nor'easter had unexpectedly roared up the coast ten days ago, bringing torrential rains, winds, and flash floods. It had flooded her childhood home. The one she was planning on moving into to begin her new life. She gripped the bridge handrail. The pretty little sky-blue, three-bedroom clapboard with white trim and wooden balconies facing the river... flooded.

Pain tore at her, but she controlled her tears. There was no time for that. She had to take action. Maddy had already taken the first photos and called their catastrophic-insurance adjuster and a flood clean-up company, but she needed something to do.

Cassie's insides churned. Her plan to stay at Pete's cottage for no more than two months while she updated the kitchen and bath had suddenly been extended. All she wanted to do was peacefully settle down, get her bearings, and slowly find a new life path. She knew moving back would stir up the pain of her childhood, her father's betrayal, her mother's lie, and her leaving Maddy behind. She had to face all of that and work through it, someday. But, dammit, now she wanted peace.

Woodenly, Cassie turned to leave—she'd talk to Pete about this mess. She stopped and looked back at the house. *I never should have moved back.*

****

"Love you, Cassie," Pete said as he kissed her cheek. She'd gone straight to the farmhouse. Pete had insisted on making her breakfast, but now she was ready to leave. "Love you back, Pete." Pointing to two Adirondack chairs on the porch, he asked, "Stay a little while longer, sweetie, please. I want to talk to you."

As if she could deny him anything. Cassie took a seat. There was no rush, she didn't have anything important to do today. *Just try to figure out my place in the universe.* She snorted at the thought. Her one errand was a trip to town to Mary's General Store for groceries. *Then, lucky me, more ruminating.*

Pete sat across from her, put his hands on his knees and leaned forward. At seventy-nine, he was still a strapping man, over six feet tall with broad shoulders made muscular through hard physical labor. His stark white hair was as thick as it had been in his twenties. Thick, unruly brows over electric-blue eyes set off a lined, hard face. But his loving smile softened the hardness.

I'm so lucky to have him in my life. He and Shirl had one son, Joe. They'd lost their infant, Lainie, over thirty years ago, and when Shirl couldn't have any more children, they'd seemingly adopted Cassie and Maddy, treating them like daughters.

"Shirl would love that you are living in the cottage."

"I miss her. She was like a mother to me."

"Ten years this November. Cassie, I know you know how I'm feeling."

She nodded.

"When's the moving van coming?"

"Seven days, give or take." Tucking a leg onto the seat, she added, "I don't have much. Sold most everything, just kept what really mattered. I already have a storage bin."

Pete's voice sharpened. "Cassie, I don't want you to move back to the house."

Her head snapped up. "Why? The flood damage will be taken care of."

"It's too dangerous." He held her eyes. "I'll worry

if you move back in. Not just for the big storms, where there's a warning, but for the damn flash floods that come up so suddenly you barely have time to get out. Just like this last one." Pointedly, he said, "Your father would not want you in that house."

Her father had been washed away in a flash flood seven years ago while saving her mother. It happened a month after Cassie had finally confronted him about his betrayal and angrily flew back to California, too stubborn to contact him.

Then it was too late.

No, her father wouldn't want her in that house. Her chest tightened painfully.

"Pete," she looked away from him. "I don't know."

"The cottage is yours. Forever, if you want it. Joe agrees with me. He loves you like a sister, so he's going to be watching over you, too."

How lucky she was that Pete, Joe, and Joe's wife Annie all loved her. They were protective. A family without DNA. Without pain.

But give up the house? Shouldn't she try to fix it up? Maddy had been first surprised and then angry that she wanted to move into the house. They fought about it. "Cassie, why do you want to live on a floodplain?" Maddy had yelled. "Haven't we lost enough?"

Why am I being stubborn about this? Cassie had been brooding about the house for months before the flood. What should she do?

"Please, Cassie." Pete broke into her thoughts. "Let the house go. Stay in the cottage. *Your* cottage. I won't sleep nights worrying about you living just yards from the river. Promise you'll think on it."

It hurt to see the deep worry on his face. "I promise, old man, I'll think on it."

"That's my girl. Come on over tonight. I'm grilling, Joe and Annie are bringing sides. Ask Maddy to bring the boys."

"I'll text her. You couldn't keep me away. See you later."

Driving down River Road toward town, Cassie's thoughts went to Marcus, who was taking up as much if not more space in her head than her house. She hated it.

What's his game? A day after she received that first text from him as she packed for California—a text she hadn't answered—he'd sent her another. There was no message, only a link to Carole King's *So Far Away*, which was on her classic rock playlist. At the Horse, he'd asked to exchange cell numbers, but she'd kept giggling and putting in the wrong number. He'd grinned, took her phone, added his number, and clearly had looked at her playlist. She hadn't answered that one either, though it had blown her mind.

Why would he send her a song about missing a lover? Marcus's reputation was about lust, not love. *This is a mistake*—he'd said it twice that night at the Overlook. And he wasn't stopping whatever he was up to because he'd woken her up at five-thirty this morning with yet another text:

MMackenzie: *Welcome back, Cassandra. I'm looking forward to seeing you soon. When we meet, we will talk about what happened at the Horse. And sorry to hear about your house, we'll talk about that, too. Rest up today.*

She was too deep into stonewalling, even a little embarrassed about it, to answer him.

Marcus shook her up, and the truth was, she had no idea how to handle him. Avoidance seemed like the best way to protect herself. *But you can't avoid anyone for long in Riverbend, there are fewer than a thousand residents.* Coming to a crossroad, Cassie slowed and stopped.

The best thing she could do for herself was to stay away from Marcus. *And somehow stop thinking about him every ten seconds.*

Cassie needed to think about getting her life back in order, not about getting laid. *Yeah, right.*

She pulled into a parking spot in front of Mary's General Store. It sold everything: coffee, beer, sandwiches, groceries, bait, and tackle. There was a small area in the back with four picnic tables that sat along the canal. The river was only forty feet away.

Cassie stepped inside. She loved the place and quirky Mary who owned it. Taking a shopping basket from the stack near the door, she heard, "Cassie, honey, you're home!" She was pulled into a tight embrace before she knew what was happening.

"It's good to see you, too, Mary," Cassie grinned.

Mary kissed Cassie's cheek, her voice gentling as she laid a hand on Cassie's face and said, "Oh, Cassandra."

Cassie beamed, "How can you be seventy-five and yet look like you're in your fifties?" Mary's snow-white hair flowed to her waist. She wore rimless eyeglasses that magnified soft hazel irises, and there was hardly a wrinkle on her sweet face. A large woman, she wore a long chiffon tie-dyed dress and looked just like the funny, whip-smart hippie that she was.

She and her then-husband, Steve, had bought the General Store in 1971. They'd renamed it Mary's & Steve's, but six years later, Steve ran away with one of their clerks, Larry. Mary took down Steve's name, but left the ampersand, so it read "Mary's &" It was weird, but it worked.

"It's been a while, darling girl, but you look lovely as ever. And I'm so sorry to hear about your house."

"Thank you. I'm trying to figure things out."

"Bet you are. Whenever Pete's been in, he's been so excited about you coming back to Riverbend, that's all he could talk about, keeping the entire town in the loop."

Just then, three twenty-something, preppie-type guys, likely from the local college, came into the store. "Gotta get to work, sweetie. See you later." She kissed Cassie again and walked away, saying loudly, "Whatever you need, guys, Mary's got it."

Cassie laughed out loud when Mary barked loudly, "A bong? You want to buy a *bong*?"

Cassie looked over and the young men were already moving toward the front door looking thoroughly cowed. "Do I look like I sell bongs? Or even know what a bong is?"

She most certainly does know, Cassie thought.

Cassie heard murmured apologies from the three men as Mary followed them with murder in her voice.

"No, I do not sell bongs. You all got one second to get outta my store, or I'll personally kick your balls up to your tonsils and turn you all into sopranos."

39

Izzy Matthews

When the front door slammed shut, applause and laughter broke out from customers.

Nothing had changed. And that familiarity felt good.

She walked through the store filling the basket, and even tossed in a bag of food for the hungry-looking gray cat lurking outside the cottage since she'd returned. Right before Ron died, they'd put down Benny, their thirteen-year-old beagle mix.

A month later, Ron was gone, too.

Shake it off. She added a few cans of wet cat food. Though she'd had no intention of getting a pet right now, she'd always been a sucker for strays.

She was reaching for a box of spaghetti when the masculine scent of river and man hit her. At the same time, Marcus's arm snaked around her waist, pulling her back into the front of his body. He bent his face right into her hair, his lips caressing her ear, and growled, "Lose your phone, Cassandra?"

Shit. "Um—" Cassie tried to pull away, but having Marcus's hard body plastered to her back was scrambling the synapses in her brain. She tried to free herself, but he pulled her tighter to him.

His voice dropped lower, "Asked you a question, baby." The tip of his tongue touched her earlobe, then traced the shell of her ear. A mewl escaped, and she felt him smile. The bastard.

"Marcus, let me go."

"I'm waiting for an answer."

"Marcus, you're embarrassing me," Cassie hissed and pushed out harder, trying to break his hold.

"Shut it, Cassie. Or I'll turn you around and kiss you right now, hard and wet. I don't care if the whole town sees us," he threatened.

40

Fuming, she stilled.

"Good choice," he said with infuriating satisfaction. Then, he lock-stepped her to the back of the store until they came to a wall. He turned her, put her back up against the wall, put his hands on either side of her head, and caged her in.

"Are you serious?"

"Deadly."

She had to change tactics, so she softened her stance. "Look Marcus, we're both living in Riverbend, and we'll be seeing each other in town."

His face closed off completely. But he wasn't backing down as he loomed over her.

"Um—" she continued. "We obviously got off on the wrong foot the night at the Horse." He scowled, but bravely she went on.

"So, why don't we go over to Pete's, get ourselves a piece of cheesecake or, if you don't like cheesecake, but who doesn't..." God, she was rambling, but she couldn't stop herself. "...their huckleberry crumb is fantastic." She kept blathering nonsense, something she did when she became nervous. "You know, the French apple pie is divine, too," she pointed to him and then herself, "and over delicious sweets we'll figure out whatever this is between us, so we can be friendly when we see each other." She forced a big smile. "What do you say?" *Gah. I must sound insane.*

Seconds ticked by like hours. Marcus stood there. Arms still outstretched, hands on either side of her head, keeping her where he wanted her. Watching her.

"Cheesecake?" She was stunned that those were the first words he spoke.

41

"Huckleberry crumb? French apple pie?"

"They're Joe's specialty."

"Joe's specialty?"

How annoying that he was repeating what she said with a stinking question mark at the end. "Marcus, look—"

In a flash, he leaned in so close that she felt his hot breath on her lips.

"We are not going to Pete's. And though I am pissed, you're also adorably nutty."

Adorably nutty? Cassie stood frozen, staring into his eyes only inches from her own.

"You are. And I like it. A lot."

"Marcus..."

He cut her off. "I contacted you numerous times when you were out west. I wanted to know how you were doing, moving back after living away for such a long time. I sent you music telling you that I missed you."

Her breath caught. He had missed her.

"And you deliberately did not answer my texts or calls."

"Well..."

He cut her off again. "I also wanted to talk to you about your house. Sorry to hear about that."

"My house? What does that—"

"I'm not finished, Cassandra," he continued sharply. "That option—to go to Pete's and have pie or cheesecake, to discuss what we have to discuss, is closed to you, right now."

Her mouth hung open in shock, but she quickly closed it when his gaze settled on her lips and his eyes flashed. "What's going to happen is this: I am going back to my office. You are going to finish your business, then get ready to go out to dinner with me. Tonight. At dinner, we are going to," he mimicked her, pointing to himself first and then her, "talk about whatever 'this' is between us. And why you blew me off at the cottage, then out west, *and* why you're still doing it now that you're back in Riverbend."

"And Cassie," he dipped his head to momentarily touch his nose to hers. "We are going to be more than friends. I'm going to be the man who will play with every inch of your exquisite body, then bury my face between your creamy thighs, stay there a long time, and then fuck you until you ache."

Heat surged through Cassie's body as he silently scrutinized every inch of her face. Being with him was like lazily floating down the river on an inner tube with a slow leak. One minute you're having fun, the next, you're swamped, lucky to be alive.

"Marcus, I don't think that's a good idea."

Ignoring her, he directed, "I'll pick you up at six. Dress casual." And with that, he removed his arms from the wall.

"I liked how your ass looked in the jeans you wore at the Horse. Wear them." His lips curled into a lazy smile when she gave him a frosty look.

Before she could reply, his phone signaled a text. He took it out of the pocket of his slacks, looked at the message and said, "Gotta run." Then, he bent, kissed her nose, and turned to leave, adding, "Six. Be ready."

"Marcus, you're not listening to me!"

He stopped.

"I have plans for tonight."

"Cancel them," he said over his shoulder, and he was gone.

Chapter Four

Pulling out of Mary's, Marcus headed toward his office in Eastbridge, a small city just four miles north of Riverbend. He pressed a button on his steering wheel. "Call Liam."

His brother answered immediately. "Hey Mac, what's up?"

"Li, Sean texted me that he won't make the meeting this morning. He's got to be there. Get yourself over to the Baylor B&B and pull him off the job. At the most, he'll lose two hours."

Liam complained, "The last time I tried to pull him off a job, he popped me in the nose. Our cousin has a hard right hook."

Marcus chuckled. "Don't I know it. You ended up wrestling each other on the floor of the Keegan Mercedes build with our workers taking bets. Lucky for us, old man Keegan wasn't around, or he'd have sacked us on the spot."

"I'm blaming this on you, Mac."

"You do that. See you both in twenty."

Ending the call, Marcus pursed his lips in frustration. The meeting scheduled for this morning about the vandalism to their projects included his best friend, Derek Prescott, who was the county assistant district attorney, but that was not a role he was playing today. The investigation was ongoing, but slowly since the police had no leads. Derek had the name of a good PI who he suggested they hire, and today Marcus would make that call.

Mackenzie Construction and Engineering was founded by his grandfather, Patrick Mackenzie. When his uncle Brennan took over, he built it into the premiere construction company in the region. Now it was his, Liam's, and Sean's. And nothing and no one was going to ruin what was their birthright. The bastards trying to ruin his company had no idea what he'd done in the Middle East, and would do again, if he caught them.

Taking a deep breath, Marcus let his company problems go and turned his thoughts to Cassandra Bennett.

She was on his mind all the time, now. Disrupting his sleep with images of taking her mouth again, while she moaned and whimpered. He often imagined what she'd sound like when she cried out during an orgasm. He was still hard after surprising her at Mary's and having the softness of her round ass pressed tight against his body. If he hadn't set this meeting for today, he would have tried to talk her into his bed, consequences be damned.

But first, he was going to romance her by taking her to dinner tonight at the Two Rivers Brewery, his good friend Jasper's place. It was a trendy microbrewery in Eastbridge that he frequented. He'd even ordered a bouquet of flowers for her, and he'd never brought a woman flowers.

He slowed and stopped at a light when a text came through. Picking up his cell, he opened the message.

Cbennett: *Marcus, so sorry but I cannot cancel my plans. We'll talk soon.*

He grinned. She was running. He drove through the intersection, pulled over at a curb, hit his flashers, and sat there thinking. She could only have plans with three people: Maddy, Rachel, or Pete. It wouldn't be difficult to find her.

He texted back:

MMackenzie: *I'm sorry to hear that. I looked forward to seeing you tonight. We'll see each other sooner rather than later. Enjoy your evening.*

Placing his cell back in the holder, Marcus pulled back into the lane. He'd waited a long time to have Cassandra Bennett. His jaw set.

Tonight was going to be fun. He was going hunting.

****

Cassie placed her cell on the kitchen table after texting Marcus that she could not join him for dinner. His words played in her head and had her arousal on a low simmer—I'm going to be the man that will bury his face between your gorgeous thighs, stay there a long time and then... I'm going to fuck you until you ache.

Absently, she fanned her face with her hand. Marcus's aggressive sensuality completely overwhelmed her. Sure, she lusted after him, but she

46

honestly liked him, too, and worried that she'd fall for him. She had to protect herself. How to handle him, if possible, was the question.

He'd rightfully given her hell for not answering any of his texts or calls. She had no excuse but her own fears. She picked up a cup of tea that she'd brewed, went out to the patio, and sat down. It was a glorious, sunny day, and she watched a pair of hawks circling overhead. Every few minutes, they dipped low and flew across the edge of the tree line.

Tonight, she'd go to Pete's, spend time with his family, Maddy, and the boys. And, just for a little while, she'd forget about Marcus and all her worries.

But she needed advice before she saw Marcus again. Getting up, she spotted the gray cat sitting at the edge of the patio, cleaning itself, obviously having eaten the food she'd put out for it. "Hey, boy," she called softly. The cat stopped and looked at her with stunning lime-green eyes. "Keep coming around, sweetie, and one day, you'll be in this house. The safest place in the world." He cocked his head, listening, and didn't run away when she slid open the door.

Grabbing her cell, she sat at the kitchen table and scrolled through her contacts.

There was only one person to call to ask about Marcus. Maddy was out. Besides the fact that she was working, she would do her usual, "Sis, you need to get laid," lecture. Yes, she did need to get laid, but she needed solid advice, first.

Rachel Wilkens, her best friend since grade school, would help her. They'd never lost touch with each other despite living three thousand miles apart.

She'd moved back to Riverbend a few years ago from Maine, fleeing from her abusive husband, and she would know all the gossip in this small town.

She'd have to tell Rachel something about that night at the Horse to find out the extent of Marcus's playboy reputation.

She'd never allow herself to be a notch on his bedpost, it would kill her. She pressed Rachel's number.

"Hey Cass, what's up?"

"Rach, are you at work?"

"No, I left early, I'm home. Something the matter?"

"Yes, nothing terrible, but I need advice."

"Man advice?"

"Yes."

"Okay, Cass. I'll be there in a few. This calls for brainstorming food. I'll stop at the diner for cheesecake, okay?"

"Yeah, I'll brew coffee. Oh, get a couple slices of their huckleberry crumb, too." Cassie remembered Marcus mimicking her about Joe's pies as if she were looney. No, "adorably nutty." She grinned.

"Got it. See you with the goodies."

What if Rachel gave her a string of women's names? What if Rachel were on it? Cassie pushed those thoughts and worries out of her head. Tonight at Pete's was going to be a no Marcus zone.

****

"So, how's it going with Mr. McHottie, sis?" Maddy asked casually, but Cassie knew she'd been lying in wait until they were alone. They hadn't had a chance to talk this week, except to check in with texts. They stood on the large patio at the back of Pete's farmhouse, standing away from the massive grill manned by Pete and Joe. Two picnic tables were pulled together to seat everyone, and another table was loaded with sides, condiments, paper plates, cups, and plastic utensils. A small fridge held drinks.

Cassie tipped her bottle of beer back, drank, and then asked in a pleasant voice, "After graduation, do you have any law firms lined up that you're interested in working for?"

"Sis," Maddy stepped closer and smirked, "stop evading."

"Darling sister, I'm not 'evading;' it's *none* of your business."

Eyes narrowed, Maddy whispered, "He hasn't fucked you yet. Has he?"

"Maddy," Cassie hissed and looked around.

"No one is listening. We look like two sisters who are just drinking beer and gabbing."

"I wish."

"You know me, sis," Maddy teased, "I'm the proverbial dog with a bone."

She was. When Maddy wanted something, she went after it with a take-no-prisoners vengeance.

Putting her hand on Maddy's arm, she begged, "Please, Mad, let it go for now." Rachel's info on Marcus's *women* had put her in a funk.

"Okay, Sis, I will," Maddy broke into her thoughts, nodding with earnest understanding. Putting an arm around Cassie's waist, Maddy gave her a quick hug. "I love you."

Cassie kissed Maddy's cheek, "Thanks."

Just then, Pete bellowed out, "Soup's on, come and get it!"

A chorus of excited kids' voices rang out as they raced to the grill.

"We got it, girls. Chill," Joe called to them as Cassie and Maddy began to move toward the grill to help. Cassie's eyes filled with the sweetness of the moment—cold beer, the smoky smell of meat grilling, the love of family on a perfect April evening. She'd missed it all, after living away for so many years.

She and Maddy stopped at the fridge, put their empties down, grabbed two Buds, and made their way to the grill. They walked to the side table, and just as they started picking up plates, Pete called out, "Marcus! Hell, boy, you're just in time for brats and beer. And I want you to meet my beautiful girls."

Cassie staggered, almost dropping her beer and plate, her peaceful mood destroyed.

Maddy softly laughed and said, "The Horse: Act Two." Cassie elbowed her, braced herself, and turned.

"Jesus," Maddy muttered as they both watched Marcus walk around the side of the house and step on to the patio, moving with determined intent, his eyes boring into hers. Her knees turned to water, and her resolve to stay away from him dissolved into potent desire.

"Beer and brats sound great," Marcus smirked as he came toward her.

"Hey, Marcus, grab a beer," Joe called out, startling Cassie out of her lustful thoughts.

Marcus read her easily, because his smirk briefly turned into a look of fierce need before he grabbed a beer from the fridge.

50

What was she going to say when Pete introduced her? Maddy must have felt her tension, because she put her arm around Cassie's waist and whispered, "Sis, what's the matter?"

"I don't want Pete to know about the Horse," Cassie muttered.

She was shocked when Pete left the grill and walked toward Marcus, who broke out in a grin. "Where've you been, boy? Avoiding me?" Pete pulled Marcus in for a deep hug. Marcus put his arms around Pete and hugged back, completing the manly ritual of slapping the other hard on the back before they broke apart.

It sure looked like they knew each other well. Pete never mentioned Marcus, even in his letters to her while she lived in California, keeping her up to date on town happenings. And Marcus never mentioned that he knew Pete, though he knew she was staying at the cottage.

With a wide grin, Pete put his arm around Marcus's shoulder and steered him to Cassie and Maddy. Cassie's stomach clenched. They stopped in front of her, and she was surprised to see Marcus's smirk gone, replaced by a soft smile.

"Marcus, you know Maddy, and this is her equally gorgeous sister, Cassie."

"Hey, Marcus, good to see you." Maddy gave him a quick hug, and his gaze dove back to Cassie.

It was ridiculous how tense she was. All she had to do was say "Hello, nice to see you again." She didn't have to say where they'd met when Pete asked. And he would ask, and he would worry because he was overly protective, and he wouldn't be happy that she was diddling with the town manwhore.

Looking over at the kids eating, Marcus said to Maddy, "Your boys have grown up since I saw them last year at the Heritage Day celebration."

"Yep, they keep sprouting up like weeds, and they need lots of fuel," Maddy laughed as she pointed out her sons, stuffing themselves with food.

Cassie's tension was building. Tuning out the conversation, she exhaled slowly, forcing herself to relax when Pete interjected, "And Marcus, here's my lovely Cassie I told you about. She's just moved back from California after being away for years. Marcus Mackenzie, meet Cassandra Bennett."

Marcus smiled, lifted an eyebrow, and put his hand out to shake. "Cassandra," his voice caressed her senses. "A beautiful name for a beautiful woman."

Breathing a sigh of relief that Marcus was playing this the way she'd hoped, her eyes narrowed at Maddy when she added, "Beauty and brains in one package. My sis is a catch, don't you think?"

True to form, Maddy ignored Cassie's warning and smiled, the brat. Cassie plastered a smile on her face. Pete's eyes narrowed at Marcus's words. *Uh oh.*

"Oh yes, I agree, Maddy." Damn, his deep, lazy voice was a turn on.

"Thank you." Cassie swallowed, reached out, and he took her hand, giving it a gentle squeeze.

She tried to pull back her hand, but Marcus held tight, smiled wider, and, ever so slightly, shook his head, no.

No? He was playing with her. Cassie pulled again. Marcus not only gave her another squeeze, but his pointer finger began to stroke her knuckle, and she couldn't stop the shiver.

"Yeah, she's a catch, Mac," Pete put a territorial arm around her shoulders, quickly pulling her into his side, forcing her hand out of Marcus's hold. Pete looked suspiciously from Marcus to her.

"Marcus," he said firmly, "Cassie is a catch, but my girl's not fishing. Understand?"

She caught Marcus's momentary flash of anger, quickly replaced with a tense smile. Maddy's expression mirrored Cassie's thoughts—what's going on?

Maddy eased the tension when she pulled Pete away from Cassie, "Hey big man, I'm starving, where's the dog you promised me?" As they all headed to the grill, Marcus put his hand on Pete's shoulder as Cassie caught his whisper, "Don't worry old man, it's all okay."

"I hope so, son, because I love you, too."

Pete loved Marcus? Marcus had moved to Riverbend only four years ago. But he had been brought up in Eastbridge—maybe they knew each other before that.

Maddy tucked Cassie's arm through hers as they walked to the grill, picking up plates from the side table. "Wow. That pissing contest between Pete and Marcus was something else."

"And I'm going to find out what it's about."

"If you need me, I'm here."

Cassie kissed Maddy's cheek, "I know you are."

Their plates loaded with food, Cassie and Maddy sat down at the table. Marcus was at her side before she could take her first bite, sitting close enough to her that the side of his body was tight against hers.

"Cassandra, nice seeing you here."

"Party crasher," she whispered sarcastically.

He whispered back, "You broke our date. I found you. I'm taking you home tonight."

"Another time, Marcus." She took a bite out of her hotdog, ignoring him.

"No, Cassandra. Tonight." He leaned into her until she could feel his breath on her neck, "As I told you at Mary's, I'm going to set things straight about..." his voice lowered, "...*us*."

Cassie gulped and stopped chewing. It was happening again. As soon as they were together, she weakened. *No,* she had to fight off her need for him, somehow take a step back, and think about this logically, and about what Rachel had told her.

Chapter Five

Marcus pulled out of Pete's driveway. He was claiming Cassie tonight, Pete's warning be damned. The old soldier would shoot his ass full of buckshot if he knew that Marcus was going to drive home, grab a flashlight, and walk to the cottage along the old footpath that connected his land to Pete's.

As he turned on the main road to his farm, Marcus wondered why Cassandra was so distant tonight. Okay, it was strained because he'd surprised her, and they were hiding their relationship from Pete. But it was so much more than that, because the bright light that shone out from her very essence—even from a photo—was out. And when he'd stepped back onto the patio after helping Pete move the fridge back into the house, she had been gone.

He'd become greedy about her. He wanted what she'd given him at the Horse—her laughter, her joy, her body, and a little bit of her heart. He could never reciprocate. He could give her his body—great sex, multiple orgasms, forbidden kink. But happiness? His heart? Impossible. He was a dark, empty man. For a moment he pictured what his life could be if he had her by his side. He couldn't have that, but he would take what he could, until it ended.

Pulling into the parking spot alongside his house, Marcus shut off the engine, took the flashlight from under his seat, and climbed out of his truck. He took off toward the path, then stopped.

Walking back to his truck, he opened the passenger side and carefully removed a large bouquet of pink and purple hyacinths. Dinner was a wash, but he was still going to romance her.

The smell of freshly turned earth filled his nostrils, as he walked on the narrow path. After his time in the desert and many years of city life, he appreciated the gift of the farm deeded to him, his younger brother Liam, and his cousin Sean when his uncle Brennan had retired. They were each given ten acres to build on, the remaining two hundred acres rented out to area farmers.

He waved the industrial flashlight from side to side to alert deer or other animals that he was coming their way. He didn't want to be crushed by a spooked 300-pound buck. The sun was just dropping below the horizon, turning the land into shadows. Overhead, he heard the squeaks and calls of bats.

Minutes later, Marcus saw the low stone wall that separated the farms and easily stepped over it. Something was brewing in the head of the lovely Ms. Bennett.

Tonight, he was going to find out what it was.

****

Walking quickly on the path to the cottage, Cassie kept looking back, afraid Marcus would follow. If he did, he would alert Pete that they were involved, and

Pete would blow. Looking back one more time, relieved there was no sign of him, she upped her pace. Ah, there was the soft glow of the porchlight. A beacon of safety in an evening that had left her nothing but confused. All she wanted to do was get home, lock up, and... what? That was the question, wasn't it: what did she want to do, and what should she do? Marcus was chasing her—it terrified and thrilled her, at the same time. If only life could be simple, again. Normal and familiar, like it had been in California—Ron alive, Eva and Abby still girls. A part of her wished that Riverbend were still in her rearview mirror. But there was no place else to go, now.

At the beginning of the walkway leading to the cottage, painted bluebird-egg blue with white trim, she stopped. Taking a deep breath, she took in the beauty that she and Shirl created years ago.

"Want to help me plant a night garden, love?" Shirl had asked, and they had. It was early spring, but beds of night-blooming flowers—Trillium, Flower Foam, and Evening Primrose that edged the walkway—were already covered with blossoms, lighting the way to the front door. With the sweet scent of Honeysuckle in the deepening twilight, nothing could have felt more like home.

Cassie walked into the house, her mind racing. Should she take the chance and be with him despite all the women that he'd humped and dumped? Rachel had told Cassie everything she knew, and though Rachel wasn't sure what was real and what was rumor, there was enough material overall to make the point moot. Could she enjoy this man sexually, then let him go? Unlikely. She was who she was—a woman who wanted a loving relationship.

She pictured how delicious he looked when he walked around the house—strong, roughly masculine, mesmerizing. *I want to be with him skin to skin, if only for a little while.* She went around the house turning on lights, sure in the knowledge that Marcus was on his way. Her mouth curved into a smile. Their hunger for each other was a force of nature. And tonight, he'd emphasized the word, "us."

Could it mean what Cassie hoped? Was he changing for her? And if he were, would it last? Moving into the living room, she sat down on the soft, navy sofa, took her cat pillow, and held it against her chest. She wasn't that young, hurt girl anymore, whose wishes were rarely granted by her parents. She could take charge and grab life. *I want Marcus as a lover. The rest, well...*

Cassie looked out the window at complete darkness. It was Riverbend, not L.A., and tonight when the new moon rose, she would clearly see that sliver of light.

The new moon meant new beginnings. Riverbend was part of her past, but now it was her future. Could she give Marcus her body, but protect her heart? *But what about all those women?*

She jumped at the soft knock.

"Cassandra, open up."

****

Holding the bouquet in one hand, Marcus waited. Nothing. He knocked again.

"Cassandra?" Was she going to lock him out? If she were, he'd take bold measures and pick the lock, a skill he'd learned while fifteen and still on the road to hell.

Finally, he heard, "I'm coming."

When the door opened, she stole his breath as the light in the room cast a bright aura around her.

He couldn't get a read on her mood, but he took in her lovely face, zeroing in on those lush, enticing lips that he wanted to consume, so he never forgot her taste. Then her expression turned wary, and right before she averted her eyes, he caught a deep sadness in them. *Why?*

"Marcus."

Cassie's soft voice brought him back. He smiled down at her and held out the bouquet. "These are for you."

She hesitated, and he wondered: if it weren't for the flowers, would she ask him to leave?

"They're lovely, Marcus. Thank you." She stepped aside, "Please, come in." Taking the flowers, she pressed her nose into the bouquet as he entered. They stood looking at each other, the tension thick. Awkwardly, she pointed to the kitchen, "I'll just put these in water."

He checked her out as he followed her. Her ass looked unfairly perfect. But as much as he desired her, he also wanted her to be happy. And he was sure that sex was the mood lifter for the occasion. He leaned against the archway leading to the kitchen, enjoying the way she moved. His mouth watered when she stretched and took down a vase. The tank top she wore rode up, the waist of her jeans pulled down, showing two dimples on her lower back. *Oh, yeah.*

Putting the vase down on the counter, Cassie turned her head to him, "Would you like coffee?"

Marcus smothered a laugh. He'd be having his

coffee with breakfast. "No coffee, thanks. Can I help you with that?"

"No, thanks," her voice was tight. She filled the vase with water and began to carefully place each flower in it. "Marcus," she said while working, "the flowers are lovely, thank you, but—"

Marcus snaked an arm around her waist and pulled her back into his front. He nuzzled her neck, drowning in her heady scent of coconut and feminine essence. She tensed and held on to his arm with both of her hands. Brushing her neck with his lips, he sucked on her earlobe, relishing her gasp.

He licked and sucked on the skin right below her ear, and she mewled, her body softening against him.

Yeah. All he had to do was keep kissing her and then move into playing with her body. Stoking her sexual heat until it ignited. Later, when she was soft and docile from two or three orgasms, then they would talk about what was bothering her and their relationship. And they had one, whether she wanted to admit it or not.

"Marcus, let's—"

"Shh, Cassie."

It took a will of iron not to immediately fuck her up against the door. He was strong enough to easily rip the button and zipper of her jeans wide open in one smooth motion—it was one of his favorite tricks. But that was for one-night stands. For throwaways. Instead, he steeled himself, turned her, and gently stroked her arms. Her hands went to his hips, and he wasn't sure if she was going to push him away or pull him closer.

Her gaze said it all. It was one of pure longing, taunting the predator in him to claim her hard and fast.

But instinct told Marcus that a few moments of caring tenderness would win this battle. His heart pounded in his chest when he asked, "Can I have you tonight, Cassandra? Earlier I made a promise to you, and I always keep my promises—to bury my face between your thighs and stay for a long while."

Her earlier wariness was gone, replaced by a determined carnal smile that made his dick jerk. He held his breath when Cassie stood on tiptoe and flicked the tip of her tongue over his lips. "Only if I get to devour that cock of yours until you scream my name."

She shrieked with delight when he picked her up in a bride carry, headed into the bedroom, and set her down on her feet at the foot of the bed.

****

"I'm crazy about you," he murmured, brushing her lips softly, though she'd felt their hard demand at the Overlook. Who knew he had this kind of softness in him? She desperately wanted to believe that she meant to him what he was beginning to mean to her—that it wasn't just the chase that excited him. And she pushed thoughts about other women out of her mind—he pursued her.

She put her hands on his waist. He straightened, stilled, gazing at her, heat building into those determined, dark-blue eyes. His erection, hard as granite, pressed into her stomach, but he wasn't grinding into her. He just held her, sharing what Cassie felt was a hot moment, but an intimate one, too. He'd surprised her because she thought by now, he'd have her up against the door, pounding into her.

What she wanted from him was hard, raw sex, so when they ended, she could handle the pain of losing him. His sweetness derailed her, made her fall even deeper for him.

"Hey, where'd you go?" Marcus asked, softly. She smiled shyly at him as he ran his hands up and down her arms. He bent, kissed her neck, "I love your smell..." he ran the tip of his tongue over the shell of her ear, "...and your taste. That coconut lotion you wear makes me crazy. Someday, I'll spread chocolate syrup over you..." he brushed his lips down her neck, licking and nipping "...and make you my favorite candy bar—sweet and exotic."

"Mmm, that sounds so good."

"I'm hungry for sweets right now, Cassie." His words were an instant turn on. *Live in the now,* Cassie reminded herself. And now, she wanted sex. She wrapped her arms around Marcus's neck and kissed him, hard. His body stiffened for a moment, but she continued working his mouth, seductively licking across his lips, reveling in the rush of his increasing arousal. When she nipped his bottom lip, he took over. Sweeping one hand into her hair, he ran the other down to her ass and pulled her into him.

"Cassie," he murmured, when she ran a hand down his stomach, those hard abs contracting at her touch. Without stopping, she headed south, touched his cock—*my god, he's big*—and began to rub up and down over the denim.

Marcus pulled his mouth from hers, shouted, "Shit!" and ground into her hand.

His entire body tensed and vibrated as if it were a viper poised to strike. He ravaged her mouth, thrusting his tongue in and out, letting her know what he wanted. What she craved. She took his kiss and continued working his cock. He pulled her even tighter, their hips grinding together.

"Stop," he pulled her hand away, took both her hands and wrapped them around his neck. "I'm gonna blow in my pants in another second. Right now, I'm gonna play with you. Shirt and bra off, Cassandra," adding in a low, menacing tone, "now."

At his command, she panicked for a moment. *My breasts sag, I have stretch marks... but Marcus wants me. And dammit, I want this.* Trying to pull out of his hold to undress, he stopped her with an abrupt, "No."

"Cassandra, stop thinking. Stop tensing up. I want you to stay right here, undress for me, and show me your beautiful body. I've been dreaming about it since the Horse."

Slowly, she pulled the tank up over her head and let it fall to the floor, revealing a lacy bra in nude. Her entire body burned, her breasts and clitoris aching, swelling in her clothes. She held back a sob at how much she missed being turned on as her body readied itself for sex. Marcus's voice was tight, "Leave the bra."

She could hear the thudding of her heart and was sure he could, too. Her head fell back when he ran his tongue over the swell of her breast. Back and forth he went, and when he took a nipple in his mouth over the silk and sucked, she lost her mind. Her hands dove under his shirt, exploring and caressing every dip and curve of his muscles.

"That's right, touch me, too."

He sucked one nipple, then the other, and her body responded, grinding into his erection.

He pulled a bra cup away and down and sucked hard. Cassie ran her hands through his hair and pulled him tight into her. Reaching behind her, Marcus smoothly removed her bra.

Cassie held her breath. Marcus put one hand on her waist and, with the other hand, slowly ran the tip of his pointer finger over her collarbone, then down in between her breasts. "You're so beautiful," he said reverently, watching his finger as he ran it around one areola, not touching the nipple. Cassie moaned and her head fell back as he did the same with the other breast. She grabbed his waist for support. Her legs shook.

"That's right, Cassie, hang on to me," said Marcus, his voice rough. Standing still with her breasts exposed while a fully clothed man played with her... none of her fantasizing had prepared her for this.

Marcus continued sucking and playing with her breasts, rubbing the scruff of his face over her sensitized nipples for what seemed like hours. Her arousal ran down her thighs until she was quivering and whimpering.

"Please, Marcus," she whimpered.

He turned hungry eyes on her. "Tell me what you want."

"Make me ache."

Chapter Six

They tore at one another's clothes, embraced, and fell onto the bed, kissing and stroking each other until they had to come up for air

"Spread your legs," commanded Marcus. When Cassie complied, his gaze turned dark and wild. Marcus pulled her down to the end of the bed by her ankles and dropped down between her thighs, spreading them wider with his broad shoulders.

Instead of his tongue, he ran his nose up and down her pussy, breathing in her scent. She placed her hands on his head, but he stopped, and ordered, "Hands above your head." When she did so, he gripped her buttocks, brought her closer to his masterful mouth, and devoured her.

"Oh! *Oh!*" she screamed, the intensity of the orgasm blinding her. He kept right on through the last jolts, then brought her down gently with licks and nuzzles, until she was soft and languid. As she lay in a swoon, he crawled up her body, trailing light kisses up her stomach and breasts. Neither Ron nor the handful of college guys she'd had sex with ever made oral sex their focus. They used it to get her ready for penetration. But Marcus... his skill, his pure *relish* in eating pussy was mind blowing.

He braced on his forearms, lowered himself onto her, ruthlessly kissing her, long and deep, her taste on his lips creating a low buzz of arousal in her body.

What she wanted with an urgency that frightened her was to feel that initial burn and stretch when his cock entered her for the first time. Because this moment wasn't just sex for her—it was filled with true intimacy, making the risk of her heart greater. There was real danger in this.

He broke the kiss, licking down her neck to the juncture of her shoulder and neck, sending her desire spiraling. "Please Marcus, fill me." She wrapped her arms around his shoulders, spread her legs, and he settled between them. The tip of his cock was at her entrance when his phone rang.

"Shit," he growled, but then it stopped. Almost immediately, it began to ring again.

Her arms tightened, "Don't answer, please."

"Cass, I'm sorry, I have to take it, we're having trouble on jobs." He reached out to grab his cell that he'd placed on the night table, not realizing he'd hit 'speaker' when he bobbled it, and it fell to the floor.

The shocking, seductive female voice that filled the room paralyzed them both. *Hey, babe, it's Ashley. I'm back in town for a bit and hungry for your big cock.*

"Fuck!" Marcus shouted, and scrambled off Cassie, frantically searching for the phone, but not before they heard, *Call me, stud.*

Every organ in Cassie's body shut down. Was this how death felt? Shouldn't she be wracked with intense heartache, instead of this... nothingness? Dazed, she laid on the bed immobile, until Marcus stood, the phone in his hand. Shame and guilt washed over his face. He shook his head from side to side, "Cassie, I'm so sorry, babe, I..."

"Babe" spurred her into action. She clambered off the bed, covering herself as best she could with her hands, bent, and began searching for her clothes. "Cassie, please, let's talk..."

"You have to leave, Marcus. Now." Her sobs were just below the surface. She had to control herself, not allow him to see her devastation, because the pain was as deathly sharp as the edge of a knife.

She watched his jaw tense, then she turned from him, found her clothes and dressed. Silently, he dressed, too. She was slipping on her shoes when his hand circled her waist to stop her. "Please," he buried his face in her hair, "I haven't seen her in almost a year. She's nothing to me. I'm not playing games with you."

She wanted to cave, to believe him. Have him hold her. Make love to her. *No*, she reminded herself, *Marcus didn't make love*. He fucked, and then he disappeared. Her mind raced with memories of the Horse, the woman who tried to stop him. Of Maddy calling him a player. Rachel's words that had hit her only hours ago pounded in her head.

He's been back for four years, and he's been a busy man. He's one night only, but he's brutally honest about it, or so Sherry who works at the WaWa told me. If they want more, and pursue him, he doesn't answer their texts or calls until they stop.

But before Rachel left, she pointedly stated, *He's never pursued a woman. He's different with you.*

She pulled out of his arms, trying not to think

about his texts, the song he sent her, the calls that she never answered, telling her that he missed her. But Marcus would never commit, and in the end, she'd be just another fuck. She had to protect herself and end it now. Unexpected anger surfaced, covering the pain of losing him.

"Listen to me, Cassandra, I want to be with you." He moved into her again and gently squeezed her waist.

She wrenched away from him. Remorse was carved into his face, but Cassie was already hurting too badly to care. "I believe you think that, but Marcus, you know that what we have isn't permanent. You do not commit. And that call..." she shook her head, "I'd like you to leave." She left the bedroom and walked to the front door.

He followed, and angrily crossed his arms over his chest. "You think I'm lying, don't you, about wanting to be with you."

"You want to have sex tonight. But... I've been told that you've been with a lot of women." Unbidden, the words shot out of her mouth. She took hold of the doorknob to steady herself from trembling.

He tensed. "Yes, I've been with many women. In the *past,*" he emphasized the last word.

"Many women in Riverbend?"

His jaw clenched, and he put his hands in his pockets, as if to contain himself. Unapologetically, he said, "Yes, Cassandra, I've slept with a few women in Riverbend. Most I met in Eastbridge and the surrounding area. I'm a single, forty-three-year-old man who likes sex. And you're being rather judgmental." He took his hands out of his pockets and stepped toward her. "We both have a past. You were married for many years. What's your problem?"

Cassie gritted her teeth and looked him right in the eye, "I was told that *all* of your women," she looked toward the phone, "like you claim *she* is, are meaningless, and that you eventually dump them."

He was surprised and looked lost for a moment. "I've never treated you like that."

"Not yet, you haven't."

Marcus moved toward her until they were toe to toe. "Asking around about me?"

She was digging herself into a bad place, but couldn't stop, "I have to protect myself."

He recoiled, like she'd struck him. Then he moved fast. He reached for her, pulling her close, holding her by her biceps. She put her hands up defensively as she fell into him.

With her hands on his chest, one of his around her waist, and the other in her hair, holding her head just where he wanted, Marcus lowered his voice. "You're not going to give me a chance no matter what I do or say. Are you?"

She stared at him, rigid with pain and anger. She was judging him harshly. But that phone call had destroyed her because she was falling for him, and when he threw her away, she feared she would break. He broke hearts all the time. And the deeper she was into him, the more she'd be waiting and worrying for the moment when she felt him changing, distancing himself, before he ditched her.

His face flushed, his lips pressed tightly together. Steeling herself, because her next question was going to end what they had barely begun, she lifted her chin.

"How do you dump a woman who you've had sex with? Do you stop taking her texts and calls until she fades away, or do it quick, after you've fucked her?" She read the shock on his face, but she couldn't stop and pulled the trigger one more time.

"How were you planning to dump me when you'd had enough of me? Or is it something you decide in the moment?"

Marcus's shock morphed into raw anger. His handsome face contorted. Glaring at her, Marcus let her go and stepped away. "This is why I don't get involved. No dates. No getting to know each other. Better to find a willing woman who I don't care about and get off. I don't need this shit, and I don't deserve it."

Guilt and remorse flooded her. She'd done more than hurt him, she'd harmed him. What was she doing? She never acted this way, and he'd said he cared about her. She had to stop it. "Marcus, I..."

Between bared teeth Marcus spat, "Shut it. If I remember correctly, Cassandra, four weeks ago, the first night we met at the Horse when I was a complete stranger, you weren't thinking about how many women I'd fucked. You didn't care a thing about having a future with me." His eyes pierced hers like blades. "Remember what you wanted from *me*?" he shouted, and his body shook, "All you wanted was a quick fuck. You wanted a wild ride, right? Is that what this is all about? Finding someone to fuck you in the way he couldn't?"

She gasped, his words battering her, in the way that the storm had battered her flooded house. "No," was all she could whisper. She couldn't catch her breath, as if there was never going to be enough oxygen in the world to keep her alive.

Cruelly looking her up and down, he strode angrily to the front door, ripping it open. Turning to her a with a sneer, Marcus spat out, "What a fucking waste of my time," and slammed the door behind him.

****

Gasping for air, Marcus bent over, his hands clutching his knees. "Okay, breathe in, breathe out." He used the technique he'd been taught years ago by the shrinks at the VA hospital on how to handle recurring nightmares. Hopefully, it would work on this nightmare, too.

"What did I do?" he wheezed. After a few more breaths, he gained control. When he straightened up, guilt punched him in the gut. Marcus looked back at the cottage door. He wanted to beg Cassie for forgiveness, but his anger was simmering at the edge of his mind, and she wouldn't want to see him now, anyway.

I ripped her to shreds. Cassie was facing major life changes, and he did have a crappy rep. Why should she believe he could stick? The image of her pale face swam before him. He shot those ugly words at her in the same way he'd laid down a line of fire from his M16. With his tainted DNA, was he any different than his sick fucking old man?

He had a life filled with regrets. But hurting Cassie tonight was one of the worst. He had to move, think, before he broke down her door and made things worse than they were. He found the flashlight that he'd left on the porch. Switching it on, he walked to the path leading back to his house. He glanced at the dark cottage, imagining her crying, her heart breaking. He knew she liked him. And he'd admitted to himself that he wanted a relationship with her, for as long as he could have her.

He'd text her later. Beg her to meet so he could try to explain why he'd screwed things up. He never apologized to women. But he'd grovel, even prostate himself, for Cassie. Marcus started down the path. He watched the sliver of the new moon rise in the sky and felt a small spark of hope. New moon, new beginnings.

He stopped. They had to talk tonight, or she'd completely close off to him. As he turned back to the cottage, his phone rang.

Chapter Seven

Three days later, Cassie rolled up her yoga mat, slipped on the thin, tight long-sleeved zipper top over her yoga tank, and followed Rachel out of *OM By The River,* Riverbend's new yoga studio. Mistakenly, she'd thought the stretch of muscles and intense concentration necessary for doing the poses would help her find balance after that terrible scene with Marcus.

It wasn't happening. Even during Savasana, the resting pose at the end of class, her thoughts raced. She'd replayed their fight over and over, like she'd been doing every day since he'd stormed out of the cottage.

Rachel stopped, "Wait a sec." Putting her purse on the bench in front of the studio she rifled through it, then held up a crumpled flier. "I forgot to give Aria the info about that Ashtanga yoga workshop in June. Be right back."

Cassie sat down. She looked at the thicket of trees and bushes along the river, bursting with new life on this beautiful spring day, but she couldn't appreciate her favorite season. Because fixed in her mind forever was Marcus's fury, firing those hideous words into her heart—*What a fucking waste of my time*—wrecking her.

The worst part was that he was on target. It stung

to admit the truth—that when they first met, she'd begged him for sex. She hadn't cared about anything. Not who he was or how he felt, just that intense need for him. The night at the Horse, she was blinded by wanting to run her hands and tongue over his gorgeous body, take his cock into her mouth, and satisfy her horny self. A need so acute it terrified her.

The memory made her cringe, but it was her own shame at how she'd acted toward him that had her tossing and turning at night. She'd badly judged him, asking him how he would break up with her before they'd even begun. They hadn't even dated, for God's sake. They'd only had a heavy make out session, and *him* going down on *her*—a scene that played over and over in her mind, like a porn flick.

She sighed deeply. She had no hold over him whatsoever, but she'd behaved like a spoiled teen crushing on a boy who she couldn't have. Now she faced another dilemma because Marcus had texted her twenty minutes after he'd left. She'd replied, but... she nibbled on her bottom lip and brought up his text for the hundredth time:

MMackenzie: *Cassie, please forgive me. There's no excuse for how horribly I acted, and I'm begging you to hear me out. I was heading back to you but got a call that one of my workers had an automobile accident. I'm on my way to the hospital now. I'll text soon.*

She'd been both relieved and regretful that he hadn't come back, and she'd paced all night before she replied:

CBennett: *I'm sorry about your worker, hope he's okay. I accept your apology, Marcus, thank you, and I apologize for my abysmal behavior, but I need space. I'll contact you when I'm ready to talk. Be well.*

Marcus hadn't responded, and she hadn't heard from him since. Maybe that was for the best.

She'd deal with her unlivable house first. Not what she couldn't have. Not who she couldn't have.

"Come on Cass, try to keep the calm vibes going for a while." She hadn't noticed Rachel come out of the studio.

Cassie shrugged her shoulders, "That's tough to do."

"Thinking about your house?"

Cassie nodded. *And the man driving me crazy.*

"Try not to worry, it will all work out."

Doesn't look that way at all.

"Let's get out of here," Rachel tipped her head, waiting.

Cassie looked at her friend. Rachel was as tall as Cassie, but without the curves. Slim as a reed with thick natural platinum-blonde hair that was ramrod straight falling almost to her waist, she was stunning. Big blue eyes and full lips on a narrow, heart-shaped face gave her cover girl looks. But it was her sweet and caring nature that radiated Rachel's real beauty.

Rachel was a ray of light that shone through the fog that seemed to follow Cassie these days. She smiled and raised her arms to have Rachel reach down and pull her up—she had her best friend back. Rachel was here to stay after escaping her abusive husband,

and now she was working as an auto mechanic in her father's repair shop.

As they walked to Rachel's truck, Cassie said, "I'm not sure about anything, the house or..."

"The man?"

"That too. I've been thinking that I made a mistake moving back. There are too many ghosts here. Maybe if—"

Rachel stopped. "The move is right," she said sharply. "You have Maddy, your nephews, your girls are close by, there's Pete, and you have me. People who love you."

"I know. I'm whining, that's all."

"Okay, sister. Enough of that. You have a flooded house and a hot man to worry about." At those words Cassie playfully smacked Rachel's shoulder.

"And I have a crazy ex that's keeping me up nights."

Taking Rachel's hand, Cassie said in a serious tone, "I'm so sorry about what you went through. Is Carl still threatening you?"

Rachel paled at the question, then forced a smile. "What did I just say about not talking about our worries? We're living near each other again, my son Jimmy is flying in from Austin next month for a week's visit, and we just finished a kick-ass yoga class. I don't want to talk about your house, Marcus, Carl, or anything negative. I need comfort food. You in, Cass?" Raising one perfectly formed light-brown eyebrow, she waited.

Grinning, Cassie hooked her arm in Rachel's, "Only if the comfort is in the form of Pete's cheeseburgers and shakes."

"What else? Let's leave my truck here and walk over."

Arm in arm, they walked giggling toward the 1950's diner, its sparkling chrome and red accents gleaming in the sunshine.

****

Marcus heard her laughter first, the full-throated sound that had mesmerized him at the Horse. Sitting at a booth in the far corner of the diner with Bret, Marcus craned his neck and watched Joe run out from behind the counter, shout, "Cassie, honey," and grab her in a bear hug.

Crazy luck. The fates were with him today. After his meeting with Bret, he'd planned to hunt her down. She'd accepted his apology, which unfortunately he'd had to text instead of talking to her. And her own returned apology surprised him, making her even more compelling. She'd also asked for space—she wasn't getting that. He'd repair the damage that he'd done to her, and they were moving on... together.

"Mac," Bret turned around, "Mmm, those are two tasty morsels—and we haven't had dessert yet."

Marcus shot back, "Do not call Cassandra a 'morsel.' It's... weird."

Bret whipped around and put his hands up in surrender, "Okay, okay. Anyway, I was really talking about blondie. A walking wet dream."

"Rachel's a doll, but not easy. You know that, don't you?" Marcus leaned across the table. "Are you going to do something about her, Hammond?"

"When did you become the poster boy for

honorable behavior toward women?" Bret returned, brusquely.

Since Cassandra came to town.

Marcus evaded the question, "Rachel's a good woman. And—she's had it rough."

"Yeah, she is, and she has." Bret crooked an eyebrow. "You have it bad, Mac, you're gone for Cassie."

He wasn't admitting to that as he peeked over and watched Karen leading them to his booth, both women still unaware that he and Bret were in the diner. One glance at Cassie, and the world disappeared. She wore skin-tight black workout pants that clung to every delectable curve, and a tight top. She'd pulled her thick hair into a high ponytail, the dampened loose ends framing her lovely face. She was breathtaking. Was there anything sexier than a sweaty woman after a workout? He smothered a groan, imagining licking every salty drop of sweat off of her.

Almost here. They were two booths away when he slid out of his seat. Cassie flinched and stopped. Rachel did too, but she smiled. He grinned back.

He overtly eyed Cassie's body. *Yeah, no bra* because her nipples hardened, poking through the material of the top. She blushed and crossed her arms over her chest, and his mouth twitched.

"Bret, look who I found."

Bret had been waiting for Marcus's cue, and stood and leaned against the booth. "Hey Rachel, Cassie." he said.

"Hey guys," Rachel answered.

Marcus smothered a smile when Cassie only nodded as Rachel slid into the booth on Bret's side, and Cassie on his, at his invitation to join them.

Putting a fist over his mouth as if he were coughing, Marcus whispered to Bret "Get Rachel out of the dinner, ASAP. I want to be alone with Red."

"My pleasure, boss. If you up my bonus," Bret grinned.

Marcus moved in close to Cassie until their bodies touched and he could catch a whiff of coconut—it wasn't enough. The need for her had spiraled into a deep ache, and not just in his dick. Selfishly, he wanted everything from her—sex, laughter, talk, and something he never cared about: he wanted her to think well of him. *Keep it light, Mackenzie.*

"This feels like deja vu, Cassandra," he stretched his arm out on the back of the seat and lightly ran a finger over her nape. She sat forward quickly and turned to him, her big brown and gold eyes scolding. He loved jousting with her.

She looked away, but not before her expression softened. Was that a sign that she might forgive him? Hope bloomed, he had a chance. The diner was neutral territory, a perfect place to work things out, as soon as Bret got Rachel out of the way.

Karen bustled over to put placemats and utensils in front of Cassie and Rachel. "Guys, are you done or want refills?" she asked Marcus and Bret.

"Another Coke, Karen, thanks," Bret handed her his glass.

"Thanks, water is fine." Marcus handed her his empty coffee mug.

"Be back in a sec to get your order, ladies," and she took off.

Cassie picked up the menu. Marcus watched her,

worried and unsure how to begin to fix things between them... then she took the lead.

****

Cassie studied the menu that she knew by heart, feeling the heat of the side of his body plastered to hers. She missed him with an ache. Cassie believed that he was as remorseful as she was. And despite his reputation, they'd experienced moments of beautiful intimacy, so maybe he did want more from her than a quick screw.

Forgive him and take the risk. Her gut was adamant.

Cassie turned to him, "Deja vu again? Yes, it does feel rather familiar."

His lips curled into that damn lazy smile, but she couldn't miss the relief on his face.

"Shall we begin at the beginning? Let's see, 'Hi Cassandra,'" Marcus playfully bumped his shoulder into hers.

Cassie laughed out loud, and every cell in her body eased. They were back. To what, who knew, but she'd take these precious moments with him.

It made her happy to see him relaxed and playful, eyes dancing with mischief. It was as if they'd hadn't fought. "Well hello, Marcus, and how are you?" she teased.

He chuckled, then lowered his voice, "I'm sorry that I didn't get in touch, but I was swamped with work after Tony's accident, and thankfully he only suffered minor injuries. After I finished with Bret, I was going to call you, but lucky me, here you are."

His mouth twitched with mirth, then he carefully brushed the back of his hand over her cheek. "You look mighty temping after a yoga workout. If we were alone, I'd lick every tempting drop of sweat off of you."

A wave of heat washed over her, and she closed her eyes. But they popped open when he unzipped her top and stroked the rim of her tight tank, just above her breasts. He pulled her closer to him, put his lips near her ear, "How have I been, Cassandra? Besides sorry," he placed soft kisses on the shell of her ear, then nipped her lobe, "hard. Horny. Impatient."

She fell into his molten gaze as he lifted one of her hands by the wrist, then placed the palm of his hand over the back of hers and guided her hand under the table over his erection. *Yes.* He was beautifully long and thick and rock hard, just for her.

"This is what you do to me. Every time." She was caught in his sexual web again, when he bent toward her lips, and her heart raced. She wanted to taste him, feel his tongue sliding along hers.

"Open your mouth," he mumbled.

"Jesus, Mac, are you serious?" Bret snapped, bringing both of them back to earth.

Cassie quickly pulled her hand away from Marcus's fly and they both sat up. She could feel the flush on her cheeks from both arousal and shame. All Marcus had to do was whisper dirty things in her ear, run a finger over her breasts, and she was groping him in the diner.

Flushed with embarrassment, she saw that Bret was smirking. Rachel was holding both hands in front of her face trying to hide that fact that she was cracking up with laughter. And—oh, no, Karen, was standing in front of the booth, paralyzed with shock, holding Bret's soda and Marcus's water.

Play it cool. "Oh, sorry, Karen, we didn't notice you. I had something in my eye, and Marcus was helping me." She ignored Rachel shaking with laughter and falling into Bret's chest, and Marcus's hand on his neck, looking down at the table, shoulders shaking.

"Thank you, Marcus," she looked at him sternly when he lifted his grinning face, "My eye feels much better now."

"Karen, it's just that Cassie, gets a little cock-eyed once in a while," Marcus choked out. At those words, Karen practically threw the drinks on the table and took off like the hounds of hell were on her heels.

"Marcus," Cassie sniped, punching his arm. He grabbed her hand and held it fast, still quaking with laughter.

"Really, Marcus? Was it that funny?" Cassie tried to pull her hand away from his grip, but he held fast and brought her fist to his mouth, giving it a kiss.

"Yeah, it was," he grinned from ear to ear.

"Priceless," Bret chimed in.

"Hilarious," Rachel agreed.

Pulling her hand from his, Cassie looked at Rachel, who looked mighty happy leaning against Bret, his arm draped around her shoulders, fingers toying with her hair.

"Guys," Bret broke into her thoughts, "Rach and I are going to change her order to take-out," his hand clasped Rachel's on the table, whose smile was a mile wide. "Mac, I'll call you tomorrow to coordinate plans for the Riverbend Picnic next Saturday."

Marcus chimed in, "There will be fundraisers going on all day for people who need relief from the flood, my admin is getting our contribution together."

"I saw the posters about the picnic up at Mary's. It's been years since I've been to one, it'll be fun," added Cassie

"Karen," Bret called out to her behind the counter. "We're going to need the Black and Blue, medium, with fries to go, right, baby?" he grinned at Rachel.

Baby? He called Rachel baby? They needed girl time, stat.

Rachel gathered her purse and yoga mat. "I'm taking Bret to my place. He wants to see the '67 Mustang Stallion dad are I working on." Rachel looked over at Bret as if he could part the Delaware like Moses, "And Bret is restoring a '68 Shelby convertible."

Bret pulled Rachel to him for a hug, "Who knew there was a grease monkey under the cover-girl looks?"

Bret slid out of the booth, taking his soda. Rachel followed, mouthing "I'm sorry" to Cassie through a smile. Cassie winked at her, "Have fun, guys."

Marcus turned to her, resting his knee on the edge of the seat, and she found herself backed into the corner. He placed a hand on the wall next to her head, the other holding her hand.

He'd boxed her in. His lip curled up at the corner as he gave her a covetous stare that simmered like banked coals.

She matched his gaze, and he bent his head until his lips kissed her ear. "I lose my fucking mind when I see you, and after you stroked my dick, it's hard as steel." He sucked on her lobe, "Are you wet for me?"

83

Chapter Eight

*W*et? Her panties were soaked with liquid heat. Every cell in her body had ignited with an alarming demand for his touch, his mouth, his smell, his cock—his power.

Pulling away from him, she watched his eyes morph from dark stormy blue to hard pitch black. "Marcus," she choked.

"Karen," he called out, their gazes still fastened on each other, "we need Cassie's burger to go. You'll eat it in the car, baby, because we're going to my place, and as soon as that door closes, I'll be on you." He kissed her lightly.

"Marcus, Cassie, what the hell?"

They broke apart as if they'd been hit with a taser. There was Joe standing at their booth, hands on his hips looking shocked and pissing mad.

Oh.

"Joe," Marcus had moved away from her, but kept his arm around her.

"You two making out in my diner? Cassie? You're with... *him*?" Joe's expression was filled with reproach.

It was Joe's expression that started a burn of anger inside of Cassie. *So we're together. And?* Cassie looked Joe straight in the eye and calmly and quietly stated, "Joe, you need to stop right now." She was going to take a chance and see if things worked out with Marcus—that's how much she wanted him. And no one, including Joe, was going to tell her that she couldn't. Joe was being ridiculous. *To put it kindly.* He'll tell Pete, but she pushed that worry away. "Marcus," she looked into his wary eyes, "let's go." His face lit with a beautiful smile. He moved out of the booth, helping her out while Joe stood watching them with a scowl. Marcus turned to Joe, "Go back into the kitchen and cool off." He threw money down on the table, took her hand, and they left.

****

Cassie stared silently out the window as they bumped along the drive to Marcus's house, barely taking in the beauty of his farm. They hadn't said much on the drive, and she needed the silence. They had to have a talk about their fight, but she desperately wanted to put that off, as did he, obviously. She just wanted to have her day with Marcus—she missed him terribly.

"By the time we get to my place, I'll have my anger at Joe under control." He broke into her thoughts, took her hand, and reassured her, "It will be okay, I'll make sure of it. And, just saying, the way you laid into Joe—impressive."

"I shocked myself, but his reaction was dead wrong." Pete would be angry about her seeing Marcus, but it wasn't his business.

"Cassandra, I know you're worried about Pete. And Joe *is* going to tattle on us."

She turned around. "Tattle?" Her mouth curved into a smile, "Are we back in grade school?"

Marcus pulled into a large circular drive that ran in front of a massive log cabin, the wood burnished to a warm golden shine. He parked and shut off the engine. She saw a barn set back yards from the house and a road on the left that led to a grove of trees.

"Cassie, you don't seem as upset, are you...?"

"I am, but what I want, Marcus, is to have our day. I want to push Joe and Pete out of our minds, and everything else, and I want to see your magnificent house," she pointed at it.

Marcus brightened, "I want that, too." He came around to her side of the truck and helped her down to the sound of barking. Taking her hand, he led her up the porch steps, decorated with pots overflowing with spring flowers. A wooden swing hung from the porch ceiling, and Adirondack chairs painted light blue and green were scattered around. A vision of she and Marcus on the swing, his arm around her shoulders, warmed her heart.

Letting go of her hand, Marcus unlocked the front door and said, "I hope you like dogs."

"I love dogs."

"Brace." He opened the door and three dogs shot out, barking, jumping, and wiggling around Marcus. Cassie stepped back and held onto the porch railing. A mixture of warm affection, searing desire for him, and something else—more powerful than either—swept through her as Marcus crouched down, saying, "Hey guys, I missed you, too."

All the dogs looked like they'd had rough lives. The rottweiler and one of the pit bulls had facial scars, and another pit bull only had three legs. Here was a kind, tender Marcus. Suddenly, Cassie's breath caught in her throat.

Oh my god. I love him.

****

Marcus laughed when Cassie knelt, patted her thigh, and clucked for the dogs. They whirled on her, knocking her on her butt, licking her face and arms as she giggled.

I knew she would like animals.

As each dog competed for the pets and rubs she gave them, she tried to split her attention: "Aren't you handsome," "You sweet thing," "I like you, too."

"Ok, you guys, get off the lady." Cassie roared with laughter as the three-legged dog dove into her lap, licking her chin and neck.

"Honeybun, you'll get more pets later." He gently took the dog by the collar, pulling her off Cassie. "Sit," he commanded in a deep voice. Immediately, three butts plopped down.

Sitting, her arms around her knees, Cassie said, "Impressive. But they look like they're jumping out of their skin."

"Yeah, they are, but they need to remember their manners. They'll stay put until I free them. Let me introduce you, though you've already met." Pointing to each dog in turn he said, "The rottie is Diesel, the male pit bull is Trouble, and here's my three-legged girl pittie, Honeybun."

"Oh Marcus, they're amazing, but they've had a hard life, haven't they?" Her eyes glistened.

She's a softie. "Yeah. They've each had a brutal past. But they're mine now."

His breath caught when she whispered, "Lucky them."

She was so lovely that it hurt to look at her. With her big smile, mussed up hair, and paw prints on her pants—he'd never seen beauty like hers. And he'd never wanted another woman in the way he wanted Cassie. Not for just a quick lay. She was getting under his skin. But how would she react, when she learned about his history? He was his father's son, after all. Marcus had killed for his country, his father had killed because he was a raging maniac. Still, killing ran in his blood. As did the temper that he'd inherited from both his fucked-up parents.

Marcus sighed. *Live in the moment.* That was the way to manage. Today, being with Cassie had to be enough.

"Marcus? Are you okay?"

His obvious distraction had wiped the joy off of her face. It bothered him that he'd done that to her.

Forcing a smile, he lied, "Just thought I might have forgotten to take care of something today. No problem."

Cassie beamed when he held his hand out to her to help her up. She took his hand, and he pulled her into his arms. Holding her tight against him, he felt her soft body melt into his, and he buried his face into her neck, inhaling her intoxicating scent. He nibbled and kissed her behind her ear, then down her neck. She whimpered and caressed the back of his head.

He'd been hard since he spied her at the diner. All he wanted right now was to pull her into the house, push her against the front door, pull down those skin-tight yoga pants, wrap her legs around his waist, and bury himself into her tight, wet heat—what he'd wanted for what seemed like forever.

He held her hips, keeping her in place, and brushed her lips with his, then ran his tongue over her bottom lip and nipped it lightly.

"Marcus," she breathed, and opened her mouth to him. He ran the tip of his tongue over her top teeth, and rolled his hips into hers. She made a noise in her throat, and he brought one hand to her face, cupping her jaw and deepening the kiss. He was losing himself in her, again.

A sharp bark ended the kiss. Turning his head he saw that Diesel was tired of waiting. Crap. One taste of her, and he'd forgotten where he was. Resting his forehead against hers, he sighed. Her throaty laugh made him sharply aware of his aching cock. *You have to wait, you fucker... as I do.*

Pulling away, he took Cassie's hand, said, "Good job, guys," as the dogs wiggled, waiting for his command. "Free." Barking, they shot off the porch. When he draped an arm around her shoulders, she leaned against him and caressed his arm. He liked how naturally affectionate she was.

Together, they watched the dogs smell, pee, and romp, and he wondered if he could have this natural domestic scene in his life.

A sense of sweet contentment stole over him, something he'd never experienced with a woman.

He'd never invited a woman into his home. He always went to their place, and promptly left after they'd finished—just a lonely parade of empty pussy, year after year. The thought depressed him.

89

"They're amazing, Marcus. You've shown them that love is possible."

With an adoring gaze, she brought him out of his thoughts. *Love?* He never said that word. But he supposed she was right. He loved his dogs. But it was different with animals. They needed him and would never deceive him. People, on the other hand...

He felt himself tense when she raised her hand to his face. *Shit.* He stilled, waiting, as she tenderly cupped his jaw, running a finger gently over the scruff, raised onto her toes, and softly brushed her lips over his. "You're amazing, too."

Whoa. A stab of pain pierced him inside, in a place that he never wanted to uncover.

He was momentarily frightened. His steely control was crumbling. He was under her spell, right now, and he was lost. He had no idea how to manage this, what to do or say in this moment.

Suddenly, the dogs burst onto the porch. Cassie pulled away and reached down to pet them. He let out his breath and took her hand. "Let me show you the house and make us some lunch, since we left your burger behind when we fled the diner."

"I'd like that."

He led the dogs down the porch and opened a gate on the side of the house, ordering the dogs inside. "This leads to a fenced-off part of the yard, so they can get out of our hair and be safe." Taking the steps two at a time, he opened the front door, holding it for her to precede him. As she passed into the house, he sensed that he'd dodged a landmine a moment ago. But this time, instead of relief, he felt a loss.

****

Cassie wiped down the kitchen counter after lunch, while Marcus started the dishwasher.

Before they'd eaten, he'd given her the tour. The house took her breath away. One incredible room flowed into another on the first floor. The kitchen was large, a dream for someone like herself who loved to cook—granite counters, white subway-tile backsplashes, oak cabinets, and hardwood flooring created warmth and old-world charm. High-end stainless-steel appliances made her envious. When she ran her hand over the professional stove, Marcus asked, "Do you like to cook?"

"I do," she nodded. "In fact, I think I'm in love," she caressed the stove.

"Looking forward to your cooking," he grinned at her, then explained how he took a log house kit and customized it for himself. The cozy breakfast nook overlooked a back patio. There was a dining room and a great room, each with fireplaces and vaulted ceilings.

The great room was part media room, part library, with two huge walls covered in bookshelves.

She walked over to them and noticed that one section was devoted to poetry, something that was dear to her heart, too, she told him.

He stood with her, pulled the ponytail holder out of her hair, and brushed through the waves with his fingers, thrilling her as he opened up a little about his past.

"By ten years old, I was running away from home and found the Eastbridge Public Library. The librarian kept giving me books to read, and I began to go there to dive into other worlds, other lives, anything to get away from my house. One day she gave me a book of poetry. I read Frost's 'The Road Not Taken.' I was hooked.

She desperately wanted to know more, but after he spoke, he tensed, said, "On with the tour," and took her upstairs. His office, three guest bedrooms, three baths, the master with a sauna, were surrounded by a balcony that overlooked the first floor living space. The furnishings were all luxurious exotic woods, soft leather, and natural fabrics, perfect for this stunning house of burnished logs. But it somehow felt sadly empty, all this space for one man. She much preferred her simple cottage.

Cassie spotted the old black-and-white photo as they walked back to the kitchen for lunch. It sat prominently on a side table surrounded by other photos of a young man, who must be his son, Aiden.

But it was that one old photo that intrigued her. She picked it up and gasped. *Oh my god, this is Pete, at least twenty years younger when this was taken, standing in front of the farmhouse with his arm around a boy I've never seen. And there's their old, sweet beagle, Boomer, lying at their feet.*

But what piqued her curiosity was that the boy wasn't looking at the camera—instead he was gazing up at Pete, as if he'd found heaven.

She looked closer at it, "Oh, it's..."

"Yes, that's me. A few weeks after I met Pete. I was sixteen."

Puzzled, she looked at him. "He never mentioned you to me."

"I'm not surprised." Marcus took the photo from

her and placed it back on the table. "It's a long story, and I'll tell it to you. But not today. Okay?" His voice turned husky.

She was dying to know the story, a piece of the puzzle about Pete and Marcus's relationship, but his emotions were high, so she gave him what he needed—time. "Whenever you want to tell me, I'm here."

Taking her in his arms, he kissed the tip of her nose. "Cassie, you're..." she waited, not daring to breathe, but a lightness infused every cell in her body. He was on the verge of saying something big, something monumental, for the both of them.

But he veered into safety, saying, "Let's get you fed, because you'll need your energy for what I have planned." She was a little disappointed. She knew how difficult this was for him, but she was more hopeful than ever that they were slowly moving into a loving relationship.

Now it was after lunch. Cassie placed the sponge on the side of the sink and spread the dishcloth over the drainer, her heart pounding because conversation had stopped a few minutes ago.

Her back was to him, but Cassie felt his intense gaze. The air was heavy with sexual tension. She turned.

Leaning against a stool, Marcus sipped iced tea from a glass, watching her over the rim. She gulped, as he put the glass down on the counter and prowled toward her. Grasping her upper arms, he pulled her into his body, cupped her jaw, and slammed his mouth down over hers.

Chapter Nine

Cassie wrapped her arms around his neck, his wicked tongue enticing hers into a decadent dance. One rough hand held her head for a deep kiss, the other swept down and caressed her ass. She jerked when he skimmed a finger down the line of her ass and muttered into her mouth, "I like ass play, Cassie. I hope you do, too," as he stroked up the cleft. She shuddered at his next words, as a secret, dark and dirty fantasy of hers filled her mind. "I want to rim your pretty hole with my finger, fuck it with my tongue, and, someday, bury my cock deep into that forbidden place and watch as you discover that you love it."

She gasped, "Yes."

"But first," he plundered her mouth, thrusting his tongue in and out, imitating sex, rendering her breathless. She moaned deeply, so close to shattering, when he pulled her into his body tighter, bent his knees, and ground his erection into her clit.

"Take me," she panted out the words. Arching into him, Cassie ground her hips into him. She ran her hands under his shirt, stroking smooth skin over tight muscles. Scoring him lightly with her nails, she ran her fingers up into his soft, thick hair and pulled.

"Fuck," and he was off the leash. She held on

94

while he roughly explored her mouth, greedily fondling her breasts, tweaking her nipples until they ached. He ran his hand all the way down her back, squeezing and stroking her butt. Arousal ran down her thighs when he cupped her vagina, pressing the heel of his hand onto her mound, circling it.

Sex had never been this fierce. This primal. Only with Marcus. She writhed against him. He lowered his head, sucking a nipple into his hot mouth over the fabric.

"Oh, oh," she panted, bowing her body into his. She shrieked when he pulled back, picked her up and sat her on the granite counter. His eyes were dark, ravenous. Spreading her knees, he made a place for himself, and ordered, "Top off."

Her arms raised, he yanked it off and threw it on the floor. "God, you're lovely." She arched into him when he gently but firmly took a nipple between his teeth until the exact moment before the pain became too much, then switched to her other breast. Back and forth he went, tightening the pink tips into hard sharp points.

Overwhelmed with need, her pussy softened, readying itself for his cock. "I need you inside of me, Marcus. Now." She bucked her hips into his erection. He rolled his hips into hers, his eyes lidded, dark. Then his lips tipped up. "Bossy much?"

"*Please*, Marcus."

"Oh, I'm gonna fuck you, Cassandra, but since we're in the kitchen..." his expression turned fierce, determined, "I need another taste of you."

Yes.

He laid her down on the counter, "Lift your hips." He tore off her pants, taking her flats along with them, and tossed everything aside. Leaving on her thong, he spread her thighs apart, staring at the patch of silk covering her pussy.

All of a sudden, she felt vulnerable. *I'm pretty much naked, and Marcus is fully dressed, again.*

Instinctively she tried to close her legs.

"Don't you hide from me," he warned, and spread her legs wider. "You know the expression, 'Eat with your eyes first?' Well..."

He let go of one of her legs. "Keep them spread." The order came as he began to play with the strip of pubic hair peeking out of the top of the thong, left after her waxing. "I like this," he mumbled, lowered his head, and nuzzled the hair with his nose. When his hot breath blew on her clit over the silk, she whimpered, and put her hands on his head.

"Uh-uh." He glanced at her, "Hands above your head." He raised an eyebrow when she hesitated, and his demand shot her craving for him into shameless need. She raised her hands over her head and heard, "Keep them there."

Then Marcus descended, maintaining eye contact until the last possible second.

He blew her mind when he held her thighs open and touched his nose to that damp triangle of silk, pushing against her clitoris. Pleasure shot through her body. Taking a deep breath, he murmured, "mmm," and ran his nose over the silk, pushing it into her opening.

Cassie bucked her hips into his face when he tongued her clit, the silk causing a delicious friction as he sucked and licked on the increasingly wet fabric. She panted. *Almost there.*

Then Marcus tore her panties off, pulled her hips

forward until they were hanging over the counter, spread her legs even wider, bent her knees, pushed them toward her head, and held her there. Cassie squealed and almost flew off the counter when he ran his nose from her clit down the length of her pussy, and then went further. She couldn't believe what she was feeling—he was rimming her asshole with his hot tongue, again and again.

It was dirty and wicked, and so taboo—she moaned and writhed in his hold. He licked back to her pussy, licking the slit with the flat of his tongue, and sucked on her swollen lips. A light sweep of his tongue over her clit had her chanting, "Oh, oh, oh."

So close. Lick. A flutter with his tongue over her clit. Another lick. A flutter. She was losing all sense of time and place. There was only Marcus and his clever tongue. Gently inserting a thick, callused finger into her vagina, as if he knew she hadn't had sex in a while, she felt the delectable stretch she'd been dreaming about for months now.

"You're so tight." Carefully he added a second finger, slowly fucking her as he took her clit into his mouth and sucked. He paused, lightly rimmed her anus with his pinky, and oh-so-gently pushed inside her. She clenched her cheeks. "No, no." Breaching that tight ring of muscle with this finger, there was a slight burn, and nerves that had never been explored were shocked to life.

She was at the very edge when he pushed to the first knuckle of his finger. She shattered—drowning in sensation, screaming, twisting, and thrashing as Marcus held her down hard, eating and fingering her, to completion.

Removing his fingers, he gave her pussy another

lick, making her jerk, leaving her depleted and limp. Moving up her body, he took her face in one hand and kissed her deeply. Tasting herself on his lips, she pulled back and looked into his blazing blue eyes.

"Marcus," she mumbled, "you put your finger up my ass."

"I did, and you screamed so loud, my ears are still ringing."

"It's dirty."

"And you're my dirty girl. Wait until my cock breaches your ass. I'll make sure you're ready, and you'll never want me to leave."

"I don't know about that, you're a lot bigger than your finger."

"I am, but I'll prepare you. But not now. Just lie here, because after I clean up, we're on to round two." He washed at the sink, then wet a dishtowel, spread her legs, embarrassing her as he cleaned between them.

"I can do that," she began to sit up.

He held her down, "No, let me take care of you." He tossed the towel across the kitchen into the sink and pulled her into a sitting position. She put her arms on his shoulders, and he bent his head and ran his tongue down to her breasts, flicking her nipples. "Christ, I could suck on these all day."

Five seconds after a mind-blowing orgasm, he's playing with her nipples, and she's hot all over again. But now she wanted to give back to him, blow his mind like he'd blown hers.

Grabbing his cock over his jeans, Cassandra squeezed and ran her fingers up and down his hard length. "That's right Cassandra, touch me, stroke me," he groaned and kissed her hard.

She stroked him harder, and he pulled away, "No baby, I'm ready to shoot my load any second, let's go upstairs."

No, that wasn't what she wanted. She wanted raw sex, and she didn't care one damn bit that he was all alpha. She was taking control, now.

"No. I want you to fuck me right here, Marcus. Take me now, on the counter," she ordered.

His eyes blazed, and his lips curved into a feral smile. "You want it here? You sure?"

She nodded.

"My girl really *is* dirty," he grinned devilishly.

"Yes," she hissed, reached out, and pulled down his zipper. Quickly, he shucked off his shoes, pulled his jeans and boxers off, and kicked them away.

Cassie took in Marcus's powerful, well-defined body, won through hard, physical work. She hid her shock when she saw several scars on his chest, she thought likely from his time in the army, but nothing could diminish his rough beauty.

And then there was his cock. Long and thick. And hard. The plum-shaped head almost reached his belly button. Gorgeous. When she ran her hands up and down the hard velvet, his head fell back in a groan.

She imagined the pleasure as he entered her—and maybe pain, because she hadn't had sex for a long time. She wanted the thrill of feeling him inside of her as they connected in the most intimate way for the first time. "Hurry, shirt off, I need to touch you," she panted the words as he took her hand away from his cock and ripped off his shirt. "Stop, or I'll be spewing on your tits."

"Almost forgot." Marcus grabbed his wallet out of his jeans, pulled out a condom, ripped it open with his teeth, and suited up. He took her lips in a hard kiss, then lay her down on the counter, and brought her hips to the end. "Spread."

She did, waiting for that first sweet burn. Guiding himself to her entrance, he bent over her, rested one forearm near her head, and slowly pushed in, gently rocking back and forth, "You're so tight, but your pussy is so wet for me. Beautiful."

"Marcus, come in." She pulled him tight into her body, her hands caressing his back.

He was big, and the stretch burned. But he was being gentle, controlling himself, stopping, waiting for her to adjust to his size. Tears welled at having a man inside of her, after years of emptiness. Finally, he filled her, his balls hitting her ass. Taking her face in his hands, he uttered, "You're breathtaking."

Her hands were on his back, and she pulled him into her body, tighter. Their closeness, overwhelmed her. He noticed, kissed the tip of her nose and said, "You're so damn sweet."

Suddenly, she was frightened because just looking at her, he had to know that she was falling in love with him. She hid it from him, fearing he would bolt if he knew. Raw and dirty, that they could have with each other, so she ordered, "What are you waiting for? Fuck me, like you promised."

He responded with a wicked grin, creating a heat wave in her belly. "Whatever the lady wants." He groaned, placed his forearms on either side of her head, pulled out almost all the way, and drove back in.

"Yes." Wrapping her arms around his back and her legs around his hips, Cassie met his thrust with her own.

"Cassie," his voice strained, "you're so tight."

"More," Cassie bucked her hips. "Harder," she demanded.

"My bossy girl gets what she wants," he teased. Marcus kissed her hard and unleashed himself. It thrilled Cassie to feel the power in his legs as the slap, slap, slap of their feverish thrusts added to her moans and his grunts as he wrapped his arms around her and deepened the kiss. He shortened his thrusts, powering into her and *yes* hit a spot that had her erupting in a short, intense orgasm. He tightened, groaned his release, and buried his face in her hair. Her arms and legs were still around him. She hugged him tight and let her legs relax onto the counter.

Picking up his head, he studied her carefully, his affection unmistakable. He held himself up on his forearms, and stroked her cheeks with his thumbs. Tentatively, he began, "Cassandra, I want to—"

Bang. Bang. Bang. They gasped in shock as the pounding on the front door destroyed one of the most exquisitely intimate moments of Cassie's life.

"Mackenzie, open the fucking door." The bellowing revved up the dogs in the backyard, who began barking furiously.

"Oh, no," Cassie hissed.

"Fuck," Marcus looked down at Cassie with fury in his eyes, "Pete."

****

"Wait a damn minute," Marcus shouted at the door, making her jump.

"Pete..." He looked down to see Cassie's lower lip quivering.

Pete was scaring her. Marcus felt adrenaline course through his body, spiking his heart rate, as if he was facing a firefight—in a way he was. *Don't lose it.* Her heart pounded against his chest as he carefully pulled out of her.

"Yeah, Pete," he echoed angrily, pushing off of the counter. Cassie quickly closed her legs and sat up, covering herself, one arm over her breasts, the other over her core. In an instant, she'd changed from the adventurous woman who'd opened her body and heart to him into feeling exposed, vulnerable, and embarrassed.

He could kill Pete.

"Oh, god," she hid her face in her hands.

He wanted to hold and comfort her but couldn't, because to control the dangerous rage that was threatening to engulf him—even Cassie, if he wasn't careful—he had to become ice.

He picked up her clothes, handed them to her, and barked, "Get dressed." Guilt washed over him when her face paled. She grabbed her clothes and jumped down from the counter. He grabbed a paper towel, disposed of the condom, and dressed quickly.

She turned from him, pulling on clothes as fast as she could, all intimacy gone.

Curb your shit, asshole. She needs you. Taking a deep breath, he gentled his voice, "Cassandra."

She looked up. Worry strained her face, "Guess he heard about us at the diner."

"Cassie, I'm sorry that I snapped. It'll be okay."

She shrugged and finished getting dressed.

Being inside of her tight, wet pussy, clenching his cock like a hot fist, was incomparable to any sex he'd ever had. He'd been about to come so hard it might have broken a few blood vessels in his brain. But it'd been much more than getting off, because he cared about her, and for the first time in his adult life, he wanted to protect a woman. He was about to tell her that when...

Bang. Bang. Bang. "Mackenzie, open this fucking door, or I'll break it down."

Marcus shouted, "Stop banging on the door and wait a goddamn minute."

Cassie squeezed her eyes shut.

Pete must know she's here. Is he out of his mind?

She was unusually quiet. That unnerved him, and his anger at Pete sizzled like hot grease in a frying pan. He went to her, wrapped his arms around her, and was relieved when she held him around his waist and rested her head on his chest.

"I'll take care of this. Promise." He would, even if he lost Pete's friendship.

She nodded, pulled out of his arms, and stared out of the wall of windows, with a strange expression on her face.

"I mean it, Cassie."

She didn't answer, but looked at him, studying him as if they weren't in a crisis situation. She muttered, "So be it." A minute ago she was freaked. *Now, she's weirdly cool, and we're up against a man who's like a father to her.*

Bang. Bang. Bang. She called out, "Pete, you either wait, or go home!"

Whoa. He took in her flushed skin, stiff posture—she looked pissed. He had to calm himself down and help her instead of doing what he wanted to do—throw

103

open the door and beat Pete, a man whom he loved like a father, to a bloody pulp.

"Cassandra, grab your stuff and go upstairs. This is going to get ugly. I'll take care of Pete."

"Not alone, you won't."

His head whipped around. She gathered her hair in both hands, smoothing it back and securing it in a ponytail. Her eyes blazed. "Open the door."

He couldn't keep up with her mood swings, but he wanted her out of the line of fire. "Cassie, do as I say."

Her brows snapped together. Walking right up to him, she rose on her toes, "I was momentarily shocked, but do not treat me like a child, the way Pete is. I'm a grown woman."

"Yeah," his mouth twitched, "You are."

Flinging out her arm, she pointed, "Open the door, Marcus. Now."

Ready for anything, Marcus went to the door, unlocked it. Before he could open it, Pete pushed through the door forcibly, his face red with fury.

"Calm down—" Marcus began and stepped back. But Pete, pushed up against him yelling in his face, spittle flying, "I warned you about playing your fucking sex games with her. She's like my own daughter. Sweet. Pure. But you... you piece of shit."

Pete's words struck such a painful blow that Marcus recoiled as if he'd been stabbed in the heart. He actually looked down for a moment, half expecting to see himself bleeding out.

Pete was pulling out the big guns. He'd spill Marcus's sordid history, show Cassie his unworthiness. His dirty, stinking DNA—he'd never overcome it. When she heard his story, she'd run and never look back. *Stop saying that to yourself. Trust her.*

And suddenly Cassie was pushing in between them, up on her toes, facing Pete and shouting into his face, "Stop! Stop this *right now*. Don't you *dare* talk to him like that."

Pete's face drained from wrathful crimson to stunned, pallid white, and he stopped as if he hit a wall. But the moment passed, and Pete's expression hardened. Marcus knew that the old soldier was shifting the battle lines.

Pete placed his hands on Cassie's shoulders. Marcus braced. *Here it comes.* "You don't know who he is. What he is. I do. Now, get out of the way so I can deal—"

"Enough of this!" Cassie said, flinging Pete's hands away, "Maybe I don't know who he is yet, but I'll be damned if I let you take away my right to find out for myself, and furthermore, my right to get hurt in the process if it happens! You seem to think that Marcus is unworthy of me, but so far, the only one who's acted unworthy is you, Pete. I love you like a father, but this is *not* how you love a grown daughter, not by treating her like a child. Do you think I don't know what it means to be hurt? Do you think I don't know exactly what you risk *every time you love someone?*" Her face grew even redder, eyes even wider, as she seemed to realize what she'd said. She made an involuntary move to cover her mouth with her hands, but stopped herself, crossed her arms, and stood firm in the silence.

Marcus shuddered, his chest rising and falling in rapid breaths. If he tried to move, his knees would buckle. Nobody in his entire shitty life had ever stood up for him. But there was his woman, and damn she was his, going up against her beloved Pete—her father figure.

And she told Pete that she loved me. It was one of the singular experiences of his life.

Though Pete wasn't throwing physical punches, for a moment he flashed back to his father in a drunken rage, destroying everyone and everything in his path. A wave of nausea hit him hard, but she was his to protect.

He squared his shoulders. *Take action, Mackenzie.*

"Stop," he raised his voice. "Pete, calm down." His sharp words startled Pete, allowing Marcus to easily pull Cassie away from him. He held her around the waist, her back to his front, and prayed she wouldn't fight him about the message he was sending. His hopes rose when she leaned back into him and covered his hands with hers, a telling move—she'd made her choice.

Pete froze, studying them. "I see," Pete spat, the disdain written on his face. "You've seduced her. Tricked her into believing that you're a decent man, that you're going to commit to her, care for her." Pete leaned toward them and mocked, "You, the manwhore of the county, are going to love her?"

Every word ripped at Marcus.

Pete was cutting him to shreds, and Cassie gasped, her body jerking in his arms.

He'd been knocked around his whole life, he'd even taken a bullet during the war—he could handle pain. But Cassie in pain, no. He would shield her.

He took a deep breath. "Pete, you're hurting Cassie."

"Not as much as you will. We both know that you'll use her, then destroy her."

Marcus simmered with anger, trying desperately to control it, when Cassie pulled out of his arms and stood toe to toe with Pete.

"Pete, I love you. You're the father mine couldn't be." Pete closed his eyes, his pain palpable, and Marcus felt the burn of it.

"But please, go home. I'll come to the farmhouse tomorrow. We'll talk then." She reached up and stroked Pete's face. "Please."

Fear clawed through Marcus. Pete would never give up. He'd work on Cassie, and maybe he would persuade her to break with him—and he'd be helpless to stop it.

"Honey," Pete took her hand, and begged, "Please, Cassie, come home with me right now. He's no good for you, Cassie. He *will* hurt you."

Elation filled Marcus when her voice steadied, "Maybe he will hurt me, but that's a chance I'll take. I'm not your little girl anymore. And Pete, we all have scars, problems. Think about it, before you trash a good man. He's worth the risk."

I'm worth the risk? She was killing him, but what a way to die.

Pete shook his head in defeat. He walked to the door, and turned to Marcus, his lips curled with disgust. "You're a piece of shit. A disgrace. I helped you, cared for you. But now? You're just shit." He pulled open the door, then spat over his shoulder, "Like father, like son," and slammed it shut behind him.

Neither of them moved. Marcus took a few deep breaths, trying to get his racing pulse to slow down. His body shook. God, he had to touch her. He pulled her to him, and they held each other, gently rocking back and forth. She raised her hand and gently touched the side of his face, the tip of her finger tracing his scar with a sweet caress. "Marcus, I'm so, so sorry about Pete. He had no right to say those terrible things to you."

Marcus looked down at her, "You know, right before you moved back, Pete warned me away from you."

Her eyes widened, "Why did he do that?

Smoothing her hair back from her head, he said, "Partly because of my sketchy reputation, and that he sees you as his daughter. But there's more—it's a long story."

"I want to hear it. I need to hear it. You can trust me."

He could—a first for him. "You're going to talk to him tomorrow. I'll have to wait awhile, get my head together, then I'll contact him after you do. Maybe I can get him into another headspace. We'll see."

Marcus ran his hand down her back and rested it on her waist, she held his hips.

"I hate to leave you, but I've got another meeting at my office with the PI I hired to investigate the vandalism. But I'll cancel it if you want to stay here."

"No, go to your meeting. I'm shocked at Pete's behavior, but yes, I'm okay. Anyway, Maddy called last night and asked if I had a few hours to talk today while the boys were at a birthday party. So this plan works out for me, too. Her ex is giving her trouble again."

"Anything I can help with?"

"I don't know yet."

"Okay, if you need me, let me know."

"I will." Raising herself on tiptoe, she kissed him sweetly.

"And one more thing, baby, before I take you home, though we didn't talk about it because we were busy... and by the way, I love your pussy, Cassie." Her blush burned beet red, and he loved that about her—one part sweet and shy, the other a sex siren. "I'm taking you to dinner tonight. I want to talk, tell you some things about myself that I don't have time to do right now." *Like my fucked up past.*

"I want to hear it all, Marcus."

He would tell her some of it, but not all, and before Pete built a case against him.

"You will. But first, dinner, so dress up. I'll be by at six-thirty."

Placing her hands on his chest, the corners of her eyes crinkled, "That sounds like an order."

"It is, and you like it." He took her mouth in a hard, fast kiss. "Let's get going."

"Oh, one more thing Marcus—I love your cock too. And I swallow."

"Shit!" He grabbed her hand and led her out to his truck to her laughter.

Chapter Ten

That evening, Cassie sat on her bed in a black lace bra and panties, getting ready for her date. She listened to her daughters' excitement on speaker, her cell propped on a pillow.

"Mom, I got the summer internship at NYU's Center for Neural Science!" Eva screamed. "The email just came in!"

"Oh, sweetie, I'm so happy for you."

"And mom," Abby cried out, "I was accepted into NPR's program. I found out yesterday, but we wanted to tell you together."

"My girls rock," Cassie whooped and hollered along with them.

"Mom," Eva's voice quivered, "Dad would be doing handsprings."

Her throat tightened, "I'm sure he is, baby."

"He is," Abby declared, "I know he is."

"Yes, darlings." She let it go at that, hearing other voices in the background.

"We've got to go, but as soon as finals are over, we're coming for a long weekend," Eva warned.

"And mom?"

"What Eva?"

"Please, make your mac and cheese."

"Will do."

"Love you mom," both girls called out.

"I can't wait to see you both. Love you. Bye."

Her girls were the best. No, their girls. Cassie looked up. "We did good, Ron. We did good."

Shaking off the bittersweet memories, she began pulling on nude thigh-high stockings, attaching them to a black lace garter belt. She'd purposely worn the belt because it made her feel sexy, and it would drive Marcus wild.

As she dressed, her thoughts wandered to seeing Maddy for a few hours after Marcus dropped her off. Ray Bristow, Maddy's ex, was taking her back to court, again, trying to lower her child support payments. He kept pleading poverty while his latest woman drove around in a new BMW. Thankfully, Rachel had been there, and next week, Maddy was meeting with Rachel's divorce attorney. "Tamara Rambo is expensive, but a killer in black stilettos and a red power suit," Rachel said.

And Cassie was paying, finally able to help her sister, easing some of her guilt for abandoning Maddy all those years ago.

She checked the time, Marcus would be here in a few minutes. Taking a simple aquamarine silk sheath out of the closet, she slipped it on and looked at herself in the full-length mirror hanging on the inside of the bedroom door. The sleeveless boat-neck top with the hem a few inches above her knee fit her perfectly, showing off her height and curves—yes, Marcus would definitely like.

But worry nagged at her about her girls. Would they be upset that she was dating? And when they visited, should she introduce Marcus to them? She'd avoided mentioning him when they'd spoken. But she had weeks to decide what to do, and by then, she'd see if her relationship with Marcus was still progressing.

Those thoughts led her back to the shocking situation with Pete. And, just as shocking, that one tender moment with Marcus, who she'd been sure was going to confess his feelings for her. *Damn it, Pete.*

But, she reminded herself, she'd also been the recipient of Marcus's powerful anger and his ability to coldly shut down. Had he changed his ways? Could he commit? Those thoughts dragged down her good mood.

"Stop it," she said out loud. *What will be, will be.* Living in the moment had become her motto to help her handle all the loss in her life, so, that's what she was going to do. Her cell buzzed:

MMackenzie: Be there in 5.

Her heart thumped as she confirmed and hoped he came to her tonight in a better mood than when he'd left. Cassie put on a pair of silver hoop earrings, then stepped into black slingback kitten heels, with a matching leather clutch and pashmina. She began to pace. *Am I nervous because of Pete? Or maybe... because we had raunchy sex hours ago, and I have no idea how to act right now.*

She jumped at the light knock. *Here goes.* Opening the door, she stifled a gasp. Marcus looked amazingly masculine in a fitted white button-down shirt with the top button left open, black slacks with black boots and black sport jacket. He'd shaved, so no scruff tonight, and had obviously tried to tame his unruly hair.

"Hi," she said shyly.

For a second, Marcus didn't answer, just stood there and did a slow head to toe. Before Cassie could say another word, he stepped into the house, pulled her into his arms, and closed the door with his foot. He ran his fingers up her back into her hair, and took her mouth.

The kiss started slow, but when Cassie opened to him, his tongue thrust into her mouth, kissing her deeply. She grabbed his biceps and held on because she was drowning in him—his spicy taste, the clean, citrusy smell of his aftershave, and the power of his hard body crushing hers. She was running out of air when Marcus pulled back, panting, rubbed his forehead gently back and forth over hers, and echoed, "Hi."

She laughed, her worry was gone. He stepped back, spread his hands over her hips, and murmured, "I love this dress, baby."

"Mmm, I guessed you would."

He took her hand, "Let's get out of here."

"The restaurant is only a little over twenty minutes from here and—"

Marcus, ran a hand down her back, over her crack to her ass and squeezed. "I love your body and how it looks in this dress, but we'd better leave now," his voice husky, "or we'll never make it out of this cottage."

Playfully, Cassie parted her lips and stroked his steel-hard cock over his slacks.

He pulled her hand away. "You're a she-devil, turning me on when we have to leave. Now stop, or I'm going to lose control, rip that dress off of you, and fuck you against the front door."

Cassie's face lit up, "Oka—"

"Don't finish that," he warned with a finger over her lips. Putting his hand on the small of her back, Marcus guided her to the door. As she grabbed her purse and wrap, he whispered in her ear, "But after dinner," he nipped her earlobe making her squeak, "all bets are off."

****

"You're quiet, Cassandra," Marcus took his eyes off the road for a second as they drove back to the cottage after dinner. He reached over, clasped their hands, and placed them on his thigh.

She smiled. "I was thinking how wonderful dinner was."

"Yeah, it was, and you're dazzling tonight," he brought their hands up and kissed her fingers.

"And you were the hottest guy in the place."

"Hot? Okay, I'll take it," he chuckled. "But it's you I burn for."

"You do?" she asked with mock surprise.

He quickly glanced at her. "Yeah. And you know it. I told you that every time I saw your lips wrap around a shrimp, all I could think about was your lips wrapped around my cock."

"That was *incredibly* romantic," she said dryly.

"I'm a regular Romeo."

"And when I offered you a shrimp, you insisted on eating it from my fingers, then proceeded to suck and lick my fingers for a full five minutes while dining at the historic River Bank Inn. That was a bit much, don't you think?"

"Nope. Not when I enjoyed watching you get turned on."

Turned on. Hell, she'd wanted to get on her knees and suck him off right there.

"Yes, I admit I was, but you're too much, sometimes."

He traced her knuckle with his thumb. "I watched you wiggling around in your seat, and I almost came in my own damn pants," his voice deepened, "and right now, I'd like to go down on you and find out how wet your pussy is."

She ran her finger up and down one of his to tease him. "I guess you'll have to find out yourself."

"I don't have to touch, I can smell you perfuming up my car. My dick is straining to get to you. Think I'll have zipper marks on it for a week. But right now, I'm going to take care of you before we get to the cottage. Because I'll be on you the minute we get inside."

"Take care of me? But, you're driving, and—"

Steering with one hand, Marcus unclasped their hands, placed hers in her lap, and put his hand on her knee, caressing it with his pointer finger. She held her breath as he slowly moved it up under her dress to the lace top of her stocking. He fingered a garter and moved it to stroke the belt.

Her breath released as she looked over at him—his jaw was tight.

"A garter belt?" It was after eight o'clock and the road was empty. He gazed at her for a moment, scorching her, then quickly looked back to the road.

"When we get to the cottage, I want you to undress, take off everything but the belt, stockings and shoes. But now," he rumbled, "I want you to pull your dress up over your hips, place your hands over your head, hold on to the headrest, and spread your legs."

She whipped around to look at him, "What?"

"Do it."

Oh, the man wanted to play.

"Cassandra," he growled. "I'm waiting."

Putting her hands on the hem of her dress, she pulled it up past mid-thigh. Marcus was looking back and forth from her to the road.

"Higher. I want it around your waist," he demanded.

Her heart raced, her legs shook, and her clit throbbed like a toothache. Cassie lifted her hips and slid the dress up. She faced him, and he stole a quick glance.

"Now turn toward me as much as you can and spread those glorious long legs."

Cassie turned and spread. When she did, she heard his soft pants.

"Wider." Wantonly, she spread. "Fuck." He braked slowly, looked up and down the road, pulled across both lanes into a small rest stop carved into the base of a rocky hill, and turned off the engine.

"Marcus." She closed her legs and took her hands off the headrest as he unbuckled his seatbelt, leaned over her, and did the same to hers.

He was right in her face when he directed, "Don't move. Hands above your head, keep your legs spread." She was already soaking his leather seats.

"Good, sweetheart," he praised, sitting up as she moved back into place. Having her restraining herself was a completely new thrill.

"Now, I'm going to watch you come. You're going to stay still, just like this. If you do as I say, you'll get what you want."

116

Moaning, she closed her eyes. She was so close to coming, already.

"Look at me, Cassie." She opened her eyes. "You got me?"

Swallowing hard, she nodded.

He watched every expression as he touched her clit over the drenched panel, tapping and stroking lightly with just the tip of his finger. She writhed on the seat.

"Stay still."

Pleadingly, she looked at him whimpering in between her words, "Oh, oh, I can't."

He pulled his hand away. "Please, Marcus, make me come."

"Ssh, be still. I'm playing now. Playing with my pussy. Obey me, Cassandra."

She was dying with need, and spread her legs as wide as she could and locked her hands around the headrest.

"That's it. My baby wants what I can give her." He began to stroke and tap her clit again. Torturing her. Tap. Stroke. Tap. Stroke. Her head whipped from side to side but she kept her torso still.

"You're being so good." She wanted to buck her hips to meet his finger. Wanted more. More pressure. If he'd only press a little harder, rub a little harder, she could find it.

"Please, Marcus..."

Then he pushed aside the thong and slid his middle finger inside, fucking her with it.

"Cassie, come." He pressed his thumb on her clit and rotated it over the silk while he bent his finger inside, stimulating the bundle of nerves in the front of her vaginal wall.

She exploded—thrashing and bucking while he kept stroking, slowly bringing her down until her body was soft and loose.

Leaning over, he lightly kissed her and helped her straighten her dress. "We'll be home in ten minutes. Prepare." He put his fingers in his mouth and sucked them clean.

"That's so dirty."

"And I love that my woman likes dirty." He checked for traffic and pulled out onto the road.

His woman. Taking his hand in hers, she kissed his knuckles, surprising him by his expression when he glanced at her before turning back to the road.

****

Marcus pulled Cassie down onto him, her head resting on his chest. She'd ridden him like a cowgirl to an orgasm that was so intense he'd entered another dimension.

"Your pussy gripped me so hard, it felt like you were putting it through a wringer—what kind of muscle control do you have?" During the exquisite finale of his release, he felt like every drop of fluid in his body had pooled into his dick. He actually thought there may be some wisdom in taking a break to hydrate.

She put her hands on his chest, rested her chin on them, peering at him. "For your information, Mackenzie, I do fifty Kegels a day. They keep a woman's vagina in good shape. I had twins, you know."

"Keep practicing, my dick loves it, and I don't want your muscles to get flaccid anytime soon."

"Flaccid like your cock right now?" she snickered.

"Yeah, something like that," he grinned. "Cassie, roll off," he nipped her bottom lip and chuckled at her mewl, "I'm gonna clean up."

He came out of the bathroom, and she was sitting up in bed with a sheet covering her lap, her lovely breasts on display. She was breathtaking, with the glow of a satisfied woman.

"Honey, throw me one of your tees." Her calling him "honey" was a punch in his gut. He was trying to get used to how much she cared for him. Casually, he pulled open a drawer on his dresser, took out a black tee, and threw it to her. Holding up the shirt, she said, "This is hilarious." The white illustration was of a gloomy Edgar Allen Poe with a raven on his shoulder, under the words, "I Need A Hug."

Marcus watched her pull the shirt over her head, unfortunately hiding her delicious tits. "Poe's a favorite of mine. My best bud, Derek Prescott, gave me that shirt as a joke."

"You've mentioned Derek before. Maddy has, too, since she works as a clerk at the courthouse. She told me she takes her breaks in his courtroom if he's prosecuting, says he's mesmerizing to watch. Have you known him a long time?"

"We met in seventh grade in a debate class. He argued against me and won. We continued it after school, pushed each other around, and became best friends. We even enlisted in the army on the same day. Derek wears the same serious expression on his face as Poe, and one day I teased him about it. Two days later, I got the shirt in the mail."

"He sounds like a fun guy."

119

"Fun? Not exactly. He's dark. But he has a wicked sense of humor."

"I'd like to meet this serious friend of yours."

"He said he's coming to the Riverbend Picnic on Saturday. He hasn't been there in a decade, but he said he'll be there. By the way," Marcus pointed at the tee, "I think that shirt looks better on you than it does on me, and I like that you're braless."

"Cool it, I need a break, big guy."

He pointed to his cock, as he pulled on his jeans. "I'm almost forty-four. My dick needs a longer rest than your pussy."

"Thank the lord," she laughed, while propping two pillows against the headboard.

He climbed in next to her and pointed to Poe, "If you haven't read Poe's poems, you're missing out. If you'd like, I'll read some of them to you."

"I read 'The Raven' in high school."

"Most people have. But you need to hear Annabel Lee," and staring into her eyes, he quoted:

And neither the angels in heaven above,
Nor the demons down under the sea,
Can ever dissever my soul from the soul
Of the beautiful Annabel Lee.

Her eyes glowed with affection, "I love that."

"It was his last poem before he died, and about his favorite themes: the death of a beautiful woman and unrequited love. He suffered the loss of many women—his mother, his foster mother, and later his wife."

"Unrequited love. Heartbreak. It's a universal

120

theme in poetry, literature... even country western songs," she grinned.

"Yeah, love can get messy."

Chapter Eleven

Marcus wasn't sure how this conversation had gone from Poe to the elephant in the room: love. Cassie gave herself willingly to him, body, mind, and heart, and he was damn lucky that she'd chosen him to be the first man she'd given her time and attention to since her husband's death.

"Honey, I would love you to read poetry to me."

What was he going to do with her? Every time she called him "honey" or showed him how much she cared about him, it created a dent in his protective walls—it scared him. She was also well-read and curious, and their intellectual connection was as powerful as their sexual one.

But he was clueless about relationships, how could he give her what she needed—pure and simple love? *Man up, Mackenzie.* He held his arms out to her, "Let's talk." She hesitated, then slid over to him. He had to touch her while he spilled his poison and hoped she would understand. He patted his knee, "Lay your head down on my lap, Cassie, and I'll massage your head."

"How did you know I love to have my head rubbed?"

"I have a head that loves to be rubbed, too," he waggled his eyebrows.

She playfully put her thumb in her mouth and sucked, "If you do a good job, maybe later."

"Keep doing that and—"

Her expression softened, "Tell me." She laid her head on his thigh, and sighed when he ran his fingers through her hair.

"Since Pete said those things about me, I need to explain them to you."

Turning onto her back, Cassie looked up at him, "I'm still shocked at Pete."

"It's okay," he stroked her hair.

"It isn't," her voice rose as she sat up. "Until the BBQ at Pete's, when I saw you together, I had no idea you even had a relationship with him, and apparently a deep one."

"You're his little girl. Months before you moved back, when I was at the farmhouse, he warned me away from you. He called me a player, said you were a good girl."

"Oh, Pete," her eyes glistened with tears, "you sweet, foolish man."

"I promise to connect with him at the picnic. He means a lot to me, too."

"We'll work it out with him somehow, but Pete had to have hurt you so much. Tell me about your past. Please. I want to know it all."

"I'm going to give you the abridged version for now, and then let's move on to the next topic, one you're gonna like."

Gently pushing her head back onto his lap, Marcus knew that it would be easier for him if she wasn't looking at him. He wouldn't give her all the dirty details, but he had to give her something.

You're just shit. Always will be. Like father, like son. Pete's words scored into his skin, all over again.

She took one of his hands in hers and ran her thumb over his knuckles, as if she could read him and knew he needed courage right now.

"I met Pete the day my father was convicted of first-degree murder for killing my mother's boyfriend, and attempting to kill her. I had driven to the Overlook to... *to drown myself in the Delaware...* I was sixteen."

"Marcus," his name came out abruptly. She sat up, shock written on her face, after he finished.

"Yeah," he looked into her eyes, "I'm the son of a murderer."

Shifting so she sat crossed legged, her knees butting up against his, her face changed from shock to anger. She took both of his hands and held them in hers, "Pete knew this, and he threw that ugliness at you? He accused you of being the same kind of man as your father?" Her voice was rising with each word until she was yelling and squeezing the fingers of his hand.

He put a palm gently on her chest, "Cassandra, calm down," his heart was pounding because he never expected this reaction from her. He knew she'd be shocked, but he thought she would want the details and be repulsed by his history. Instead, his warrior queen was defending him again—and also breaking his fingers, if he didn't stop her. He changed their hold so their fingers were entwined and he had control.

"Calm down? He's holding you accountable for your father's terrible deed," her voice raised again.

Father's deed. It sounded like a line from Shakespeare. He wanted to laugh in the face of this tragedy, but he banked it because that would really set her off.

"What Pete said is so very wrong. And why? Because we're spending time together?"

It would kill him to lose Pete. Could he convince Pete that he could be—was—a better man with Cassandra?

"And what about your mother?" she asked in a whisper.

Her face was filled with softness and compassion, and it was all for him. The shame he'd buried as that lonely, angry teen was floating to the surface, but he tamped it down. "My mother..." he said bitingly, "right after the trial, she left me and Liam with my uncle Brennan."

"She left you and your brother? She abandoned her sons after the trauma you and Liam had suffered through?" He'd edited out the lifetime of abuse that Nolan Mackenzie had rained down on him, Liam, and his mother. He couldn't face that conversation.

"Yeah. It's another long story, Cassandra, for another time." *She'll never hear that horror.*

"Are you in contact with her?"

"No. I haven't heard from the bitch in eight years."

"Eight years?"

"Yeah. And Cassie," she looked at him, waiting, "it's good that we don't."

"But..."

"I'm done talking about it," he said gently. After spewing just a small part of his childhood ugliness to her, it was as if his skin had been excoriated and every nerve ending was exposed and throbbing. Time to change the topic and the vibe between them.

Marcus shut it down by pulling Cassie into his arms and kissing her. As she always did, she kissed him back, giving him everything he asked for: her lips, her mouth, her taste, her soft body pressed to his.

Lifting his head, he looked into her heavily lidded eyes. Kissing the tip of her nose, he situated her on his lap and said, "Next order of business."

Leaning into him, Cassie kissed his neck, moved her hand down onto the zipper of his jeans, and began to stroke him through the denim.

"Hmm, I'm good with that, too." He took her mouth in a wet, deep kiss as his hands roamed under the shirt, playing with her breasts until she was squirming.

Pulling away, Cassie murmured, "I'm craving your cock, and you didn't let me suck it. Instead, you impaled me."

He laughed. "It wanted your pussy."

"But I wanted your cock."

"As soon as I recover," he lifted her hand off of his dick. "Remember I said two things to talk about?" Taking her chin in his hand, he studied her. She was thirty-eight, and had slight wrinkles in the corners of her eyes and forehead, a testament to having laughed, loved, and cried—of having lived. A few strands of gray glistened in the soft copper waves. Cassandra had pure natural beauty, and in this moment, he imagined living the rest of his life with her and growing old together—could he be enough for her? Tightening the hold on her chin, as if she'd suddenly disappear, he began, "Let me make this short. You are mine, Cassandra. We're an *us*: exclusive. I don't care who likes it or not. And if any man dares to come on to you, tries to touch you, or tries to claim you, I'll shove his dick up his ass. You hear me?"

Her eyes widened, and then a glorious smile lit her face, increasing her beauty tenfold.

"I hear you, honey."

"Say it Cassandra. Say what I need to hear."

Taking his jaw in her hand, she rubbed it with her thumb, and gazed lovingly at him, "I'm yours, Marcus. But…may I ask if you've ever had an *us*?"

He watched his hand stroke her face before he answered, and a line etched between his brows. "No, I never have. Even when I was married, we weren't really together. Kelly got pregnant when I was on leave. We'd only gone out a few times. I was young, twenty-two, she was nineteen, we didn't think it through. So we eloped, found a cheap apartment, and then I was away almost all the time. After a year, she wrote me a 'Dear John' letter, and we moved on. And since then... no, Cassie it's only with you."

She tilted her face, drew his mouth to hers, and gently kissed him.

"Enough heavy stuff." Grinning, he moved her off of his lap and lifted the hem of her shirt. She raised her hands, and he pulled it off, throwing it on the floor. She began stroking his cock hard over the denim, "And, just saying, if any woman flirts with you or puts her hands on you, I'm going to bitch slap her." She raised a brow, "You hear me?"

"I hear you," he grinned and saluted her.

"So stop stalling and give it to me."

"Yes, ma'am," he laughed and tumbled her backwards onto the bed.

127

****

The next morning, Cassie was floating in delicious twilight. The dream was so real, she could feel Marcus's big hands holding her thighs apart, feel the rasp of his overnight scruff on the inside of her thighs as he kissed and rubbed his face between her legs. And his tongue, oh god, he used it like it was another digit. She moaned when just the tip of it poked her clit hard and then fluttered over the throbbing pearl. When he puckered his lips and sucked hard, she exploded.

Her eyes popped open as the orgasm caught her up like the swift currents of the Delaware. But wait, she couldn't be tossed around because... Cassie tried to put her hands on his head, but she couldn't move. His big hands held her legs widely apart, but her hands? When she tried to sit up, to twist her head around to see what was happening, she couldn't.

He'd tied her to the headboard.

"Marcus, oh my God," her voice was breathy as she struggled to get free, and yet, being tied down—a long-time fantasy of hers—was so hot that desire roared through her body. But he hadn't asked, he'd just done it. And she hadn't woken up? He'd driven her to three orgasms last night, after their dead-serious talk. Dinner, drinks, incredible sex, and then she'd slept like the dead. It was the first time that they'd slept together for an entire night. Progress. And what a good morning, but now he was still lightly sucking... his mouth was too much, she was too sensitive.

"Good morning," he murmured, as he kept licking and nuzzling.

If she didn't have to pee, maybe she'd let him stay there as long as he was using that talented mouth. "Marcus, stop, please." She looked down her body at the top of his head between her legs—that was hot.

He lifted his head, his lips glistening wet. "You tied me down."

"I did," he grinned.

Her hands strained at the ties, "Uh, why?"

He leaned over and kissed her belly, then looked at her with a smirk on his handsome face. "I woke up early, you were sleeping, and I was hungry. You know, breakfast is the most important meal of the day."

"And honey, you know how to eat. But why didn't you wake me? I love when you go down on me."

"I know you do, but I wanted to restrain you, see how you react, because you like me to take control. And having you lying there spread out for me to do..." he ran his lips over her belly and she squirmed, "...whatever I want."

"Oh—"

"You like it, don't you? I see it in your eyes whenever you struggle."

She tried to twist her head so she could see what he used.

"I took the tie-backs from the living room curtains," he said reading her mind again.

"So nothing is safe from you."

Sitting up he said seriously, "You're always safe with me. I would never hurt you or do anything you don't like or are afraid of."

"And I trust you, but I have to pee. Badly."

Brushing a kiss over her breasts, he climbed off untied her. Hopping off the bed, as she walked to the bathroom, he called, "Cassandra."

She turned to him, and my god what a delicious creature he was, sitting on the edge of the bed, naked, his legs splayed while he stroked that big cock of his. "Make it fast, it's payback time. If you're not back here in under five minutes, I'm going to turn you over my knee and spank you until you learn how to follow instructions."

Her heart rate kicked up. He wasn't kidding when he said he liked to play. Pushing open the bathroom door, she turned her head and poked at the hungry lion, "Is that a threat?"

His smile turned feral, "That's a promise."

Laughing, she went into the bathroom. When she came out, Marcus pounced on her, kept his promise, turned her ass pink, and rode her right into bliss.

****

Cassie bent to stroke Grey's head as the cat rubbed against her hand. "I knew you'd end up with a name. Guess you're here to stay, my friend." She filled his food bowl on the patio while he wound himself between her legs. Squatting so she could talk to him eye to eye, Cassie held out her hand, and he came right to her. His eyes closed, and she heard just a hint of a purr when she stroked his face with her thumbs. "Hey buddy," the cat opened his lime-green eyes, "now that you're sleeping in the cat carrier on the patio, I can trap you easily. So, Monday, you're going to see Doc Warren to get examined and vaccinated. And baby,

130

sorry to tell you this," Grey bumped her hand when she stopped stroking him, "but those gonads of yours are going to get snipped. Then, sweetie, you're going to become an indoor cat."

He blinked at her, she smiled at him, stroked his head, whispered, "Grey," and stood up.

Walking to the edge of the patio, Cassie looked out over the lawn and wooded area. God, she loved this place like no other on earth.

It was a week later, the Friday after she'd been with Marcus after their dinner—and after they'd cemented their commitment to exclusivity. He hadn't said he loved her, and she hadn't spilled her feelings for him, but it seemed like he loved her. She had hope anyway.

She had to stop thinking about him all the time. *I have a million things to do today.* First was the house. She'd mentioned meeting with the catastrophic insurance inspector last Wednesday in passing to Marcus and was shocked when he'd shown up, following the inspector around, pointing out damage that might have been missed. After, Marcus had kissed her hard in front of the inspector, whispering, "Mine," then he'd gone back to work.

Secondly, she'd reached out for freelance work and had two article proposals due by next Tuesday for Claire Curran, an editor she'd worked with in the past.

And she was presently making ten pounds of potato salad for tomorrow's Riverbend picnic. The guys were bringing meat to grill, and she, Maddy, and Rachel were making the sides.

There would be seven of them in their group, maybe eight if Derek showed. But instead of heading into the kitchen and getting to that to-do list, Cassie sat down on a patio chair. Grey rubbed against her legs, then lay down next to her feet as the sun rose in the sky. Closing her eyes and putting her head back on the chair, she thought back on how remarkable the last week had been.

A day hadn't gone by when they weren't in touch. Marcus had said, "I have a crazy, busy week, but I'll be in touch whenever I can." And he'd kept his promise, either texting or calling, even just to say hello and tell her how much he missed seeing her. On Tuesday he'd called from his car: "I'm on my way to meet with an architect, but all I can think about is your body under mine."

"Are you hard now, Marcus? Hope your meeting *goes down* the way you want it to," she'd teased.

"I'm as rigid as a two-by-four, just talking to you. But Cassie, you teasing me is going to get you in trouble."

"More like a two-by-eight," Cassie shot back before they said their goodbyes.

A half hour later, he'd texted her a link to Springsteen's *I'm on Fire,* with a direct order, "Don't use your vibrator or get yourself off after listening. That's my job. Get ready."

Cassie had never realized exactly how sexually aggressive that song was. And Marcus had kept his promise about getting her off that night by having them up on their knees on the bed, her back to his front. While he'd taken her from behind, he'd played with her breasts and used her vibrator on her clit. She'd never had sex in that position, but it was stupendous, and her throat was raw from screaming out her orgasm.

Sure, sex between them was fantastic. But it was more, so much more, from cooking dinner together, debating politics, his reading poetry out loud while they lay in bed, or talking on the phone about their days if they couldn't be together—talks often ending with phone sex.

Cassie smiled when her phone rang with Marcus's ringtone.

"Hey, whatcha doing?"

"Oh, just sitting on the patio instead of working."

"Wish I was there for a quickie. Or maybe a long quickie."

"I wish you were, too," she whispered.

"When you whisper like that, I want to turn around and speed back to you. But I'm calling because I'm headed out to that project in Jersey I told you about, and the customer wants me to stay for dinner. I'll be back very late, the guy likes to talk and drink, but after, I'm heading home. Hector and Marissa have the day off, so I have to take care of the dogs, and Liam's coming over to spend the night."

"Of course. I'm just getting ready to start cooking for tomorrow, and then I'm working on my proposals, so I'll meet you at the picnic in the morning."

"Wish I was picking you up."

"Me too, but it makes more sense for Maddy to pick me up."

"Yeah, because we're going to be spending the night on my boat—one of my favorite places."

"I can't wait to see it."

"I can't wait to fuck you on it, from bow to port, to starboard to stern."

"Marcus—"

133

"It's gonna happen, but the boat ride will be fun too."

"I'm looking forward to the picnic first, so you'll have to contain yourself."

"I promise to behave. I'll be bringing my horseshoes and frisbees."

"Horseshoes and frisbees?"

"Yep. Me and Bret, and Derek, if he shows, are champs at both."

"Maddy's boys will go wild. A bunch of hunky men to play with." She sighed. "Their father is an awful man and spends no time with them."

"Your hunky man and his friends are going to make those boys happy."

"Thanks, honey."

"Gotta go, but I'll text at some point today."

"Bye, see you tomorrow, Marcus."

It made her nervous just thinking about it, but tomorrow Pete and Marcus were meeting at the picnic, after Marcus had talked to Pete on the phone. He'd told her the call was tense, but she hoped they could mend the break. She'd met with Pete the day after the fight, and Pete's remorse for his actions had them hugging each other and promising that they'd never fight like that again. Change was hard for Pete, but he was trying.

She stood up, time to get back to work, and Grey got up, too. He stretched before jumping onto the chair, curling into a ball on the seat cushion, and going back to sleep. She gave him a rub on his head and walked back into the house.

Tomorrow, she and Marcus were coming out as a couple to the entire town at the picnic. It felt surreal.

Ordering her Echo to play Jim Croce's station, Cassie began to sing along with *Time in a Bottle*, those poignant, prophetic words piercing her soul as they always did. *I want time with Marcus*, she thought, taking a large pot out of a cabinet to begin cooking.

I love him, and it's growing stronger every day. Could he ever love her back? He hasn't said the words, but he shows it. Sighing, she filled the pot with water, and set it on the stove to boil.

Chapter Twelve

W*here the hell is she?*
    Marcus sat on a picnic table, his legs splayed, feet propped up on the seat, holding a travel mug of coffee. He took a sip. Too bad she was coming with Maddy. If he was picking her up, they could have had a quickie, since it would be hours before they were on his boat.

Damn, but he missed her the past week.

He'd never been hung up on a woman like this before. Even Liam and Sean both noticed his distraction at work. Bret's words played in his head: "You're gone for Cassie." Yeah, he was addicted to everything Ms. Bennett, and he didn't care what anyone thought about it.

Sipping from his cup, Marcus scanned the park from one end to the other—a perfect location for the picnic. It boasted a massive lawn with an area for grills, picnic tables, sandboxes, and space for horseshoes. There were two tennis courts at the far end of the park and three docks on the river. His boat, *Nevermore*, was already tied up there. He couldn't wait for Cassie's reaction when she saw the name.

Tonight, he'd take Cassie to a cove up the river where he often docked to fish, and sometimes to think and stargaze. Add hot sex to the night—what more could a man want?

He checked the time again. "Marcus Mackenzie," he heard, smiled and looked over to see Mary. Riverbend's resident hippie didn't disappoint, with her long, flowing gray hair and filmy tie-dyed dress. Large peace-sign earrings hung from her ears. She was guiding four strong young men who were steering a large cart piled with sandwiches, canned goods, and pet foods across the grass to the donation tables. Area businesses had opened their hearts and pocketbooks for those in need—one of the things he loved about living in Riverbend. His company had purchased hundreds of dollars' worth of gift cards for area stores that would be handed out today.

"Nice donation, Mary," he gave her a thumbs up as she followed the cart.

She called out, "Come by next week, handsome, I need you to look at the foundation in back of the store, we're taking in water in the basement since the storm."

"Will do, sweetheart. Need help?" She shook her head no and hurried after the cart.

Marcus checked his watch again. Cassie said she'd be there around eight. *Around eight, asshole*, he scolded himself, *does not mean eight on the dot. Stop obsessing about her.*

Spotting Liam and Sean turning into the park, Marcus put his mug down, hopped off the table, "Hey, Liam, Sean."

Sean grabbed Marcus for a hug and back slap, "Hey, cuz." Hitting Sean in the shoulder, Marcus teased, "You clean up well, Sean. Looking to get some today?".

"Yeah, old man. Watch and learn. There's a new stud in town."

"I thought you were taken by the very hot Shannon Powell." Marcus put him in a friendly headlock and they grappled for a minute. "I'm very taken, cuz," Sean pulled away laughing.

Liam was silent, watching, his mouth set in a flat line. *He's pissed. What's with him*? When Marcus pulled Liam in a for a hug, he could feel the tension peeling off of his brother. Quickly pulling away, Liam asked sarcastically, "Waiting for someone, bro?"

"Yeah," Marcus nodded carefully.

"Marcus," Sean said, "Liam tells me that you're still seeing Cassandra Bennett, and that she's taking up all your free time. What gives, Mr. One-Night-Stand?"

Hell no. Marcus turned toward Liam. "Talking about me behind my back, bro?"

"As I hear it," Liam said, smirking sourly, "you were seen making out with her at Pete's diner a few weeks ago. It's all over town."

And what you don't know, dear brother, fucking her for weeks now.

This shit from Liam was just that: shit. He hadn't been spending as much time with Liam as usual. When the hell would his brother grow up? When would he stop leaning on Marcus? He wasn't his damn father. "Yeah. So what? Have a problem with it, Li?"

"Marcus, are you gonna hang out with us today or not? Drink beer? Maybe play horseshoes like we did last year?" Liam threw the words at him like they were daggers. Marcus could see the anger in his brother's eyes, but also a wounded little boy begging for attention. Hell. He could invite Liam and Sean to hang with him and Cassandra, but when Liam got needy, he turned into a nasty little thirty-seven year old boy with mommy and daddy issues. *And damn, can't I spend time alone with Cassie? With my friends?*

He sighed. Guilt weighed heavily on his shoulders. "Liam, I'm waiting for Cassandra, but you and Sean can—"

Sean interrupted, "She's not your usual type from what I heard about her—gorgeous, though I haven't seen her yet. Big surprise that she was kissing you at Pete's, since I overheard someone at Mary's store asking, 'What happened to Cassandra, the good girl?'"

"Sean..." Marcus began, but Liam spoke over him in a sneer. "Cassandra, a good girl?" He snorted. "She must be a kinky bitch underneath the goody-goody, if my raunchy, controlling, fuck-em-and-leave-em brother is tapping that piece of a—"

Exploding with rage, Marcus reached out with both hands, took Liam by the collar and pulled him up until they were face to face. They were so close that Marcus could feel his brother's short breaths on his face. "Never, *ever,* say a fucking thing about her. You hear?" He shook Liam.

Eyes wide in shock, Liam struggled, but Marcus's hold was tight.

Then Liam stilled, calmly articulating each word, "Go on, hit me. Dad would be proud."

Shocked by Liam's words, Marcus's chest heaved as he loosened his hold and pushed Liam away. His brother looked thunderstruck as he found his footing on the grass. People had stopped to watch. *Great, something else for the town to talk about.* He hoped Cassie wasn't here yet.

Unclenching his fists, Marcus tried to calm down. Ever since he'd begun to pursue Cassie, the control he'd established over his life, over his emotions, was fracturing. And what was the big deal? So they were together. So what? They were single, adult, and free.

But it was beginning to feel like a shitty Greek tragedy, with all three fates against them. First, it was Cassie who had misunderstood him. *Yeah because of your great rep, asshole*, his ego reminded him. Then Pete. First warning him off of "my Cassie," and then going ballistic on him, taking him down verbally, which still rankled.

And now Liam was comparing him to Nolan? Couldn't he try to have a normal relationship with a woman? And now, he'd attacked Liam. Daddy's DNA was a potent undercurrent, embedded in his cells. Liam was softer than Marcus, needier. Marcus had to protect him, had to make it right with Liam.

The "making it right" list was growing exponentially.

Stepping toward the brother he loved, whom he'd practically raised, Marcus reined in his anger at Liam's words. He put out his hands palms up and begged regretfully, "Please, Li, I'm so damn sorry. I just—"

Scowling, Liam spat, "Forget it," with a curled lip, and stormed away.

Watching Liam, Marcus, almost went after him, but instead asked, "Go to him, would you, Sean? He won't want me now." It hurt just hearing himself say the words.

Putting his hand on Marcus's shoulder, Sean asked, "What gives with you two?"

"I think it's because I haven't spent as much time with him since I met Cassie."

"Cuz, I've never known you to chase a woman before. To stay with one woman."

"No, I haven't." Marcus looked out at the park, where two couples entered, holding hands, and one of the men stopped to give his woman a quick kiss. A pang of envy hit him. What would it be like to have a woman he could rely on to walk by his side? "I don't know, man, Cassie is different." *Or maybe I'm different.* It was a revelation he'd have to think about.

Sean punched Marcus's arm, "Good for you, Marcus. About time you stopped dicking around." He grinned, "Sorry for the pun."

Marcus forced a smile. Sean's voice lowered, "Go for it. I've been with Shannon for a year now. And Marcus, it's sweet having a girl I like and who likes me. Never felt anything like it."

"I'm glad for you, Sean."

"She'll be here later. I'll introduce you to her."

"I'd like that."

"I'll take care of Liam. Since I met Shannon, I haven't seen Liam as much, either, so I'll make more time for him. Marcus, go enjoy your day and your woman." With a wave, Sean walked toward Liam.

My woman. He liked the sound of that. Checking his watch, he was tempted to send Cassie a *Where are you?* text. He'd give her another ten minutes.

He started back to the picnic table to retrieve his coffee when he heard a sultry, feminine purr, "Marcus, there you are."

What else could go wrong today? It was Amanda Terkel. He hadn't seen her since she'd tried to stop him at the Horse as he'd walked toward Cassie. Turning toward her, he forced a smile. She was with

141

her side-kick Jen Walter. At least he hadn't fucked her, too.

"Hey Amanda, Jen."

Immediately, Amanda closed the gap between them and put her hand on his arm. Gently but firmly, Marcus moved away. Her expression was pained. *Crap.* Ten months ago, he'd taken her out, and they'd fucked. Then she wanted more, texting and calling him repeatedly. He hadn't answered, and distanced himself after that. He'd disappointed and hurt her, though he'd been honest about one night only from the get go. Eventually she'd gotten the message. Or had she?

Smiling slyly, Amanda ran her finger over her low-cut neckline—so low-cut that her tits were hanging out—reminding him of her augmented D's. She wasn't an interesting woman, and she was a lousy lay—a taker. Why had he gone out with her?

"Jen and I were wondering if you had your boat, would you take us out on the river?"

No fucking way. "Sorry, ladies, but I'll be busy all day," and off he went. He looked toward the park entrance, and there was Cassie, standing with Rachel, Maddy and her boys, Danny and Jason, the town librarian, Regina Wilson, and her assistant, Sue Johnson.

Her clenched jaw told him that she'd seen the byplay between him and Amanda. Playing it cool, he gave her a big smile as if nothing had happened while walking backward to get his mug, Marcus held up a 'one minute' finger.

Her smile was frosty, and it chilled him. Here was another mess to clean up. They'd just made up after the *"hey stud"* phone call, and now another woman crawled out of the woodwork. If the shit around him got any higher, he'd need a shovel. He'd explain to Cassie who Amanda was because it had to be obvious that they'd had sex. His manwhore rep was coming back to haunt him again.

Jogging to the table, Marcus picked up his coffee, and slowly walked back to Cassie who'd turned back to the group. Was she angry? He'd grovel, but he was also going to claim her today.

He eyed her sweet, heart-shaped ass in the faded jeans she was wearing and the dark green tank top that emphasized her pretty tits. He'd never been with a sexier woman.

Marcus desperately wanted Cassie to acknowledge him. He wanted her eyes to light up when she saw him. But Amanda had pulled her shit and maybe ruined the day. *No*, that damn voice in his head said, *it's not Amanda, it's your years of dicking around that are biting you in the ass.*

****

Cassie half listened to Maddy talking to Regina and Sue as she watched the byplay between Marcus and another woman—the same woman who'd tried to stop him at the Horse. That bitch had teasingly touched Marcus's arm and emphasized her tits—that were practically falling out of her too-low top—with a sly smile. She might as well have used a laser pointer, "Remember these?" He'd obviously slept with her, but he'd shrugged her off and abruptly walked away. *Calm down. He's done nothing to make you angry. You know his past.*

143

And Marcus had looked worried when he'd seen her watching, and was on his way to her right now. *You're exclusive, in daily contact, and sleep together whenever you can.* But she was falling hard for him, so handling his past was more difficult than ever. She had to let go of it—either trust him, or stop seeing him. She couldn't bear the thought of breaking with him, but his questionable reputation was smacking her in the face.

Right in the face, because Big Tits and her buddy were heading her way. As they passed her, the woman whined, "You know I'm a champ at blowjobs, Jenn. Rudy told me I had a mouth like a Hoover. So, I thought Marcus would want seconds but..." She noticed Cassie, threw her a look that could kill, and flounced off.

Gross, Cassie shivered. "So Cassie, will you come speak to our high school seniors who want to be writers? It's no more than an hour, and that includes Q&A."

"Of course, Regina, I'll be happy to do it. I'll come to the library on Monday and we can set up a date and time."

"Wonderful, Cassie."

At that moment, Maddy looked over Cassie's shoulder and muttered, "Incoming."

An arm circled her waist, pulling her back into his front. She quivered when his breath whispered in her ear, "Mornin', Cassandra."

His hard body against her, the potency of his masculine scent, and god, that deep, gravelly voice melted any thoughts about his reputation or that she was pressed into his body in front of the town librarian.

"Marcus," she answered in a breathy voice.

That's all she could manage, his virile sexuality scrambling her brain.

He lifted his face from her ear, "Morning, ladies, boys." Regina and Sue greeted him, taking in the scene with amusement.

"Nice day, Marcus." Maddy's eyes sparkled with mischief, "I see you finally found the right group."

"And the right woman," he kissed her on the cheek, then draped his arm around her shoulders, "It's going to be a fun day for the town."

Maddy's son Jason whined, "Mom, I'm hungry." Before Maddy could answer, Marcus stepped away from Cassie, and ruffled Jason's hair, "I am too, bud, so you go grab a table and grill, and we'll get you some food. You're gonna need energy for Frisbee because you're both on my team." Jason gazed at Marcus, hero worship written on his face.

"Come on, Jay," Danny raced to the picnic tables, and Jason took off right behind him.

Her breath caught. He was being wonderful with the boys, and today the boys would get a little of what they needed.

Regina brought Cassie back to the conversation in a no-nonsense voice, "Sue, let's go help set up." But a moment after she said goodbye, she turned back, "Marcus, the library cannot begin to thank you enough for the job you did on its roof, and before our insurance check even came in. We're overwhelmed by your generosity."

"Regina, my company is here to help the town in any way it can."

She beamed at him, "You're a good man, Marcus." Then she turned and caught up with Marge.

145

"What a wonderful thing to do for the library," Maddy chimed in. "I hear you repaired Mike Sloan's auto shop, too. And that you wouldn't take money from him, since his deductible was so high. And," Maddy continued, "that you're working non-stop on a slew of other houses and businesses on the river."

His humble reply, "I have a company that can help. Anyone else with my resources would have done the same thing. It's no big deal," had Cassie bursting with pride.

It was a big deal. She went on tiptoe and kissed him lightly on the lips. She saw his surprise, then he took over, kissing her back. Her head spun when he whispered, his breath caressing her ear, "Be careful with your kisses, Cassandra before I put you over my shoulder, carry you to my boat right now and eat your pussy until you scream. I can still taste you on the back of my tongue after a week."

Wet heat surged through her body, but Danny's gagging sounds and loud, "Gross," broke them apart. Oh no, the boys were back and had seen their hot kiss.

"You don't like kissing girls, Danny?" Marcus teased while Maddy and Cassie laughed.

Danny shook his head hard from side to side. "Honey," Maddy, looked at her son, "I'll ask you that question again in seven or eight years."

"I don't get it, mom." Danny looked puzzled.

Before anyone could answer, Jason, scooted close to Marcus, grabbed on to Marcus's leg and asked, "Is Aunt Cassie your girlfriend?"

Marcus released Cassie and crouched down on his haunches, making Cassie's stomach dip.

He rubbed Jason's head and said, "Yep, she sure is."

Danny moved in and asked plaintively, "Does that mean you can visit us and play games with us?" Her nephew's desperation hurt to watch. Cassie realized with a jolt that Maddy had married a man who was unavailable, just like their father had been.

Still crouching, he had both boys leaning up against him, his arms around their waists, "Yeah, we'll have lots of playtime."

"Cassie," Maddy whispered, "He's so good with them. Look how my guys are leaning into him. I'm tearing up, wishing they had a dad like that."

"Marcus is enjoying himself, and he's a parent, you know. His son, Aiden, is in college in New York, like Eva and Abby. He's close with Aiden now, but he wasn't always. I don't know all of it."

Maddy nodded, but she jerked liked she'd been slapped, when Marcus told the boys, "When my friends Bret and Derek come later, we'll teach you how to play horseshoes, so grab those bags over there and carry them to the table." Marcus stood and grabbed the handle of a large cooler as Maddy's face flushed, "Derek is coming to the picnic? Derek Prescott?"

"Yeah, Bret and Rachel should be here any minute and Derek within an hour. Why?"

"Nothing, just surprised," Maddy mumbled and busied herself gathering bags, as Marcus followed the boys.

"Spill now sis," Cassie demanded as they both picked up supplies and walked to Marcus.

"Cass, another time, okay? "Maddy's expression made Cassie back off. "We'll have a girls night, and soon."

The boys ran back with Marcus following, "Mom, I'm starving," Danny shouted.

"Okay, okay," slowly Maddy followed Danny, who yelled out to Jason, "Mom says we can have a snack now."

"What's up with Maddy? Her face went beet red when she heard Derek was coming." Marcus pulled another cooler as he walked with Cassie.

"She knows Derek because she works as a clerk at the courthouse. I think she likes him."

"Too bad for her. Derek will never go there."

"Guess we'll find out when he gets here." Cassie gave him a quick peck on the lips, "Let's get this picnic started."

Chapter Thirteen

It was near dusk, the setting sun streaking the western sky with ribbons of orange and gold.

Marcus sat on the picnic table, his feet on the bench, watching Cassie, Maddy, and Rachel pack up the food and supplies. Bret had gone to the parking area to get his truck and drive it to the park entrance so they could load up. He was driving everyone home, so Marcus could take Cassie to his boat, and finally ease the ache in his cock that had begun the moment he saw her this morning.

"Ready for me to jump in here and help you out, ladies?"

"Cool it, big man. We pack, you guys haul," Maddy ordered.

He leaned back on his arms, thinking back on the day, when his stomach knotted as he spotted Pete and Joe walking toward him, Joe holding Pete's arm. He'd seen Joe in the morning, when he'd carried in donations, and like two brothers they'd punched each other's shoulders and hugged. "I've been a jerk, and we'll talk later," Joe said quietly. But Pete had been busy at the diner for the morning rush, so he hadn't had a chance to talk to him. Cassie spotted Pete and moved toward him, but Marcus shook his head. She nodded and resumed cleaning up.

It was reckoning time. Marcus jumped off the table and walked to them. They stopped inches apart from each other. Then Marcus wrapped his arms around Pete, who murmured, "Son," pulling Marcus tightly to him. It was dead silence around them, except for a few sniffles.

They broke apart, Marcus controlling the burn in his eyes. "Old man, next week, you and me at the Horse, beers and pool."

His voice heavy with shame, Pete tried to lighten it to a teasing, "Best out of five, and prepare to owe me."

"You wish."

"Mac..."

"Not now, Pete. You look tired, get some rest and kiss your girls on the way out."

"Okay, but we'll talk then."

Marcus breathed deeply, feeling his muscles loosen with relief, and watched the two men he loved as much as Liam and Sean leave. *Yes, I do love.* The joy of it overwhelmed him.

"Marcus?" Cassie called as she wiped her eyes with a tissue.

"It's all good." Maybe it was. "Finish up ladies, Bret should be back with the truck any minute."

He jumped back on the table thinking back on the day. Thankfully he'd mended things with Joe and Pete, and he thought about everything that had changed, recently.

Bret and Rachel were sleeping together, no one could miss that, though Bret had recently told Marcus that he had no plans on getting serious with a woman. "You found Cassie, and I'm happy for you. But I'm taking your place in little old Riverbend—one fuck and done for me." Looked like Rachel was in for a heartbreak.

But the shocker of the day was Derek showing up at all, and when he did, he wheeled right over to Maddy, who was sitting at a picnic table watching her boys play catch. Derek and Maddy's attraction to each other was on full display—their intense flirting even turned him on. Wheelchair bound with a spinal cord injury from over twenty years ago, when he, Derek, and Bret found themselves in a firefight in the Gulf war, Marcus knew that Derek would never become serious with a woman.

Years ago after a night of drinking, Derek spilled to Marcus, *No woman wants a man in a chair, but I have a few women on the side who know my limitations, and how I need it. Raw, dominant, and no fucking entanglements. Ever.*

They never spoke of it again, but with his history and mindset, what was Derek thinking, coming on to Maddy and even spending time with her sons? After a few hours, Derek's M.O. surfaced, and he'd abruptly cut himself off. Marcus couldn't miss the hurt on Maddy's face when Derek left. Cassie would surely be up his ass about his best friend.

One incident had pissed him off, but it also started him thinking about the vandalism.

It was when Frank Warner, lowlife and sleazy small-time contractor, who was somehow bidding against him for the University dorms, had come on to Cassie. It had severely tested Marcus's control.

He'd been playing horseshoes with Bret, Derek, and the boys. He'd looked over at Cassie, and there

151

she was talking to Frank, who was standing close to her. Too close. She looked uncomfortable, and Marcus could see the tension in her shoulders as she took a card from Frank's hand.

Marcus had gone ballistic. "No way," he'd said and was about to take off to stake his claim when Bret had stopped him. "Calm down, Mac. You look like you're going to kill Frank."

"Ease up, buddy." Derek commanded.

"I'm good" Marcus took a deep breath and quickly walked over to Cassie. He was good, unless Frank tried to touch her—then he was a dead man.

As he slipped an arm around Cassie's shoulders, pulling her to his side, he lifted his chin, "Warner."

"Mackenzie," Frank unhappily assessed the situation.

"Never seen you at the annual picnic, Frank."

"I decided to be more neighborly. See if I could help people who were swamped by the storm."

"I'll bet you were."

Frank's face darkened at the dis. Then he smiled smugly. "Call me any time for an estimate, Cassandra, or house repair, or anything else you may need." Without waiting for an answer, he turned away, stopped, and threw back at Marcus, "See you at the university bidding wars."

"What a creep," Cassie shivered as they watched Frank stopping people and handing out his cards. "Is he a competitor of yours?"

Leaning down, Marcus nuzzled her hair. "He's an ass-wipe. Forget him." But something was off about Frank. That smug smile taunted that he had a secret. Marcus's instincts were good. They'd saved his ass throughout his life, and right now they were screaming at him not to ignore Frank's threat. Did he have something to do with the recent vandalism that could take Mackenzie Construction and Engineering out of the bidding? He wouldn't put it past the scumbag who had skirted criminal behavior for years. A few more acts against Marcus's company, and their reputation for superior workmanship, completing projects on time, and finishing within budget would be in tatters.

Monday, he would set up another meeting with everyone, including Derek, and figure out how to legally investigate Frank. But that would wait. He had a hot date tonight.

As night descended, turning the sky to vivid purples, his mind turned to Cassie.

Very soon she'd be playing naked first mate to his captain.

With his arm around Cassie's shoulders, and her hand around his waist, they watched Bret's truck drive away.

"You're all mine now," Marcus pulled her around to face him, ran a hand up into her hair, gripped her ponytail and tilted her head up to meet his eyes. He read her raw need, and heat and desire percolated between them.

She held onto his arms, then skimmed her hands up under his tee shirt to his back, stroking and kneading his muscles, drawing him closer into her willing body. He rolled his erection into her belly, and the low hum in her throat created a heavy ache in him.

Wrapping an arm around her, he tugged her tightly into his body and slowly nibbled and flicked his tongue over her parted lips. She whimpered when he

153

ran the tip of his tongue back and forth over her jaw, then nipped it.

Sliding her ponytail holder off, Marcus ran his fingers through her hair and buried his face in the soft waves, breathing in her addictive aroma, "Every time you bent over one of the ice chests, and your glorious ass wiggled, all I wanted to do was pull those shorts off, bend you over a picnic table, and take you from behind." He nipped her lobe, she squealed, and he growled low, "I've been brutally hard all day. Think I set a Guinness World Record for blue balls."

She pulled away, passion radiating between them. "Maybe," she teased, "if you behave, I'll drop to my knees and ease your suffering."

"Oh lass, you'll be sucking my cock before the sun fully sets." Before she could answer, Marcus was holding her captive by her biceps. His face was stern, but his eyes danced with mischief.

She smiled, but there was a wariness on her face. He loved playing with her.

"The first mate on my boat is actually a maiden that was captured on one of my raids. She's my prisoner, my sex slave, and she will obey me in everything."

Marcus tightened his grip. Cassie laughed, and wrenched out of his arms. She took off running, taunting him over her shoulder, "You have to catch me first, Captain Blue Balls."

"Captain Blue Balls?" Marcus bellowed, "You brat," and took off after her.

Cassie squealed. She was fast, but he was faster. His thundering footfalls had her screaming in delight. He caught her arm, and in a flash threw her over his shoulder.

Shrieking with laughter, Cassie banged on his back. Marcus swatted her ass and warned, "Aye, lass, stop that or you'll get a good spanking as soon as we get to my boat. Before I have you tied and on your knees so your fuckable mouth can turn my balls from blue to white, your ass will be red."

"Please, please, oh mighty Captain Blu—I mean Captain Hottie." She laughed so hard she was stuttering as she begged, "Please, Sir, let me down."

"Captain Hottie is it, wench? I like it, but I like 'Sir,' much better." He never had fun with women, but Cassie had a shining life-force that pulled him into a joy that he'd never experienced.

I won't ever let her go.

She pounded on his back, bringing him back to the present. "You better be good, I mean it." He swatted her butt again.

"Ow, ow! I'm good with my mouth, Sir."

"Are you now? If you don't please me, I'll give you a good spanking like I promised." He tortured himself by turning his head toward her and catching the scent of her spicy arousal, with that underlying hint of the coconut lotion she wore. He took a deep breath, "I can smell how you burn for me," and nuzzled the side of her ass.

"You're a dirty, pervy man, Captain."

"I am, and I'm going to spend a good part of the night between your legs eating my fill of you."

"Eat away, Captain, any time you like."

Chuckling, he came to the path to the river. From there it was only a few yards to the dock and his boat.

"We're here." Gently, he slid her down his body onto the dock.

"Oh, Marcus, it's a beauty." The hull was white and sleek with a thin blue stripe running across the bottom, just above the water line. Portholes ran along the slide, right above the stripe.

"It's a twenty-three-foot Bayliner, the best boat to sail on the river."

"I've never been on one. Seen them of course. We had a boat—who didn't when you live on the river—but my dad only had a small motorboat. Oh, you named it *Nevermore*."

She shone her bright light at him—he loved how she sparkled when she was happy.

"I thought you would get a kick out of it."

"I love it."

His heart was full of Cassie tonight. He was showing her a private part of himself. He rarely invited Liam—he preferred to sail alone. When he sailed, he was free of worries about the past or the present. Being on the river was magical. He loved the wind in his face and the power of the boat as it cut through the deadly currents. The scent of brine and sediment, and the thrill of seeing a heron taking flight, were carved into his senses.

But with Cassandra, the prescribed rules of the way he lived were being swept away, just like the river eventually swept the land clean after a flood. He couldn't give her the kind of love she needed, the love of a good man, but he could give her this part of himself—his love of the river.

"Come on board." It was ridiculous how much he wanted to impress her. They stepped onto the deck and he watched her awe as she looked around, then showed her the cockpit, pointing to a chair facing the controls. "This is where the captain sits. Let's go," he took her hand, and took her below deck. "In this one small space," he swept his hand from bow to aft, "is the galley, head, and storage."

"Oh, this is beautiful," she ran her hand over a cabinet front.

"All the wood appointments are teak, the best wood for boats. And over there," she turned as he pointed to a large triangular mattress that took up almost the entire front of the boat, "is the sleeping area, a V berth. It also converts to a table and benches for eating. But you're not going to see the table anytime soon." He licked below her ear and promised, "You're going to become acquainted with every inch of that bed. You'll be screaming so loud while you're coming that you'll scare the damn fish to death."

"Just saying Captain, you'll be doing some screaming yourself."

"Maybe I will, baby. Let's sail."

Back in the cockpit, he pulled up the anchor, sat in the captain's chair and turned to her, "We're going to a quiet cove, but first, it's time to get you into uniform."

"And that is?"

He enjoyed her wariness, and lowered his voice, "Strip."

Her eyes narrowed, "Are you serious?"

"As serious as a flood warning."

She cocked an eyebrow, " Marcus, really?"

"Be careful, disobedient first mates have to walk the plank." He crossed his arms over his chest.
"I'm waiting."

Cassie hesitated. But when she remembered that she was free to explore her sexual needs, be wild, without judgment for the first time in her life—and that Marcus thought she was beautiful—she let go of self-doubt.

Smiling slyly, she began to dance, slowly removing her top and bra, shaking her shoulders, then holding her breasts out to him as an offering—his laughter morphed into dark, molten lust that left her breathless. She lowered the zipper of her shorts one millimeter at a time, pulled them off along with her thong, and boldly put her hands on her hips. "Does this uniform please the captain?"

He raked her over, his chest rising and falling with rapid breaths. When he twirled his finger for her to turn, her knees wobbled, but she did as he ordered. "You've a beautiful body, lass."

"Captain," she looked around and spotted a padded bench-seat across from his chair, "where does the first mate sit?"

He grinned slyly, and pointed between his legs.

Her heart hammered with anticipation. He crooked his finger, and she eagerly went to him.

Pulling her to him, he ran the tip of his tongue around her belly button as he stroked and squeezed her ass, the calluses on his hands catching lightly on her skin as they would with silk cloth. His other hand played with her breasts, stroking and tweaking her nipples. She needed to touch him, too, and she ran her hands through the thick waves of his hair.

"Hands at your sides, Cassandra," the command was mumbled as he licked her belly, then held her hips with both hands and sucked around the top of her mound. She bucked her hips into his face, her skin hot to the touch. "Marcus, I want." If only he would lower his mouth just a bit, and suck.

"Do as I say, and you'll get what you want—later." He pulled back and looked up at her.

"But first, you're going to use that pretty, ripe mouth on my cock as I take us to the cove." He let go of her and reached for a cushion that he threw on the floor between his splayed legs, then turned his chair to the controls.

She crawled onto the cushion, kneeled, and placed one hand on his thigh. With the other she stroked his cock over the soft faded denim and tilted her head up. "Is this position pleasing to my captain?"

His nostrils flared as he started the engine and pulled away from the dock. "Get to work."

She unzipped his pants, and when he hiked up, she pulled them off with his black boxers, down to his ankles.

His delicious cock bobbed in front of her, and when she took hold of the smooth silk over steel and stroked him twice, he pressed his hips into her hand. His balls were already drawn up, ready to blow.

Primal musk assaulted her senses, as she bent forward and licked the salty drops from his slit.

"Suck me," he hissed and spread his legs wider.

Playing her tongue on the vee underneath the head, she took him in her mouth as far as she could, and began licking and sucking him like she was lapping up water, while the hand at the base of his shaft played counterpoint. Saliva pooled on his balls, and she dove down, rolling his balls in her mouth, while she jacked him. She reveled in his groans as he ground his hips into her hand. She was close, too, and she freed a hand to rub her clit.

"Stop, stop," he grabbed a handful of hair and pulled her off of him.

"Are you crazy?"

"We're here. I'm not coming in your mouth. I'll have us docked in a sec. And then I'm going to bend you over that bench," he tipped his head to the padded seat, "and fuck you—hard." He stood, pulled up his pants, pulled her up to stand, and placed her on the side of the controls. "Do not move."

The bold taste of him on the back of her tongue and his stern order created a searing hunger for him. If he didn't hurry, she'd jump him and ride them both to peak. But with lightning speed, Marcus docked, dropped anchor, and turned on the sidelights.

He turned to her, his chest pumping for air, and his face, *my god*—his lips curled in a silent snarl, and greedy, lidded eyes ravished her. She blinked, and he was on her. Rough hands rushed into her hair, holding her head, tilting it as his mouth met hers.

Cassie held on to his biceps to keep herself from drowning in him as he tongue-fucked her mouth. She sucked on his tongue, and when he pulled away, one hand holding her head, watching her, he slid two fingers into her pussy. She arched into him.

"You're drenched." He finger fucked her for a few moments. He pulled out, and heat curled down her spine when he sucked his fingers into his mouth, "Pure, fucking, honey."

She shrieked when he picked her up and carried her to the bench. He faced her away from him on her knees. "Lean on the back, spread your legs, and tip up your ass." She heard his pants drop, and a condom wrapper tear.

"Oh my god," his tongue licked from her pussy to her anus, the tip rimming her until she was panting, every nerve sizzling with a direct line to her clit.

"Yeah, you like when I play with your ass."

160

"It's dirty," she stammered.

"You're a dirty girl under all that responsibility."

Her reply was silenced when Marcus ran his tongue to her ass cheeks, and sucked on each one, then said, "Oh, I forgot something." She yelped when he wrapped a hand around her waist, and began to spank her, "You're still a beginner, so five it is." Leaning against the back of the bench, she buried her face in her hands as he peppered each smack across her butt, never hitting the same place twice, as he'd done a few weeks ago. Then held his hand over the burn.

The spanking sparked every molecule in her body into a raging fire.

He caressed her back, "Cassie, are you okay?" His voice was taut with worry.

She began to laugh and looked at him over her shoulder. Her body thrummed for sex, and when she ordered, "For god's sake, Marcus, fuck me," lust glittered in his eyes.

"Hold on, baby." Rough pubic hairs brushed over the backs of her legs. He leaned over and began playing with her breasts, his weight and the heat radiating off of his body had her right on the edge.

"I'll go slow since I haven't taken you from behind, but baby, I'll be buried so deep, you'll feel me in your bones." With one hand on her butt, the other guided his cock to her entrance. Slowly but relentlessly, he penetrated her until he was seated at her womb. She basked in the intense fullness of being completely dominated by the raw strength of his body as he held still to allow her to adjust.

She ached for that intimate connection with him, that first hard thrust, "Marcus, move."

"Bossy girl," and he began to thrust and *yes* he hit that spot, and he laughed when she mewled. "Got the g-spot. Now, let's add..." and he reached around one hand to press and tap her clit, the other tweaking a nipple.

"Oh god, oh god," he pounded into her, his chest hair tickling her slick back. "More." She tipped her ass back to meet him stroke for stroke. The room filled with the slap of their bodies, grunts, moans, and the musky smell of sweat and sex—the best aphrodisiac ever.

"Oh, oh, oh," he probed her anus with a finger and slowly entered her until he was knuckle deep, and fucked her ass in sync with his cock. A brilliant burn began, building and building, she surrendered to a vivid white peak of inexplicable ecstasy, and came screaming his name.

She collapsed, but Marcus held her up with one hand around her waist, shortened his thrusts, hammering his release into her, and roared "Cassandra." He melted into her, burying his face in her hair, his heart thudding into her back.

Not sure how long they lay like that, she finally roused and muttered, "I need to pee, but I can't move."

"Let me get rid of the condom, then it's all yours. That's if I can get up." But he climbed off, went to the head, came back, and it was Cassie's turn. She exited the toilet, and Marcus was at the controls, bare chested, jeans back on but not fully buttoned. Lucky her.

"Come here." She went to him, naked and a little less insecure about it after the mind-blowing sex. Taking her in his arms he kissed her deeply, cupped her ass, and pulled her into his hips.

"That was incredible, Cassie," he muttered on her lips, "thought I'd busted a blood vessel or two."

She pulled back a little to gaze at him and gently smoothed his hair back from his forehead.

"It was amazing, my throat is raw from screaming. Poor little fish, hope they survived. And you stuck your finger in my ass, again."

"I love playing with your ass, you know that, and it took your orgasm to new heights. Wait until it's my cock."

"I'm not quite ready for that big boy just yet."

"Then soon." He handed her a tee shirt. "Put this on, then I'll help you onto the bow, and we can stargaze for a while. But no panties, baby, I may want to play while we're out there."

She put on the shirt, gave him a sexy once over, "Do not button your jeans, I may want to play, too."

He laughed out loud, "Anytime, my cock is all yours." He hooked her by the nape and kissed her fast and hard. But his lips softened, and she heard him sigh before he pulled his head back, and gazed deeply into her eyes with an expression she'd seen before. It was the look of love. Her breath picked up. Would he finally say those three little words to her? "Cassandra, what we have is more than I've ever..."

Her hopes rose. Yes, he was going to say it, *I love you,* or something close to it.

The loud ringtone from his cell broke the spell like glass shattering, and stopped him cold.

Her heart fell. *It's happening again. Every time he's ready to say something special that damn phone rings or a crazy man breaks the moment.*

The call ended, and immediately rang again.

Marcus let go of her and stepped back a little too quickly, as if he'd pushed her away. A sense of dread crept up her spine. "What's the matter?" She placed a hand on his arm.

Her stomach knotted when he pulled away. "It's Liam. It's trouble."

Chapter Fourteen

"Trouble? How do you know?" He didn't want to have a conversation, he wanted to find his damn phone. "One ring, stop, one ring, then repeat is a signal we use when there's an emergency," his tone sharp as a blade. *Christ,* it wasn't her fault that this was happening, but every muscle in his body was strung tight because there was only one reason that Liam would call at this time—vandalism.

"What can I do, Marcus, please—"

"Nothing," he brusquely cut her off, found his phone, and hit Liam's number. "Tell me," he ordered.

He'd shut down. Cassie stepped away from him.

"It's the Mayfield, Mac. Fire. But it's out, and the police—"

"I'm on the boat, gonna dock and be there within the hour. Wait for me."

He speed dialed Bret while he went to the controls, and told him to meet them at the dock. "Get dressed," he spat, and watched her face pale.

Ice. He had to become ice. He couldn't care about her now. Being cold and frozen were old survival mechanisms. Cutting off everyone and everything was the only way he could contain his fear and control his rage—the killing rage.

165

****

Cassie's limbs felt leaden. The shock of Marcus's clipped, "Get dressed," hit her like a stun gun. It was an emergency, and she knew all about emergencies, but she'd never hurt those around her when things were going down.

The real Marcus had shown up again. After he'd thrown those words at her, he'd started the engine as if she weren't there. Why couldn't he allow her to be there for him?

Cassie had heard Liam yelling through the phone from across the room—fire in the Mayfield build. Terrible, yes, but Marcus's reaction was to aim his worry and anger at her.

They'd had a fantastic day, had come out as a couple, and Marcus and Pete were good.

And they'd made love, and though they'd had raunchy sex, to Cassie, it was intimate, too. And my god, he'd lovingly held her and was on the cusp of admitting his feelings for her. Until that phone call.

She took a deep breath and began to dress. She found her top and shorts but couldn't find her panties. After thoroughly searching the floor, she gave up. They would dock any minute now.

What should she do? She stood near the bench and watched him. His hands were steering the boat, but they looked disembodied because his head and body were rigid and unmoving. It was as if he'd calcified into solid concrete.

He didn't turn her way, not even to give her a quick look, or a head tilt, or apologize, or tell her to sit down. Nothing.

It was as if she wasn't on the boat.

Tears welled in her eyes, and she stifled a sob. Why couldn't he communicate with her? That's what couples did. *But remember, Marcus is clueless about relationships.* She was who she was, and a big part of that was being a forgiving and loving woman. Her feelings for him ran deep. She wanted to comfort him, put her arms around his stiff shoulders, tell him it would be okay, that he could lean on her.

Heart pounding, Cassie walked up to his chair from the back. He was so focused on steering the boat that she was sure that he wasn't even aware how close she was to him. Softly, she put a hand on his shoulder and stilled, testing him. "Marcus," she whispered.

Without looking at her, not even giving her an eye flick, Marcus dealt her another blow when he roughly shrugged her hand off of him so hard that she jerked back a step.

"Sit. Down. Cassandra." His barbed words pierced her.

Keep control. Keep control. She chanted the mantra to herself and forced her tears back. Quietly, she walked to the seat and sat at the edge of the cushion. Clasping her hands in her lap, she waited for this tortuously slow sail to the dock to end. Though she ached for the funny, sexy, caring Marcus who'd been present today, this brutally cold-hearted man was not worth the heartache.

For weeks, she'd worried about him breaking it off with her, but right now she couldn't wait to get away from him.

****

Monday morning, Cassie sat on the patio, drinking a cup of coffee and eating a snickerdoodle. Last night, when she couldn't sleep, she'd looked through a closet that held some of Shirl's things and found her sewing basket, which led to a long crying session.

The basket contained an unfinished canvas of a picture of the cottage. It was lovingly wrapped, and the date on the design was almost eleven years ago, just before Shirl was diagnosed with cancer. The basket now sat next to the sofa, where she'd spent many days as a girl with Shirl, doing needlepoint, eating cookies, being loved.

She'd also stumbled upon Shirl's box of recipes and cried out with joy. And sure enough, there was the one for snickerdoodles, written out in Shirl's beautifully slanted hand. It was their special cookie that Shirl always baked when Cassie was having a rough time at home. After trying to fall asleep, unable to turn off her racing thoughts, at one o'clock in the morning, Cassie had surprisingly found the ingredients in the kitchen, remembering that Annie used the cottage and often baked there. Baking had helped—a little.

I miss you, Shirl. Cassie took a sip, broke off a piece of cookie, and nibbled on it. If Shirl were alive, Cassie could talk to her, tell her everything that was happening, and take in Shirl's wisdom. She was an intuitive woman, a great listener, and always on the mark about what to do when life sucked.

Cassie sipped coffee and a memory came to her. She was a senior in high school and was complaining bitterly to Shirl about her mother, who wasn't involved in any way to help Cassie attend New York University, her first college choice. And worse, her mom had actually told her to not bother applying, that she wouldn't get in, and if she did, she and Cassie's father wouldn't help her financially.

"Cassie, I know it's hard for you to understand her, but you cannot make her into the mother you want instead of her being the mother you have," Shirl had told her as Cassie sobbed in her arms. "You cannot change another human being." Shirl wiped Cassie's eyes with a soft hankie. "All you can do is cope with it and make sure that you live a full and rich life. Pete and I will always be here for you. You can always lean on us. And sweetie," Cassie had looked up at Shirl, "You will be going to NYU." And she had, with their loving help.

Cassie gazed out over the lawn to the beauty of spring on the farm. The copper beech was beginning to blossom, the fields were being plowed, songbirds were busy building nests, and the scent of early blooming bulbs filled the air. But Cassie didn't take in any of the beauty before her because her mind was filled with Marcus. "I cannot change him," she whispered sadly.

Their goodbye was brutal. Bret was waiting on the dock when they arrived. He'd tied off the boat after Marcus threw him the line. Marcus stiffly took Cassie's elbow without a word and helped her off of the boat until Bret could grab her.

The tension on the dock was thick as river fog. Marcus didn't look at her or say one word to her, but to Bret he'd barked, "Hammond, I'll keep you posted, get her home," and then he was gone.

Get her home. Not get Cassie home, not an, "I'll

see you later," not one indication that she meant anything to him. Bret was silent on the drive to the cottage, as was she. When they'd pulled up to the cottage, she unbuckled her seatbelt and jumped out of his truck before he could move. Giving him a hasty, "Thanks Bret," and without looking back at him, she ran up the path, as he called out, "Take care, Cassie."

Now, it was a day and a half later, and Marcus hadn't called, texted, or emailed. She'd phoned him on Sunday. "Hope everything is okay." No response.

She'd texted him again, later that evening. Nothing. She had to try one more time, so this morning, she called his office. A kind woman told her that Marcus was out, she didn't know when he'd return, and transferred Cassie to his voicemail.

Marcus's silence was loud and clear. He was done. So was she.

Marcus was who he was, she wouldn't contact him again. Taking a deep breath, she whispered, "Let him go." Sighing, Cassie finished her coffee and felt Grey begin to weave back and forth through her legs, something he'd begun to do a few days ago.

"Hey, pretty boy," she reached down to scratch his head, "I was lost in my head and didn't see you come onto the patio." He was still living outdoors, but today she decided to lure him into the house. The cat pushed his head into her hand and for the first time, he began to purr. Cassie bent, and gently held his head looking into his stunning green eyes. "Aww, you're purring." He blinked at her, as if he agreed.

She pushed back her chair and stood, picking up her mug and paper plate that had a few cookies left on it. Looking down at the cat, Cassie told him, "It's time to man up and come inside, and not behave like another man I know who is too damn scared to do that." She already had a litter box set up in the tiny mudroom, and bowls in the kitchen with kibble and water. An old soft quilt was folded on the floor near her bed.

"Hey Grey, come on in. It's time to see your new home." She slid the glass door open, walked through it, left it open and looked back at him.

"Come on baby," she clucked softly when her phone rang. It was Pete. She'd successfully warded off Rachel and Maddy coming over yesterday. Thankfully they'd both been busy, but they were all meeting for dinner this coming Friday. By then, she'd be able to talk about it. Maybe.

But she couldn't put off Pete, so she answered the call.

"Hey, whatcha doing?"

She looked back at the open door and Grey was as few inches inside. He stood there, watching her. Not wanting to spook him, she went into the kitchen.

"Just drinking coffee, Pete."

"What's the matter, Cassie?"

Pete could read her well, but she didn't want to talk to him, and certainly not about Marcus. Not right now.

"Uh—it's nothing."

"Nothing, huh? I'll be there in a sec."

****

The snickerdoodles were eaten, and the mugs of coffee were empty. Heart aching, Cassie watched Pete wistfully hold the needlepoint canvas in his hands as if it were a delicate piece of lace.

"Yes," he said, staring at the canvas, "my lovely bride loved her needlepoint."

"That she did. And she taught me well."

"She often told me how much it meant to her that you were interested, and that she could teach it to you. Maddy, no. That girl only wanted to plow the fields with me. But you?" He put the canvas down on the table. "You, were all about Shirl."

"I was. She was the mother mine couldn't be."

"She was that. I loved your father like a brother, but he and your mom," he gave a half shrug, "they were troubled."

It felt like a door had opened. *Troubled?* That was an understatement. The ghosts of her past were no longer buried like they were when she lived in California. *No, this is not for now.* Cassie focused on Pete, "You look tired. A little pale. Are you feeling okay?"

"Think I'm coming down with something. For the last few days. I'm tired, and my back hurts. Maybe it's the flu, or just the change of the season."

"Going to see doc Taylor?"

"Yeah, Annie forced the issue. Appointment is tomorrow at ten."

"Good. You have to take care of yourself, or no more cookies," she laughed.

"You and Annie are bossy girls."

"We are," she teased. She picked up the canvas, "If you don't mind, Pete, I want to finish this."

"She would love you to do that. My Shirl hated to leave something undone, but she was too sick to even thread a needle, at the end," his voice cracked.

172

"When it's finished, I think instead of a pillow, I'll have it stretched and framed."

"You were always a kind and loving girl, Cassie." Yes, he still thought of her as a girl, and that had led to problems, but right now she needed to be that for him. And maybe for her, too, because she was feeling a little lost since Saturday night.

"I love you, old man."

"Instead of calling me names," he chuckled, "how about you pour me another cup of your excellent joe."

"Aye, sir," she laughed, put the canvas down, picked up their mugs, set them on the counter, and began to fill them.

Pete pointed at Grey who had hesitatingly come into the house, but now was peacefully sleeping on a sunny spot on the floor. "So you finally got him in, I see."

"Yeah, right before you called."

"He's home now," *Just like me.*

Cassie poured coffee and brought the mugs to the table.

"Snickerdoodles, needlepoint, and memories. What's really bothering you, Cassie?"

Her head snapped up, and she was caught in those perceptive blue eyes. "It's nothing, Pete."

"I don't see *nothing* when I look at you. I see something. Not something old. Something fresh."

Her voice shook, "It's... I'm still getting settled, you know. The insurance agent will be giving me their estimate, so I can start that process, and..." She had to detour Pete away from worrying about her, about her house that he didn't want her to move into, and about why she was so sad. "And guess what?"

173

"What, baby," he said softly, his words hit her hard, because that's what Marcus had called her a few times.

"I reached out to an editor I'd worked with before and she's interested in getting a proposal from me, and I also talked to Andy Hartwell, a few days ago. He was an editor at the L.A. Times. I'd worked freelance for him from time to time, writing articles about new psych research. Well, he moved to a woman's lifestyle magazine a year ago, and I'm sending him a proposal for an article. Or maybe a series of articles."

He smiled, lifted his mug to his lips, said, "That is so good to hear, Cass. So what's it about?"

"The working title is, 'Finding Home Again.'"

His eyes flashed with surprise and interest. "Go on."

"I'm writing my story, but it will include research, too." Cassie picked her mug up, then cradled it in both of her hands. "The theme is, how do you find a way to begin a new life, without a roadmap, when your partner dies? Your love was your real home, not necessarily the physical structure that you lived in. So how do you begin to find home again in all the grief?"
Pete held her eyes and she saw his tears well to the brim, but the big man controlled them. When a tear rolled down her cheek, Pete reached across the table and wiped it away with his thumb.

"Know what you're feeling, girl, but the farm, the rhythm of the seasons, the hard work it takes to keep it up—that helped me to weather that battle."

"I know it did. Living in LA, after Ron died, I was..." she hesitated, but found the word, "untethered."

"Just saying, Cassie, I'm no expert, and I hope I

don't upset you, but honey, you were untethered for a longer time than that."

She lowered her eyes, yes, she'd been disconnected for years. The decision to move back to Riverbend had many facets. One was that she hoped to reconnect with people she loved.

Pete let her hand go and sat back on the chair. "Cassie," he pointed to himself, the canvas, and his arm swept the room. "Me, Shirl, the farm, and this cottage have always been your home. Your tether."

She forced a small smile, "Did I ever tell you how smart you were?"

"You better believe it. Now, you've got man troubles, and I can guess who that man is."

She sighed, "Yes, of course it's Marcus, smartypants. I'll tell you what happened, and maybe you can give me some insight into him, but Marcus and I are finished."

"Tell me."

Thirty minutes later, they moved outside to the patio. Sitting across from each other, they were so close that their knees touched.

"I like him Pete, even though he hurt me. But I'm also angry. Years ago, Shirl gave me good advice, and I'm trying to live it. 'You cannot change or fix another person,' she told me. So, I'm doing the best I can, by moving on."

He hadn't said a word as he listened to her story. But now, his face was thoughtful, as if he were trying to come to a decision. Cassie waited. He was a man who didn't jump into conversation but had to think things through, except of course when he'd banged their door down while she and Marcus were banging each other.

175

"I've known Marcus for a long time. I'm not going to say how or when we met, because that's for him to tell."

"I know some of it. I saw a photo of you and Marcus taken in front of the farmhouse. He said he was sixteen."

Pete stood and walked to the edge of the patio. "Yes, I met him two weeks before Shirl took that photo." He turned back to her. "He doesn't trust easily, men or women, and his reasons are good ones. He's badly damaged, Cass. He acts out, especially toward women, and uses them. That's why I lost my ever-loving mind when I found out that you were with him."

"Pete," Cassie stood, walked to Pete, bent, and kissed his cheek. "No worries. Marcus has been pushing and pulling at me since we met. I know he's a troubled man."

"He is."

"He told me that his father is in prison for life for murdering his mother's boyfriend and for trying to kill her."

Pete's forehead creased, "I'm surprised he gave that much away. He holds his past close to his chest. His parents are a great source of shame for him."

Shame. Is that why he can't commit to a woman or take comfort? Because he believes he's unworthy? "He broke up with me, and I'm pretty sure for good. And maybe it's best from what you're telling me."

"Cassie, I—"

"I'm good Pete, I am. I only met Marcus a little over a month ago, so it's not a big deal."

Pete snorted and raised an eyebrow, "Not a big deal?" His gaze pierced her. "You love him, don't you?"

Cassie's mouth fell open. "I did fall for him."

"And I promised I would be here for you when he hurt you, remember?"

She hugged Pete, "I do, and you are."

A text sounded on his phone. He opened it. "There was a time that no one could reach you easily, but now... guess I'm going to head down to the diner, Joe needs help."

"You take care and see the doc. I'll check in with you tomorrow."

Pete walked to his truck, slower than his usual jaunty gait, and that worried her. He climbed into the driver's seat and called out, "I'm a phone call away," as he drove off.

Sighing, Cassie picked up the mugs, slid open the door, and went into the house. She cleaned up and gave Grey some love. Picking up her laptop and notes for the article and set up at the kitchen table.

You love him, don't you? But he couldn't love her, so hoping things were different was a waste of time. She had to get her head together. She had to stop thinking about Marcus and instead start thinking about herself, and her new life path.

Chapter Fifteen

After Pete left, Cassie sat down at the kitchen table and bent to her computer when she heard Maddy's ringtone.

She sighed. After this call she was muting her phone. "Hey Mad."

"What did that prick do to you?" Maddy shouted.

"Maddy, really, you just blew my eardrums out. And didn't we agree to meet this coming Friday?"

"Yeah, and we will. But I ran into Rachel this morning on the way to work, and she told me that Bret told her that Marcus was ice cold toward you when the boat docked. He didn't talk to you at all, and that the tension was deathly thick. He worried that you looked pale, like you were in shock."

"Maddy, take a breath and quiet down. I'm okay."

"I'm on my coffee break, so I only have fifteen minutes, but no, you're not okay, from what Bret said."

"Maddy, please, let it go now."

"Oh crap, that shithead Derek Prescott is wheeling my way."

"What? Maddy?" There was no answer. "Maddy?"

"Tell your motherfucking BFF to leave my sister alone, counselor, or I'll kick his balls into his body cavity," Maddy shrieked.

"Maddy! Stop talking right now and get on the phone," Cassie yelled.

"Hang on, sis."

"Madeline Harper," Cassie yelled.

Cassie jumped out of her chair when she clearly heard Derek's deep voice. "Maddy, instead of cursing at me, I can think of better things for you to do with that luscious mouth of yours."

Did he say what I thought he said? She had to stop this right now.

"Maddy, get back on the phone," Cassie yelled while she paced around the kitchen. She'd seen them flirting at the picnic, so there must be more going on between them than Maddy had let on.

"Maddy," she hollered, and Grey jumped off the windowsill.

"Sorry, boy." Then she heard Maddy tease back provocatively, "Promises, promises."

What?!

Derek's deep voice came through the phone, "Maddy, I'm sorry I said that to you, I shouldn't have. It was inappropriate, but when you cursed, it angered me."

Angry? Derek hadn't sounded angry at all, but turned on. "Maddy, I heard you say 'sis,' so may I please talk to Cassie? It's important, or I wouldn't ask."

Cassie held her breath. She was in a terrible predicament, listening to her sister's intimate byplay. She should hang up, but she wasn't going to. She had to know why Derek wanted to talk to her—it had to be about Marcus.

"Yes, it's Cassie," then Derek was on the phone.

"Cassie, hey, I'm sorry to bother you, but is Marcus with you? It's important that I talk to him."

Not a word from him apologizing to her about what he'd like to do with her sister's mouth. Okay, she could play the game that nothing was weird about what was going on during the courthouse coffee break.

"Sorry, Derek, but I can't help you. He's not here."

"Ah. Do you have any idea where he is?"

"No, I haven't heard from him since Saturday night."

She heard Maddy cut in, "She hasn't heard from the jerk because, from what Bret said, Marcus took off after they'd partied on his boat, leaving Bret to take her home. Looks like your buddy is done with her. Nice guy."

"Derek, please tell Maddy that I'm asking her to be quiet. Thank you."

"Your sister says, 'shut up.'" Did Cassie hear humor in his voice? Was any of this funny?

"What did you say to me, counselor? Shut up?"

Cassie couldn't help herself, "Sounds like the two of you are fighting in a sandbox."

"Hmm, yes, your sister does pull me into a space that is uncomfortable. Sorry."

Derek Prescott sounded anything but uncomfortable, to Cassie.

"What space are you talking about, counselor?" Maddy snapped.

"Yes, she can do that, but please ignore her for a moment, Derek. Marcus was upset and took off because of the fire at one of his buildings."

"I know, and I have important information for him. But he's not answering my calls or texts. His admin told me that he is out for the day."

"I'm sorry I can't help Derek, but as I said, he hasn't contacted me either, and I'm pretty sure that—"

should she tell Derek the truth that she and Marcus were finished? "That I won't be hearing from him."

"Are you finished with my sister, bigshot?"

"Cassie, if what you say is true, then he is truly a stupid man. But thank you, here's Maddy."

Marcus is a stupid man? What does he mean?

"Hang on again, sis, one more sec," Maddy clipped.

Cassie didn't want to hang on, she wanted to ask Derek what he meant by "stupid man."

Then Maddy let fly, "When you find your friend, Derek, I don't want that bastard near her anymore. He's playing her. You hear me, counselor?"

Cassie groaned.

"I don't think so Maddy. Not in the way you think he is."

"He is. Of course you're going to defend him, he's your bestie."

"Calm down, little girl."

"Maddy, enough," Cassie yelled into her phone.

"Little girl? Nice. And Derek, you're no better. At the picnic you flirted and played with my boys, taking them for rides. They keep asking me when they're going to see you again. Yeah, nothing to say Derek, after making my boys like you? Making me like you and then kicking us to the curb? And now you're playing me, just like he's playing her, telling me the dirty things you want to do, but of course you'll just sit in your chair and—"

"I think you've said enough, Ms. Harper," Derek's voice chilled.

"One more thing. You made me think you were into me. Everybody who saw us thought the same thing. Then this morning, while I waited for you in the courthouse parking lot, you were back to the old Derek. The cold Derek."

That's how I felt when Marcus wouldn't acknowledge me on the boat. She had to stop her sister from tearing herself up over a man who wasn't worth it.

"Maddy," Cassie yelled as loud as she could without stripping her vocal cords, "Please stop right now, or I'm hanging up."

"Sorry, Cass, I'll waste one more second on this a-hole. Counselor, go fuck yourself."

"Ah, Madeline, you know that's not how it works. And..."

"And what, big boy?"

"Yes, it is rather," Cassie heard him snicker. "But right now, I'd like to turn you over my knee, pull up that pretty dress you're wearing, pull down your panties and spank those dirty words right out of your sexy mouth."

What did he just say?

Maddy's bitter laugh brought her back to the present, "Spank me? Sure you will Derek. You're all talk and no action. I'm done with you."

"Holy shit," Cassie whispered.

"And Derek," there was a pause, "FYI, I'm not wearing panties."

"What," Cassie screeched, but heard a deep chuckle and, "You dirty girl."

You dirty girl? Derek and Maddy and... dirty?

"Cassie, I'm sorry." Maddy said, breathless, as the fast click-clack of Maddy's high heels skittered down the sidewalk.

"Maddy, what the hell is going on with you and Derek?"

"Nothing but four years of sexual frustration."

182

"Wha—"

"Coffee break is over, Cass, gotta go. See you on Friday for man bashing," and Maddy hung up.

Cassie looked at the phone in her hand. *What the hell just happened?*

****

"Crap," Marcus sat at the desk. He'd been at work by six this morning because he hadn't been able to sleep since Saturday's fiasco. And he was dragging ass. He'd checked emails but hadn't answered any. When the phone rang, he let it go to voicemail, even though Liam and Derek had called. He'd called Liam back and set up the work schedule for today. Liam still sounded pissed, but he'd patch things up with him later this week.

Of course Cassie had called to check on him. When her number came up, his breath caught in his throat, but he'd let it go to voicemail. She'd called again this morning and left a message with his admin, Janice, who told her and anyone else who called that he was out for the day.

And if he'd answered her call, what could he say? "Sorry, I was an asshole?" Would she forgive him? Take him back? He'd been a prick, and she was worried about him. He was a stranger to guilt with women. But today he was filled with it. Cassie kept messing with his head. With his ordered life. She made him think about what his life could be like, if he smashed his defensive walls to pieces.

But he couldn't really have her. He wasn't a violent man like his father, except when someone was trying to kill him. But he carried the poisonous

Mackenzie DNA, that was death to a long-term relationship. The evidence was in. Look at what happened on the boat. He'd gone inside of himself to the dark place. The place where Cassie and every person in his life ceased to exist. In that moment sailing back, he couldn't bear her touch, her comfort. He winced, remembering how cruelly he'd shrugged her hand off his shoulder. Nothing existed, only the explosive rage, which he had to control, or he might turn into the monster known as Nolan Mackenzie.

He had to clear his head and think. Today, he'd decided that he was going to hide out in his office, with Janice holding down the fort. The sixty-eight-year-old widow, who'd known him as a boy, was once a teacher's aide at his elementary school. The woman could kick ass when needed, including his, and was the best admin he'd ever had.

Marcus sat back in his chair, closed his eyes and took a few deep breaths. His body relaxed, and a vision of Cassie laughing with him at the picnic morphed into her on her knees, and how she loved sucking him off. And then, that crucial moment when he held her and almost admitted that he wanted to be with her permanently. Every waking moment since then, he thought about her, smelled her, tasted her, and then argued with himself that he'd hurt her over and over. She needed love, not a damaged man.

Reaching into his pocket, Marcus pulled out his fix—Cassie's thong, which he'd found the next day. He'd almost thrown it out, so he wouldn't have to see her. But when he'd pressed it to his nose, inhaling her scent, he'd pocketed it. Yeah, he was a perv keeping her panties, but Marcus didn't give a crap.

184

Her aroma was like a drug for his dick. One sniff, and he was hard as a rock.

He missed her, with a chronic ache in his chest. He fingered the silk unable to keep obsessing about Saturday's clusterfuck, when, "Mr. Mackenzie," Janice's voice came over the intercom. "Mr. Abernathy the fire investigator just called, but I didn't want to disturb you. He asked to see you today if possible. Should I set up an appointment for him later today?"

"Not sure, I'll buzz you in a few, J."

Marcus held the silk panel. *I have to let her go. By now she knows it's over.* A vision of Cassie hurting made his chest tighten. All of a sudden, he was suffocating from his thoughts, his emotions, her image. He had to get out. She wanted too much from him—commitment and love.

He had to focus on finding the vandals and shoring up the firm's reputation, that was his top goal. Then he'd get his life back in order. He balled the thong up, pulled two tissues out of the box on this desk, and wrapped it up. He bent and pushed it into the bottom of the wastebasket. He flipped on the intercom, "Janice, I'm going out for a while. Ask Abernathy if I can stop by his office at one, then text me with a confirmation."

"Will do boss, but may I ask if you want me to call Ms. Bennett, also? She called this morning asking for you. Sounded quite disappointed when I said you were out for the day. What a lovely voice she has."

"Thank you Janice, but do your boss a favor, and butt out of his business."

"You always had a smart mouth on you Marcus, maybe it's time for me to retire." She clicked off the intercom, but not before he heard her mumble, "Stupid man." Shit, he'd be groveling to her for days. *Got it.* A stop at her favorite chocolatier was in order today.

Okay, get back to regular programming. He felt better that he'd taken control of his emotions and had decided that he and Cassie would never work.

Her panties were gone—she was gone.

Marcus grabbed his cell and keys, walked out the door, and smiled at Janice, who promptly turned her back on him and began typing. *Bet a pound of Dilly's homemade truffles would do the trick.*

"Chocolate, raspberry, and what else?" He stopped in front of Janice's desk.

Without turning, she said, "Don't forget the toasted coconut this time, boss."

"I promise I won't, J," he chuckled.

Sparring with Janice had eased some of his tension. But when he was walking to the elevator, his chest tightened again because his brain was screaming at him that he was making a mistake he would live to regret. *I've got to get outside,* so he could breathe, not feel so damn confined. Instead of taking the elevator, he took the stairs. When Marcus reached the next landing, he put his hand in his pocket and stopped. "Well, hell."

With only a moment's hesitation, he turned, and raced upstairs, flying into his office without explanation. He dug through the wastepaper basket, picked up the tissues, took out the thong, took a whiff and put it in his pocket.

Addicted and fucked up, for sure.

Chapter Sixteen

After her call with Maddy, Cassie forced herself to sit down at her computer and continue working on her article. It had taken some effort, since her mind whirled with Pete's words, "You love him, don't you?" and Maddy's and Derek's sex game, or whatever that crazy conversation was.

The weightiest was Marcus's silence. How could he just cut her off as if she didn't exist? As if there was nothing between them. She couldn't understand how anyone could be so cruel toward another person.

Unable to concentrate, she went to the kitchen to brew tea. While she waited for the water to boil, a flash of red outside the kitchen window caught her eye. It was a cardinal and its plain-Jane mate. Both flew to the ground, then the female flew back up with wisps of grass in her beak.

She's building her nest, with her mate watching over her.

The burn of tears spilled over. *I want that.* Grey began to weave back and forth around her legs, rubbing his face on them, marking her as his. It was as if he knew she needed comfort.

Wiping her eyes with the sleeve of her shirt, Cassie bent, rubbed Grey's face, and said, "You're my sweet baby boy." She stood, put the tea bag into the cup, and poured boiling water over it, letting it steep. *Stop whining.*

She straightened her shoulders and put some force into her voice, "I've got a kickass proposal to get out to Andy by Friday, and one to Claire Curran."

Marcus Mackenzie doesn't want me? He's the loser.

Carrying her mug, Cassie sat at the kitchen table, staring at the large yellow pad that had a list of ideas written on it. She sipped, and suddenly, *Yes. I'll contact the facilitator from my LA bereavement group, maybe I can interview her and other members.*

She began to write furiously, and I have to find an area bereavement group to do the same. And show the differences between how widows and widowers cope with loss, how they move on. There must be gender differences. Cultural differences. Family and or friend support. Finances matter. Children matter. Age matters.

Ron died when I was only thirty-six. She stopped writing and nibbled on the pen. *But I don't want this to be a research article, just add stats here and there. This is a personal story. My story, and anyone else who wants to share theirs.*

She'd gone from sad and down to invigorated in under thirty minutes. *I've missed this, writing, and researching, and creating something that someone will find helpful.* Excited about the direction of the proposal, Cassie bent to her pad,

She jumped when the knock came. Her forehead furrowed. She'd been so engrossed in her work that she hadn't heard a car pull up. It couldn't be anyone she knew because they'd have texted first. Maybe it was a worker on the farm. Another knock. Cassie walked to the door and looked out of the peephole. She leaned against the door to stop herself from falling.

Marcus.

Thud-thud-thud, Cassie's heartbeat reverberated in her chest. Her stomach pitched.

"Cassandra, please let me in."

She desperately wanted to forgive him, but he'd battered her heart. Even if he begged for forgiveness, she had to let him go. *It's better to face him now, stay on the porch, and be clear that there are no more chances.* What she wanted with every cell in her body was for Marcus to tell her that he loved her. *Stop dreaming, it will never happen.*

Taking a deep breath, she opened the door, but blocked the entrance with her body. He looked absolutely delectable, his messy hair falling over his forehead, wearing dark gray slacks, black boots, and a stark white shirt with the sleeves rolled up to his forearms with the top button undone. *No,* she pushed her need for him aside, schooled her expression, and waited.

"Cassandra," he said warily. "I'd like to talk to you. And I brought this for you," he held out a small gray stone planter in the shape of a turtle. The body was filled with mini white tulips and purple hyacinths. It was a lovely gift, and that coupled with the remorse written on his face could have her falling for his charms again. She swallowed hard, steeling herself, and tried to wipe any expression from her face. She stepped out on the porch, stood right in the doorway, and crossed her arms over her chest.

"Uh," he held the turtle out to her. "I'd like to talk to you, to apologize for..."

"That wasn't necessary, but thank you," she talked over him, her hardened mask in place.

"Cassandra, please, take it." For a moment she hesitated, but took the planter, placed it on the side table on the porch, and looked him squarely in the eyes.

Closing his eyes for a moment, she watched pain skate across his face. Her heart ached for that hurt little boy that Pete had talked about. All she wanted to do was to take him in her arms and make it better. *No. You're nothing to him.*

"Please, I want to explain about Saturday. May I come in?"

"Marcus, thank you for stopping by, and for the turtle, it's lovely. But I'm very busy and now is not a good time." *Your turn buddy.*

"Ahh," his voice was tight and his jaw clenched. *Getting a little ticked because I'm not falling all over you?*

"Okay, Cassandra, when would be a good time to talk?"

Before she could answer, Grey walked out of the cottage, and began to rub himself against Marcus's legs. *Kitty, you may be out of a home if you don't stop it right now.*

Marcus squatted down immediately and rubbed Grey's head, who of course began to purr loudly. "You were able to get him into the house," Marcus looked up at her with a soft smile, and her anger faded like mist at sunrise. He gave Grey another head rub and stood. "Cassandra," he stepped closer, but when she moved back, he stopped. "Please, let's talk."

She stared at Marcus for a long moment. He was deliciously virile, with sex skills to die for. As well as smart, well-read, and funny, with a caring side, too. Seemingly a perfect match for her. Unfortunately, he was also severely damaged. She chilled remembering how cold and nasty he'd been on the boat.

You cannot change or fix another person, Shirl's voice was loud and clear. Without answering, she leaned down, picked Grey up, put him in the house and closed the door. A muscle in Marcus's jaw twitched. It took everything in her power to say, "I don't want to do that Marcus, not now."

His phone rang, but he didn't answer it. Instead, Marcus lowered his head, put his hand on his nape, and stood there looking at his boots.

Her phone that was on the kitchen table rang.

It was unbearable watching him. She had to escape into the cottage. She was about to ask him to leave when his phone rang again.

Her phone rang again, too.

Marcus came out of his funk, took his phone out of his back pocket, looked at the caller and answered, "Joe? Marcus listened and his body went rigid. He looked at Cassie, his face stricken. "Where did they take him?"

No, she screamed inside. Her chest tightened with fear, and when her phone rang again, she threw open the door and ran to get the call. Marcus was right behind her

"No Joe, I'm at the cottage with her."

Grabbing her phone, Cassie saw Annie's calls, and hit the call back icon. It rang, but went right to voicemail. Before she could leave a message, Marcus was there, gently taking the phone from her hand.

191

"Cassie," she looked up at him, her vision blurred with tears. She croaked, "Pete?"

"He had a heart attack. But he's conscious. The ambulance is taking him to Eastbridge Memorial. Get your things together, we're going there right now. Joe has you listed as Pete's daughter and me as your husband."

"Wha...?"

"While they waited for the ambulance, Pete told Joe to say that so we could get in to see him."

"You go ahead, Marcus, I'll be right behind you," she took kitty kibble out of the closet.

"No. I'm taking you to the hospital. Feed Grey, and let's go."

She couldn't fight him. Like a zombie, she filled the food bowl and grabbed a light jacket and her purse. Marcus opened the front door for her, put out his hand for her keys and pointed to his truck. Her hands shaking, she dropped the keys into his palm, and somehow made her way down the porch steps while he locked up.

She stumbled as she walked to his truck because she was crumbling inside. He looked tired and sick this morning. *Why didn't I recognize the signs? Ron had his first heart attack two weeks after we married. Not Pete. Not Pete.* Her world was falling apart again, and she couldn't hold herself up for another second.

A strong hand took her by the elbow, "Easy, baby," Marcus said quietly.

It was his 'baby' that broke her. Silently, her tears fell.

As Marcus helped her into the truck, she tried to imagine her life without Pete in it. The losses were piling up. Ten years ago, Shirl died. Seven years ago, her father died. Two years ago, Ron was gone. Her mother, fifteen months ago. She'd already lost Marcus, because her love wasn't enough.

"Are you buckled up?" Marcus asked as he turned and drove down the lane to the main road.

Her voice shook, "Yes." Though it was warm outside, Marcus put on the heat and directed the vent in her direction. "Thank you," she whispered to the passenger window.

Her life would be barren without Pete. *My Pete.* She controlled a sob, closed her eyes and put her head back on the seat.

They drove to the hospital in silence.

****

Marcus pulled into the hospital emergency parking lot, turned off the engine and unbuckled his seatbelt. He shifted his body and turned toward Cassie, who was leaning back against the seat, her eyes closed. *I want to take care of her, but will she let me?*

"I'm awake," her voice cracked.

She turned her head to him and he fell into rich brown eyes that no longer gazed at him with the warm affection that he'd become used to. Worst of all was he'd lost the right to take her in his arms and comfort her.

Cassie turned from him and sat up. "Wait, I'll help you out." Surprisingly, she didn't argue with him, her exhaustion obvious. He helped her down from the truck, and guided her into the waiting room.

"Sit for a sec, Cassie, I'll find out where he is." Without looking at him, she nodded and took a seat.

193

"Cassie, Marcus," Joe called out, as he came through an inner-door.

"Joe," Cassie scrambled off the chair and launched herself at him. Joe held her head against his chest as she sobbed quietly. "It's okay. He's conscious, it's a mild attack and he's gonna be okay. He's driving Annie and all the nurses crazy, wanting this and that." Joe looked at Marcus, his pale face belied his words. Marcus's chest compressed with fear.

Watching Joe hold Cassie was tough. *That's my job. I want her in my arms.* Marcus's instinct to protect Cassie hit him hard, but he had to bide his time. "Joe, can we see him now?"

"Yeah, Mac, he's been asking for both of you. There's something important on dad's mind, and he'll only tell the two of you."

A nurse approached them. "This is dad's nurse, Nancy. Nancy, this is my sis, Cassie, and her husband, Marcus."

"That man has been worrying, waiting to see you two. Joe, how about I send Annie out here, and you and she get some coffee and take a break. He's waiting for more tests and results. And we're waiting for a room, it will be a while."

"Sounds good." Joe kissed Cassie, and squeezed Marcus's shoulder.

Marcus took Cassie's hand and they followed Nancy.

"Joe said my girl was coming. Where the hell is she?" As they approached the curtained room Marcus said in a low voice, "He commanded men into battle, must have been one tough son of a bitch. See he hasn't lost his touch."

Cassie ignored him, softly called out, "Pete," as she slowly pushed ahead of Marcus and the nurse and pulled aside the curtain. He was pale and haggard, sitting up on the gurney. Oxygen was running through his nose, and he was hooked up to an IV and monitors.

Dark grief tore at Marcus. He couldn't bear the thought of Pete dying.

"Cassie, finally," Pete's shaky voice brought him back to the present. He watched Cassie carefully sit on the side of the gurney, then she was in Pete's arms, tears spilling down her cheeks.

"Okay folks," Nancy said, "I'll leave you alone for a bit. Do you need anything Mr. Hoffman?"

"Nope, it's all good." Nancy left and Cassie began, "I should have known. You looked tired, complained about your back hurting. I've seen this before, with Ron."

"Cassie, don't you dare take that on. No one knew."

She sat up, sniffled, took a tissue from Marcus's hand, who was standing behind her.

"But—"

"Mac," Pete motioned to Marcus, "I need to talk to both of you. No time to waste."

"Why don't you rest? We'll come back after your tests are done. When you're in a room," Cassie pleaded.

"No," Pete said in a weak but firm voice. "I must get this off my chest."

"Pete, please," Cassie put her hand on his cheek.

"It's going to be okay, Cassie. Lean in, son," Pete tipped his head to Marcus who pulled up a chair and sat down next to her. Pete took one of her hands, and entwined their fingers. He squeezed her hand, and said barely above a whisper, "We've got you." Marcus covered both their hands with his. "That's it Mac, let's keep our girl close and safe." Marcus felt warmth flitter through his body.

Cassie teased Pete, "You're as bossy as Marcus." Relief swept through Marcus when he heard Cassie tease. *Maybe she'll forgive me.*

"Yeah, Cass, that's what you get with two grunts looking after you. Now hush and let me say what I'm gonna say."

"Marcus, we never did get to have those beers and shoot some pool, so I never got a chance to properly apologize for losing my mind and saying terrible things to you. Things that are lies—because," Pete's voice cracked, "you're the best man I know Marcus, the very best."

"Pete, don't." If Pete continued, Marcus would be bawling like a baby. And he never cried. "We talked at the picnic, and I know why you were protecting her from me. I'm not angry."

"I have to man up Marcus. I'm tired and need to get this out. Cassie," those weary blue eyes met hers, "you're a woman, not my little girl anymore. When you told me you were moving back, it was as if I traveled back in time. A time when you would be my little Cassie, spending time at the cottage with Shirl. And I wanted that time back, just for a little while. I missed you more than you'll ever knew when you left for college and moved out west."

"Pete..."

"Honey, I'm ashamed of my actions, and what I said. God, Shirl would kick my ass if she was here."

"She would." Cassie laughed softly and Marcus

took a chance and put a hand on her shoulder. She turned to him with a sad smile, allowing his touch.

"Mac, what I said to you is unforgivable. I'm mortified at the garbage I threw your way. I acted like the father you have when I wanted to be the father you deserved."

"I know you didn't mean it, Pete."

"Son, don't make excuses for me. Do not protect me. I saw your face when I yelled that you were a piece of shit, just like your father. I destroyed you." The memory of Pete's words were like a knife in Marcus's chest, but Pete needed redemption, "Pete, it's all good, I forgive you—believe me."

"Cassie is my girl, but Marcus you're my other boy. You have been since that day at the Overlook all those years ago. You were standing there, a sad, angry, sixteen year old ready to bolt because your world was crumbling all around you."

Pete's words flashed Marcus back into the past.

Marcus saw that angry sixteen year old filled with despair who stood at the railing of the Overlook, contemplating drowning himself in the river. Life had become unbearable that day, when Nolan Mackenzie was found guilty of murder—life without parole.

"You didn't trust anyone, Marcus. But somehow I got through to you a little." Marcus came back to the present, and he squirmed as Pete continued.

"I not only saw goodness in you, but beyond the sadness and bluster, I saw a hint of greatness. And you lived up to it. I'm proud of what you've made of yourself. You're a true hero in every way. And son, you are nothing at all like your bastard of a father, if you can call him that. I'm so damn sorry."

197

Marcus was speechless when the curtain opened, and Nancy hustled in with a male aide. "Okay folks, time to go. Mr. Hoffman, we're taking you for more tests, so you'll be busy."

Cassie kissed Pete, hugged him tightly, and made room for Marcus, who leaned over and hugged Pete. But before he could straighten, Pete grabbed onto his shirt, "I've had a heart attack. It's mild, but it's damaged my heart. Joe and Annie and my grandchildren are doing well. I need to know that you'll take care of our girl. So stop screwing around and find what I had with Shirl." He turned to Cassie. "And I need to know that you will let him do that. I need to know that you will make each other happy."

That crazy man was giving them his blessing.

"Mr. Hoffman, you have to—" the nurse started to order.

"Quiet." For a man who'd just had a heart attack, he could bark out an order when he had to.

Marcus stood and put his arm around her shoulders. She wound an arm around his waist.
Silently they waited.

Pete raised a brow, "Say it."

"I will," came out in unison, and they quickly looked at each other in surprise.

"Perfect." A weak smile tugged at his lips, "Now get the hell out of here."

Chapter Seventeen

What is she thinking? Marcus was desperate to know. They'd driven in silence since leaving the hospital, something they were good at. Cassie's head was turned to the passenger side window on the entire drive. Deja vu.

I'll make her talk to me, listen to what I have to say. They had to work this out.

Pete's powerful, shocking words had taken Marcus's breath away. *You're my other boy. You're nothing like that bastard... I'm proud of you.* He still felt like he couldn't get enough oxygen into his lungs after that scene.

He knew Pete cared about him. *He and Shirl saved your life, asshole. Why do you think they did that? They love you.* Pete hated the reputation Marcus had earned and wasn't afraid to chew him out, "Stop being a manwhore and be a man."

And that promise they'd both made to make each other happy, and said at the same time, *I will.* Could he learn to love like a normal person? Would he know how? Or would he keep jacking it up between them until she was forced to end it with him? "Cassandra, are you doing okay?" he called to her softly and quickly glanced at her before turning back to the road.

"Yes," her voice was flat.

He was taking her to the cottage, where hopefully they could talk things out, and then, he prayed, go to bed. Sex was their main connection, and it would tie her to him. He ached to be inside of her. To breathe in her scent. To taste her. To feel her silky skin under his rough fingers. To fall into her heat and soft curves while she arched into him, calling out his name.

Surprising him, she said, "I can't believe Pete made us promise to be together."

He had an in, and he was taking it. He took her hand, twined their fingers together, and placed it on his thigh. "Cassie, Pete made us promise to make each other happy. Honestly, I'm not sure about any of this, except for one thing," He looked at her again, then turned back to the road.

****

Cassie's head and heart were in chaos. She promised Pete to give Marcus a chance, and she would. "What are you sure about?" she asked softly.

"I want you sexually, but it's more than that, and you know it. I can't get you out of my head, and I like being with you, Cassandra, and not just when we're screwing. And," Marcus gave her a quick glance, "we both know heartache and loss."

"Yes, we do."

"And now we're both worried about Pete. Terrified that we'll lose him."

He's opening himself up. Not professing his love for her, but even this wasn't easy for him. God, she wanted to comfort him and be comforted in return.

And truthfully, he'd taken over her mind, too. She rubbed her thumb over his knuckles and heard him sigh. *Yes, he cares.*

"Cassie, we're alive, and I want to revel in life, dive into it. And I'm never more alive than when my cock is buried deep into your pure beauty. I've never felt this before for another soul, and that connection is everything to me."

Her hopes sparked. She had to trust that he wasn't playing her. So, she risked, "When I'm with you, I feel that way, too. Marcus, when you're inside of me, deeply connected, it's the sweetest feeling in the world."

He lifted their hands, softly brushing her knuckle with his lips, and coasted to a stop. It seemed to Cassie like they'd first met at the Horse years ago, not weeks. They'd stopped at that same T in the road as when she was on the back of his bike, and he'd taken her to the Overlook. Now they were lovers, and hopefully much more.

****

Marcus ushered Cassie into the cottage and locked the front door with a snick. He stayed where he was, back to the door, and the raw need and hunger on his face stole her breath. "Come here," his rough command turned her knees to water. He crooked his finger at her, his mouth lifting in a wicked smile.

Cassie dropped her purse where she stood, and in two steps was in his arms. Her arms snaked around his neck as he crushed her to him, and their mouths met in a blazing kiss.

He spread a broad hand across her back, holding

201

her as if he'd restrained her. His other hand grabbed a handful of her hair, eliciting the perfect bite of pain that singed every cell in her body. He came up for air and barked, "Get naked. Now."

"Yes, yes," she panted.

They tore off their clothes, tossing them to the side. She couldn't stop giggling when Marcus almost fell over, his foot caught in his slacks down around his ankles. "Fuck it," he yelled, but saved himself by grabbing onto the doorknob.

He kicked his pants aside, branded her naked body with fiery eyes, and began to roughly stroke his dick. "You think this is funny?"

Slowly she licked her bottom lip, watching his eyes flare. She could entice, too. She held her breasts and played with her nipples, "Yes, it was amusing, what are you going to do about it?"

His chest rose with each breath. Marcus let go of his dick and moved to her. "Hold your tits up for my mouth," he ordered.

Immediately, she did. He held her hips and took her left nipple into his mouth, first teasing the tip with his tongue, then sucking hard, and she arched up with a mewl.

"Keep holding them for me," he latched onto her right breast, sucking and nipping as she whimpered and undulated, rubbing up against him.

"Marcus, please."

"Hands down at your sides and leave them there, or you'll be begging all night."

She wanted control tonight, just as Marcus did, so she took it.

His surprised "Wha...?" when she grabbed his

face and pulled him down for a blistering kiss made her smile into his mouth. The feel of the rough scruff of his face on her fingers, the soft lips of his punishing mouth, and his taste assaulted her senses.

She pressed her body against him and thrust her hips into his, whispering into his mouth, "Marcus, I want you inside of me."

He groaned deeply and instinctively took over, tightly holding her ass to him while swiveling his hips and cupping her jaw to control the kiss.

Cassie wound her arms around his neck then ran her hands up into those thick waves, grabbed hold, and pulled, just the way he liked it.

He growled and bit her lower lip, making her yelp. *Yes.* She wanted that side of Marcus. The rough side. She wanted him to nip and bite and fill her with his cock in the way only he could.

Marcus deepened the kiss, his tongue mapping her mouth, teasing her until she needed air. Breathless, she pulled away, licked his ear, and slowly ran her tongue down his neck.

He took hold of her jaw to control her and peppered her mouth with nips and licks. His other hand roamed over her body, from her nape, down her back, and over her ass. Sometimes his touch was light, using only his fingers, sometimes he stroked harder, or squeezed her ass. He stroked her collarbone and her breasts, not touching her nipples. He lightly stroked his hand up the side of her body from the side of her breast, down past her waist to her hip. And all the time he played with her mouth. Kissing her deeply, dueling with her tongue, sucking it into his mouth, then nipping her bottom lip.

When she ran her hands down his chest to his cock, he stopped her by taking them in his hand and holding them captive.

"I want to touch you," she pleaded.

"Not yet."

He continued his mastery, playing with her body, lighting up her skin, until every nerve ending was throbbing with intense need.

"What do you want?" his voice was a low growl, and his hot breath in her ear sent her reeling.

"I want you. Right now."

Her screech split the air when he grasped her in both hands right under her ass, hauled her up, and leaned her back against the front door. Her legs instinctively circled his waist, and her hands held onto his shoulders. He took her mouth hard, to the point of pain. When she opened for him, his tongue plunged in and out.

He tore his mouth away, "Line up my cock."

She reached between them and put the head of his penis at her entrance. "Are you ready, baby?" My god, he was sweet. Always taking care of her.

She growled, "Marcus, fuck me like you hate me."

He thrust into her to the hilt.

"Harder," she panted and threw her head back on the door.

He buried his face into her neck as he pounded into her. His grunts, her moans, and the sounds of flesh on flesh filled the room.

"Oh," she called out, "I'm almost..."

Marcus nipped her ear lobe while his hips drove into her, keeping pace, stroking that place inside of her with each plunge of his cock.

"Cassandra," he ground out, then swiveled his hips right onto her clit.

That was it. "Marcus," she screamed. The orgasm hit her like a seismic wave that kept her pussy clenching as it rode over her for what seemed like forever.

As she came down, Marcus planted his face in her hair, grunting as his thrusts became frantic. She squeezed her inner muscles and felt his cock thicken as he groaned long and loud.

His hot semen shot into her. They hadn't used a condom.

"What was that," he mumbled, brushing his lips over hers as he gently lowered her to her feet.

The room smelled like sex. Her back and pussy were both sore, semen leaked down her legs. She was exhausted, but at the same time every nerve in her body was thrumming with energy. *I want to revel in life, dive into it.* Marcus said it. And they had. Great sex with him was an affirmation of living.

She held on to his arms to balance herself, then raised up on her toes, kissed him lightly, and said, "I think you fucked me like you hated me."

He chuckled and wound his strong arms around her, holding her to him, her head resting on his chest, arms on his shoulders. "When I heard those dirty words come out of you, I went a little crazy. I was rough. Did I hurt you?"

He was worried about her. God, she loved him. "No... yes... you gave me exactly what I asked for." she looked at him and smiled into his eyes, "I'm a little sore, in a good way. And I'm leaking."

"Shit. Cassie, I forgot."

"I did too, but I'm on the pill now so we're good," she assured him.

"I'm clean, Cassie." Marcus added, his face serious. "I have recent results—I can show you."

"I believe you, Marcus," Cassie returned, adding with a smile, "but thank you."

"Well, then... can we go ungloved from now on?"

"Yes. But," she looked at him, unsure, "are we...?"

"We're exclusive, Cassandra. There's only you, for me. Now stay there."

He went into the bathroom and came out with a wet washcloth. Ignoring her pleas that she could wash herself, he lowered to his knees and gently cleaned between her legs to her embarrassment. He stood, tossed the cloth in the bathroom, and pulled her into the bedroom. "I texted my farmhand Hector that I won't be home tonight, so he's taking the dogs."

Two hours later, Cassie lay sprawled on top of Marcus, who gently caressed her back. She was beyond exhausted to the point of paralysis. So was he. She smiled. They were back together, and it was because of Pete. She pushed her worry about him away for now. Hope had returned.

****

The next morning, after Marcus woke, he'd pulled her leg over his hip and slipped into her from behind. He built her up slowly, kissing her nape, playing with her breasts while murmuring sweet things in her ear. Right before he came, he stroked her clit, and they released together. It was one of the most intimate, loving moments of her life.

This loving Marcus, she could easily forgive. But they had to face what happened on the boat, at some point. Her stomach roiled just thinking about it, but she pushed it to the side, not wanting to ruin the lovely morning.

They were sitting at the kitchen table, comfortably drinking coffee, when Grey bumped their legs for strokes. This was her dream for the future—love, great sex, sweet domestic bliss.

Stroking Grey's head, Marcus said, "It's as if he's been here forever."

It's as if you've been here with me forever, too. "Yes. Once he came in, he immediately adjusted. What he doesn't know is that this Wednesday, he's getting all his shots and he's being neutered."

"Poor guy." Marcus's phone sounded with a text. He opened it. "It's Joe. Pete is doing well and complaining that he's lonely."

"Wonderful, he's complaining. Marcus, how about we visit him, and then have lunch at the diner?"

He texted back, put the phone down and stood. "That's a plan." His eyes twinkled with mischief. "Let's shower together, I want to make sure that your entire body is germ free. We're going to a hospital, you know."

She raised a brow, stood, and put the mugs in the sink. "Oh no, I'm too sore from your incredibly large cock pounding into me—though I'm not complaining. You go first."

"My lips sucking on your tasty clit won't hurt a bit," he laughed and pulled her into the bathroom.

Chapter Eighteen

Marcus sat across from Cassie in a back booth at the diner. He'd ordered a cheeseburger, Cassie wanted a turkey-bacon-club sandwich. After their waitress delivered their drinks, he sipped his cola and watched her. She'd been quiet and had barely made eye contact since they left the hospital, though Pete was more energetic and should be home by early next week.

Marcus wasn't sure what to do or say right now. They had to talk things out because that huge elephant was sitting right between them, trumpeting about his cruel behavior toward her on the boat, and how he'd cut her off for days. She'd broken up with him at the cottage, and if not for Pete's heart attack, she'd be gone from his life.

The thought terrified him, because Cassandra had somehow smashed his walls to pieces and stolen his heart. She was loyal, kind, loving, and deserved the best of everything that life had to offer. And, shocker, Pete thought he was the man to give that to her.

"Marcus, are you okay?" She surprised him, that she was attentive to his mood, because she'd seemed off in her own world.

"Yeah, why?"

She reached over and took his hand, "Because this hand is clenched in a fist, and you look like you're a million miles away."

"Uh, Pete looked much better, didn't he? His color is back, and I know he's feeling better because he ordered us to go to the diner. That's the old Pete."

Coward, you're afraid of her.

"Yes, he did seem better." She raised a brow. "But Marcus, that's not it. What's really bothering you?"

Tell her the truth. Tell her you're afraid to lose her because you're not good for her.

Instead he picked up their clasped hands, kissed her fingers, and lied, "Nah, I'm just tired, it's been a rough day, except for great sex." He released her hand, picked up his glass and drank.

Her sly smile was warm and mischievous, "Yes it was amazing, let's repeat it real soon."

"Whenever you're ready, I'm there." *Stop avoiding, talk it out with her. Trust that she will listen.*

She didn't respond, but kept watching him, knowing full well that he was on edge, then she spoke, "You were wonderful with Pete today. He was terrified under all that fake bluster," her kind words stopped his racing thoughts for a moment.

"It was nothing. Just tried to take his mind off of things." His pointer finger rimmed the glass. He didn't deserve her praise, he'd been so cruel to her.

She leaned forward on the table, "It wasn't nothing. Don't you see how much you mean to Pete? He loves you like a son. And I can see why."

His chest tightened. He hated when people told him what a great guy he was, because that was only

209

surface. The rot in his soul was buried deep, but when it surfaced, it destroyed anyone in its path—like it had done to Cassie.

He shook his head, and his stomach painfully tightened. "Cassie, we have to talk about what happened..."

"Okay, one cheeseburger, one turkey club," the waitress interrupted, and he could avoid that conversation for a bit. They dug into their food, and while they ate, he veered into safety and asked her about fixing up her house.

When they finished and were sipping their drinks, he studied her. She seemed to be mulling something over in her mind, then her gaze penetrated his.

"You're right, we do have to talk about the scene on the boat, Marcus, and try to work things out, but first I'm going to say something to you Marcus, that I've wanted to say for a while now, though we met not long ago," her voice was soft, subdued, maybe a little unsure.

Uh oh. He held his breath. He could read her, and knew what was coming. A part of him didn't want her to say it, because he could never give that love back to her—and he would surely lose her. Yet, the selfish man that he was—or maybe it was the unhappy, unloved boy that still lived inside of him—was desperate to hear those words.

He barely breathed.

Then she hit him with her kill shot.

She took a deep breath, "I've fallen in love with you."

He had to stop her. "Cassandra," his voice was raw, and his eyes burned.

"Hush, please, let me finish," as she often did, she twined their fingers together. Marcus held on to her like she was a lifeline.

"I think it happened when I was in California and you sent me one of my favorite songs, *So Far Away*, and checked on me while I was there. We'd only met that one time at the Horse, and though I was pissed at you, didn't respond, acted like a bitch, you persisted. You cannot imagine what that meant to me."

She was blowing his mind. *Tell her that you fell in love with her photo, with the promise of her, before you even met her. Tell her that Pete's been talking to you about her since you were sixteen years old, and she's been rooted in your unconsciousness since then. Tell her.*

He couldn't say it. He wanted her. Desired her. But he didn't believe he was capable of truly loving her. "Cassandra, I..."

"You don't have to say it back. You don't have to love me back. But life is so fragile, and as you said, 'Dive into it.' So I am." She brought up their hands, kissed the knuckles on both his hands, then released them.

Her soft, golden-brown eyes glowed with genuine affection. "I love you."

"Cassie," he hesitated, "I'm not sure I *can* love." He stopped, swallowed. She hadn't moved, just sat there, watching him, her hands holding her glass of tea.

"You know some of my history, but I've never felt for anybody what I feel for you."

When a slow smile danced on her lips, every tight muscle in his body loosened in relief.

"That's enough for me Marcus. It is." *For now.*

211

He saw it in her expression, that she meant it. She was incredible.

Ruthie broke the moment, bringing them the check. "Anything else?"

"That's all, thanks." Marcus stood and pulled out his wallet.

Cassie scooted out of the booth and, in a sultry voice, whispered in Marcus's ear, "There's something I want, as soon as we get to the cottage, and it's not a long, serious talk. Instead, I want your long, thick dick, like a burning hot poker in my mouth."

Oh, she was a wicked tease. "Baby, prepare yourself."

They'd raced to the cottage and now, *damn it*, Marcus was trying to find the right key to the front door. If he couldn't locate it in the next five seconds..."

"Cassie, baby, you keep hitting my arm—I can't find it. You have like ten keys on this tiny ring—what the hell."

"Do it, Marcus," she bit his earlobe, then sucked on it, at the same time she was attempting without success to climb his body. "Shit, babe," he bobbled the keys, but finally found it. The key slid home, Marcus unlocked the door, pushed it open. Cassie shrieked in surprise when he picked her up with one arm holding her to his side, her legs dangling.

"Mar—" she began, but in a split second, he hauled her inside, slammed the door closed behind him with his foot, and pushed her against the door. One arm held her jaw, the other gripped her hip.

"Door sex again?"

"Yep, for round one." He swallowed her moan in

212

a deep, wet kiss. His tongue plunged into her mouth— *god* he couldn't get enough of her. "So fucking delicious," his voice was a low rumble as he licked along her bottom lip, then the top.

He tightened his hold on her jaw, and her hands dove into his hair. Ravenously, they ate at each other. Tongues clashed. Hot breaths seared their mouths. Their heads rapidly twisted back to take the kiss deeper, wetter, harder.

Abruptly he pulled away, ignored her whine, and ordered, "Everything off, Cassandra."

Clothes flew. The air was filled with pants and the heady smell of arousal. When she kicked her panties to the side, Marcus was on her in a second. He pushed her back onto the door, captured her hands in one of his, pulled them over her head, and devoured her mouth.

Cassie held on to his shoulders, then Marcus caught her where her ass met her thighs and held her as she hopped up and wrapped her legs around his waist.

"Baby, do it," his heart beat out of his chest, in perfect tune with her excited panting. One of her hands reached down, and she put the head of his cock at her opening. They both groaned deeply when he drove into her in one long thrust.

He began a hard, driving rhythm, twisted his hips and thrust deeper. His cock hit that spot, and she gasped. He rammed into her, and she lost control, bucking into him like a pile driver.

He went at her like a wild animal. She begged, "Don't stop."

"Never. That's my girl, come now."

****

"Ahhh," heat rose throughout her body, she tensed, and a giant wave of energy washed over her. Her head thunked against the door, as she wailed.

Her release sent him into a frenzy. He buried his face in her neck, and the only sounds in the room were flesh on flesh, moans, and grunts.

He lost his rhythm, and began to pound into her. *Oh god,* another orgasm blindsided her. They went at it so fiercely that the hinges on the old door were rattling. The raspy *squeak creak squeak creak* screeched in the room. The door was shaking like it was going to splinter apart at any moment.

Cassie couldn't stop a giggle at the image of them tumbling onto the porch with her impaled on his cock.

"I'm fucking you," he growled, "trying to get there after you've gotten off," he grunted, "and you're giggling?" He thrust hard again.

"It's," and she burst out laughing, "the hinges, making a racket. That door is going to break down any second. Don't you hear it? We're going to fall onto the porch."

"You're laughing about hinges that I don't give a shit about," he lifted his head and glared at her.

She grinned at him, he shook his head. When she clamped her arms and legs tighter around him, and met his thrusts, he buried his face back into her neck.

She couldn't help herself and teased, "Marcus, hurry up, those hinges are rusty, that old door is going any second."

"I will," he ground out, "if you stop talking about rusty hinges."

214

Another giggle escaped. "Uh, honey, I think that your badass dick just went a little soft."

Suddenly he stopped and his shoulders began to shake. "Are you okay?"

Marcus threw his head back and roared with laughter. The sound of it was beautiful, as if he'd gifted her with a secret part of himself—he'd never let himself go like that. And she'd never had so much fun while having sex. They were so good for each other. Did he see that, too?

Gently he lowered her legs to the floor. He kissed the tip of her nose, then rested his forehead against hers. "Laughing is a cock-blocker, you know, and my dick is unhappy about it."

"Oh, the poor baby." Cassie reached out, one hand stroked his cock, the other cupped his balls, and she rolled them in her hand.

His nostrils flared as he ground into her hand.

"Lean against the door and spread, big man," she dropped to her knees.

****

Cassie woke with her back pressed against Marcus's front, his arm wrapped around her waist. Her arms were folded over his, holding him to her. His face was nestled near her ear, his quiet breath telling her that he was asleep.

Who knew that Marcus spooned? It was a first for both of them. But the biggest shock was that she'd told Marcus that she loved him, and he hadn't bolted. He hadn't said the works back, but his words, *I've never felt for anybody what I feel for you,* sounded like love to her.

215

Marcus could shut down again, but he was worth the risk. If they eventually broke up, she would move on, but she would grieve at losing him for the rest of her life.

But, for now, they were here together. It was dark, but she knew it was morning. She tilted her head to check the time. The clock on the nightstand read 4:30, too early to get up, so she snuggled back into Marcus's body, his warmth and touch lulling her back to sleep.

At six o'clock his phone rang. Marcus stirred. He let it go to voicemail, then listened to the message. "It's Charlie Dunst, the PI we hired." Marcus sat up abruptly. "He caught the vandals in the act, called the cops, and the two teens are on their way to the station. I've got to call Liam and get down there, Charlie will meet us there to give his statement."

Cassie sat up, "What a relief. Marcus, get dressed I'll have a travel mug of coffee ready for you."

"Baby, you're the best." He gave her a sweet kiss, found his clothes, and headed into the bathroom while calling Liam.

She got out of bed, pulled on sweats and a top, relieved that instead of closing off in anger, Marcus was affectionate, loving. *Progress?* She crossed her fingers, then went to make coffee for her man.

✳✳✳✳✳✳✳✳✳✳✳✳✳✳✳✳✳✳✳

At nine o'clock, Marcus, Liam, and Charlie sat at a bistro table in the Quad, a funky coffeehouse combined with a used bookstore that had the best breakfast in all of Eastbridge. The two teens were

216

processed, Charlie had given his statement to the police, and now the three of them were discussing their next moves.

"They're not talking," Liam complained, then put a piece of Belgian Waffle into his mouth. They'd made peace when Marcus had picked Liam up two hours ago. Liam had apologized, and Marcus promised to spend more time with him.

"No, they're not," Charlie said. "The eighteen-year-old already has a rap sheet, he's bad news, but the seventeen-year-old is clean. Kid was shitting bricks when he looked down the barrel of my gun. He started shaking like he was having a seizure, and pissed his pants. But the older guy gave him a look that froze the kid into silence." Charlie pushed his plate away, picked up a large ironstone mug of coffee and drank. "He's scary, hard already at eighteen, but he's not the ringleader."

Marcus picked up the last piece of bacon on his plate, ate it, and asked, "You said you were going to contact me with new info right before this happened. Any idea who it is?"

"As I told you, one of my guys has been quietly sniffing around, asking questions, paying a few people off to find out what's really going down with your jobs, and in this town. We know that they're not random acts, but a pattern of destruction to hurt you and your company, but no knowledge why. These kids are likely being paid off and intimidated to say nothing if they're caught. They'll only charge them for this act of vandalism, unless they can be linked to the others. And maybe there are other teens involved, too." He picked up his mug, held it, and said, "There is someone pulling the strings. Someone, I believe, who has balls and thinks he's invincible."

"Yeah, it's like a gang is after us," Liam said.

"Not a gang. But it's someone who wants to not only take our business, but to ruin us and step into our place. Charlie, I mentioned my suspicion of Frank Wagner to you after he pulled my chain a few days ago at the Riverbend picnic."

"Yeah, I began investigating him immediately—he's a complete slimeball. I'm going to lay this all out in my report that I'll be emailing to you later today. But I'll tell you this, I found a slim thread that connects Frank Wagner to a man named Ray Bristow. Do either of you know him?"

Marcus sat up straight and said, "What?" as Liam's head jerked in his direction.

"Who is he, Mac?" Charlie asked.

Marcus leaned toward Charlie and lowered his voice, "I'm seeing Cassandra Bennett, Ray Bristow is her sister Maddy's ex. He's a small-time criminal. A wealthy scumbag who skirts the law as a slumlord in the city, with a shady mortgage company, to boot, but no one can find the evidence to shut him down."

"Or to put him in jail, where he and his sons belong," Liam added. "He always gets away with things. Buys people off, and rumor has it he uses intimidation, too. He drives a Mercedes while Maddy is struggling financially with his twin boys. He's taken her to court twice to lower his alimony and child support payments. Pleads that his business is failing. And the dirt bag won both times."

"Payoffs?" Charlie asked.

"Likely," Marcus said. "And late last year, he was

involved in a small construction project. A new venture, a new part of his business he said, when he was interviewed for the local paper." Marcus ran his hand through his hair, unsure about what to do with this news.

"Are you going to tell Cassie?" Liam had a worried look on his face.

"No." Marcus looked at Liam and Charlie. "We'll keep this quiet for now. Just us, Li, not Sean or Bret, Cassie or Maddy. Cassie will freak. And Maddy is a loose cannon, she'll go after Ray if she hears this. We need him thinking he's invisible and untouchable. And Li, if you see either man, or one of Frank's crew, play it cool, brother."

"I promise, Mac. I'm meeting Bret at the Mayfair site, when the cops are done with it. I'll let you know what's what."

"I'll keep digging," Charlie took out a tablet and input the info that Marcus had given him. "I'll look into the boys' friends, families, Frank Wagner, and now Ray Bristow. I'll detail that thread I found, and the next steps my team are taking, and get that report to you later today. It will likely take a while to get Bristow if he's the puppetmaster, but we'll keep digging."

"Dig deep, Charlie," Marcus bit out the words.

"You done Li? Charlie?" Both men nodded and pushed back their chairs. Marcus pulled out his wallet, took out his credit card as he moved to the cashier, and said, "Let's get the hell out of here."

Chapter Nineteen

Saturday morning Cassie sat on her patio in the cool air. It was the second week of May, and the day was already bright and glorious. Spring bulbs and dogwoods were in full bloom, scenting the air. The perennials that Shirl had spent years planting were budding in beds around the cottage. The majestic copper beech that stood as a sentry at the end of the lawn, separating it from the small wooded area and the fields beyond, was in flower.

Cassie's cell on speaker was propped up on the table. She was smiling as she listened to Eva yell out happily, "Mom, we are both finished. No more papers, projects, or finals for the next four months."

"Great going, you two. You both did so well. Proud of my girls."

"And guess what?" Abby's voice was raised joyfully, too, "Next weekend we're coming to Riverbend, from Friday night to Sunday afternoon."

Cassie's heart thumped, "Fantastic. I cannot wait to see my girls and kiss and hug them until they scream 'stop,'" she laughed into the phone.

"Us, too. Prepare, mom," Eva teased, "We're gonna jump all over you when we get there. We can't wait to see Pete and his family."

"He's been pestering me about seeing both of you. He's coming home on Monday."

"Mom," Abby sounded serious.

"What Abby?"

"We've missed spending time with Aunt Maddy and the boys. It's so good that you moved back to Riverbend. Now we can spend the weekend with them, too."

Unexpectedly, Cassie felt a lump in her throat. Because she'd run from her childhood, her girls had missed out getting to know their aunt and nephews.

"I know. Me too, baby. When Maddy hears you're both coming to visit she'll scream. You know your aunt."

Abby laughed. "We sure do, can't wait to see her, and Jay and Danny. We'll call you in a few days, mom. See you next Friday," Abby said softly, then hung up.

Cassie held the mug of tea. *I'm happy. Or maybe it's contentment, but whatever*, she thought, *it's been a long time coming*. And it wasn't all about Marcus, though being with him, loving him, was more than she'd ever imagined when she decided to move back. *I'm finding myself again. I'm writing again. No, it's more than that. I'm embracing parts of myself that I hid, or felt guilty about for my entire life—my sensual side, who likes wild sex.*

She smiled thinking back to Marcus's command when he'd called her yesterday, since they hadn't seen each other since the arrest of the teens, due to their busy schedules.

"Be ready for my call at ten. I want you naked, in bed, with your bullet vibrator charged and ready. At nine-fifty five, start playing with your tits until your nipples are rock hard. Understand? But do not get yourself off, or I'll spank you, cause I'm gonna fuck you with my words."

His sexy bossiness had spiked her arousal, and when she answered, "Aye, captain. I'll imagine you sucking and nipping on my nipples, while I play with myself. And I'll spread my legs and imagine you're getting me off with your magic tongue."

"Shit. If I had time, I'd drive over and screw you against that rickety door again. Loose hinges be damned. Ten. Be ready."

Phone sex with Marcus was fantastic. She'd played with herself and was a hair trigger away from coming when he called. Marcus had her use her vibrator on her clit and had dirty talked them both into explosive orgasms. Before they'd hung up he'd surprised her and made her stomach tingly, when he'd murmured in his sexy voice, "Oh, one more thing, tomorrow night, dress up, we're going to The Rock. Reservation is for five o'clock."

The Rock. She'd loved the high-end seafood house right across the Delaware in New Jersey. It was another landmark in the area. "Marcus, I haven't been there in years."

"New owners, and the food is even better. They've updated the place. Still classy, but more so. And babe, looking forward to you blowing my mind with the dress."

Life was good. The first draft of her article was finished, and she only had to revise and send it off to the editor. Pete was feeling better. She and Maddy and her nephews were connecting as deeply as if she'd never left town. Her friendship with Rachel was solid. She'd see her girls next weekend. The clean up on her house was finished and next week Marcus had insisted on sending over a small crew to talk to her and Maddy about rehabbing the place. Maddy wasn't in agreement about what to do with the house, but that was just a blip in her life.

Happiness bloomed inside of her because tonight she'd dress up and see her man.

Two hours later she was working on her article when unexpectedly Marcus's Expedition turned into her driveway and parked.

She went to the front door, opened it, and watched Marcus exit the truck with a paper bag in his hand and prowl toward her. *Oh boy*. His eyes speared hers, looking her body up and down, taking in her short denim cutoffs and thin tank top as he walked toward her. Her heart rabbited in her chest, and wet heat curled between her legs at the erection he was sporting.

"I thought you were meeting an architect this morning?"

"I am, and I don't have much time." He climbed the steps.

She tilted her head toward the bag. "Is that for me?"

He pulled her to him by her nape and gave her a fast kiss. "It's for your sweet-like-sugar pussy."

Her eyes widened. What the...?

"It came this morning, and as soon as I opened the package my dick got so hard I knew I couldn't concentrate on a meeting this morning, and I didn't want to scare the architect with the huge bulge in my pants."

She gasped when Marcus took the Butterfly vibrator out of the bag.

"Inside, and get naked." Then he slapped her ass and pulled her into the cottage.

****

Marcus grinned when Cassie squeaked at the sting on her ass as she booked it into the cottage. He followed her in, admiring her long shapely legs, and her ass jiggling in the tight denim cutoffs.

He closed the door and turned. Jesus.

Cassie was standing a few steps away, watching him. Her brown eyes were almost black with dilated pupils. Her face was flushed. Her nipples jutted out of her thin top, pointing at him, beckoning—calling to him, to sate their mutual desires.

When she purposely ran her tongue over her bottom lip, he could almost feel the slow slide of her eager tongue licking his dick, sending a jolt of lust to his balls. Before he could move to take her in his arms, she stepped up to him, put her hands on his chest, stroking over his shirt. Quickly, she unbuttoned it and pulled it open, caressing his nipples. "God, I love your body." She ran her nose over his chest, "I love your smell, all manly. All mine."

"Cassandra, tonight will be a long, slow climb to release, but right now it's going to be hard and fast. I have to be back in Eastbridge in an hour. But first, I have to show you why you'll love this. Get into the bedroom."

She stood near the bed while he opened the bag and took out the vibrator, letting it dangle by a strap on his finger. It did resemble a butterfly. The body had an embedded vibrator that would stimulate her clitoris, while the wings aroused the labia. Straps that wrapped around the waist and thighs would keep in place.

"I've seen them online, but never used one. And it's hot pink... nice."

"I thought the *hot* color suited you." He took the remote out of the bag, showed it to her and said, "And this controls it. Your clit will thank me while I'm pounding into you."

"Stop talking, start doing."

"You're feisty today."

"No, I'm horny."

"I cleaned it in my office, so it's ready to go. Let's get you set up, little butterfly, and see how many times I can make you come in the next forty-five minutes. Clothes off, baby."

After throwing clothes here and there in a whirlwind of need, Marcus kneeled before her, and strapped the vibrator on.

"It feels kind of weird"

"In a few minutes it will feel kind of arousing."

"Up on the bed, Cassie. Knees to the edge, chest to the mattress, arms out in front of you. And I want your ass in the air, pointing right at me." Arousal was running down her thighs. He enjoyed her mewl when he lapped it up and licked her pussy. "You taste delectable, and if I had time, I'd feast on you for a good long while, but time is short." He spread her cheeks and slid into her.

"Yes," she hissed, rearing back to take him deeper. Her wet heat played havoc with his control. He was primed and ready to fire, and he couldn't hold out much longer. But she was coming first. He picked up the remote and turned it on, then he grabbed her ass firmly and snapped his hips harder. Their ragged breaths filled the room.

"Oh, oh, yes..." Cassie wailed as she clamped onto his dick like a tight, wet fist, but he wasn't going over, not yet. He wanted her to come again.

"Once more." He upped the vibe and she came again in under a minute.

Mumbling into the mattress, Cassie barely managed, "I'm done in, Marcus."

"Don't think so," he said with a wolfish note in his voice.

Marcus turned off the remote and rolled her onto her back, keeping her ass at the edge of the bed. "Stay right there." He propped a pillow beneath her hips, spread her thighs, situated himself between them, and extended her legs up his chest.

"Marcus," her breathy whisper had him on the edge.

He held onto her hips and drove into her, watching her body arch into his thrust. Her eyes closed, her lips parted—she was stunning in her passion.

He set up a pounding pace. She opened her eyes and they gazed at each other, creating an intimacy that delivered a one-two punch straight to his gut.

"Ready?" Marcus picked up the remote and turned it on.

"Oh god," Cassie's eyes closed, her body tensed. Her pussy gripped him as if she'd used her wicked mouth.

"You're gorgeous, absolutely, gorgeous," he spoke through gritted teeth. His balls heated and swelled. Almost there. His head arched back and he came with a long groan.

His pulse slowly stopped racing, and when an overwhelming need to hold her close, to continue the intimacy surfaced, it was an eye-opener.

Is this what love feels like?

Breathing deeply at the possibility, Marcus turned off the remote and rolled them to their sides, pulling her tightly into his arms. They lay together, cheek to cheek. He peeked at the clock on the nightstand. *Shit, five more minutes.* He wanted to spend the rest of the day with her and cursed himself for agreeing to the weekend meeting.

He kissed her, then apologized, "Sorry, but I've got to get back to the office."

"Okay." She didn't move, only smiled broadly.

Marcus chuckled and pulled out of her arms. He kissed the tip of her nose and rolled out of bed.

Stretching, Cassie hopped out of bed, too, still wearing the butterfly.

"Come here." Marcus stopped dressing, kneeled in front of her, undid the buckles on the straps, and took it off. He picked up the vibrator and held it out to her. When she tried to take it, he hung it by a strap on her forefinger. "This is only for variety. And there's more where it came from."

"Can't wait," she stood on tiptoe and kissed him.

"Shit, my meeting starts in fifteen minutes." Marcus opened the front door, smooched her on the lips, and took off.

****

It was the next morning, and as Cassie prepared breakfast for herself and Marcus, she thought back on last night. Dinner at The Rock was amazing, as was the night of sex, but not as lovely as this morning. Marcus had woken her up before dawn, rolled on top of her, clasping their hands on either side of her head. After he'd tenderly kissed her until she was aching with want, he'd slowly entered her, keeping his thrusts slow and rhythmic. They didn't speak, but gazed deeply into each other's eyes the entire time. When he picked up the pace, and hit that *spot*, he'd moaned softly, as they exquisitely came together.

After, he'd held her back to his front and stroked and petted her body bringing her arousal down. In his deep, rich voice, he'd murmured, "My beautiful Cassandra." It had sounded as powerful a statement of love as when Pete called her "My Cassie."

"So your daughters are coming to town next Friday?" Marcus startled her out of her reverie. He picked up a glass of fresh-squeezed orange juice and drank, while he scratched Grey's head, who had jumped on Marcus's lap as soon as he sat down.

She'd mentioned that Eva and Abby were coming to visit when she began making breakfast, and he'd asked questions about them. But as time went on and she hadn't asked him to meet them, the mood in the kitchen had changed from playful to subdued.

"When did you last see them?"

"It's been months, I can't wait."

"Aiden said he'd visit with Mal, his boyfriend, sometime in June. I'll let you know when he's coming."

Oh no, he's fishing for an invite, I should have

228

kept my mouth shut. Cassie bent, opened the oven door, said, "That would be nice," pulled out two plates that she'd kept warming and dished out scrambled eggs, bacon, and added buttered toast.

He was hurt that she hadn't invited him to meet the girls, but she hadn't told them yet that she was dating.

"Cassandra, coffee?" Marcus interrupted her thoughts again.

"Yes, please."

He filled both their mugs, then sat back down, sipping his coffee. "Any special plans with your daughters?"

He's not letting this go. "We'll be visiting Pete, he'll be home by then. And they want to spend as much time as possible with him, Joe and Annie, their kids, and Maddy and the boys. Likely, Joe will BBQ, but Pete's also been bugging Joe to take him to Tina's for her lasagna on Friday. He figures he'll be out of the hospital for four days, enough time to heal. If the doc clears him, we'll go there. Mostly we'll just hang out, but I think Pete's going to overdo it."

"Likely, he will."

Cassie bit into a slice of toast and looked at Marcus. He wasn't looking at her. He sat there holding his mug, seemingly studying the slant of morning sunlight that lit up the table. But his forehead was creased, and it wasn't from smiling.

She'd thought about introducing Abby and Eva to Marcus but she wasn't sure how they'd react to her dating. They'd loved their father deeply, as he did them. She and Ron had a loving relationship, if not a passionate one, but they were a close, loving family.

229

You're in love with Marcus, that's why you're hiding this relationship from them. Casually mentioning dating was one thing, but they were perceptive young women, and wouldn't miss that she'd lost her heart to Marcus. She'd worried that they'd be shocked, and maybe even angry, believing that she'd forget Ron. It would be best to tell them after this visit, and maybe she and Marcus could go to the city and he could meet them there for the first time.

Why are you avoiding telling him how you feel? He's unhappy that you've left him out. But it all felt too new, and though they were a couple, she was still a tad distrustful that in the end they wouldn't last. But it wasn't that as much as it was the raw guilt that her girls would be unhappy.

Marcus finished his food and pushed the plate away. "Ah, I see that you'll be busy," her attention came back to him at the flat sound of his voice.

She smiled at him, but when he smiled back, it never reached his eyes.

Chapter Twenty

Five minutes later on the drive home from Cassie's, Marcus's frustration had him so wound up that he almost missed the turnoff to his farm. He slowed to a crawl on the long narrow drive to his house.

She doesn't want her daughters to meet me. That stung. But he got why she wouldn't. They were new. *Nah, be truthful.* It's likely her mistrust, because he continued to act out and shut down when things turned bad. Of course, there was his fucking rep. Cassie was understandably wary.

Maybe he should ask her to meet them and see how she reacts. He was holding back from doing that. *Why?* He was always brutally blunt with women. *"It's been fun babe, but the night is over. See you."* He cringed at the memories. *Admit it. You're afraid to push her and have your shit come up again and have her leave you.* But dammit, he wanted that invite. He wanted to be part of her... *say it, "family."* And he couldn't wait to introduce her to Aiden and his boyfriend, Mal.

He parked in front of his house, and even with his windows rolled up, he heard his dogs barking with excitement. He was so wrapped up in Cassie that he'd been remiss with his time and attention to them. And

Liam. And Sean, too. He'd hung out with Liam last week, and they were good. He'd make plans with him and Sean, to go to a minor league ball game next week.

Marcus turned off the engine and sat, deep in thought.

What was he going to do when her daughters visited, and he was home alone, feeling sorry for himself? *I'll obsess about it, become resentful. But Riverbend is a small burg, remember how you hunted her down at Pete's BBQ?* Marcus tapped a finger on the steering wheel. Then it came to him. He hit a button on his steering wheel: "Call Aiden."

"Hey dad, how's it going?"

"Hey kiddo, I'm good, how are you doing? How's Malcolm?"

"You really aren't ever gonna stop calling me that, are you, dad?" Aiden said with the warm exasperation of a lovingly harassed child.

"Never, *kiddo*." Marcus chuckled along with Aiden

"We're great. Celebrating that school is over for the next ten weeks."

"Well I hope you're not celebrating too hard. You're halfway there. I'm proud of you."

"Can't believe I'll be a junior in the fall."

"A junior at Columbia with a 4.0 GPA and an incredible internship for the summer."

"Yeah, cannot wait. I'll actually be helping design new products, *and* I'm getting paid to boot. Don't forget that."

"So I can stop paying the rent on your apartment?"

232

"Hey Mal," Aiden held the phone away from his mouth, "my dad's cutting off my money because my internship is paying me."

Marcus heard laughter coming from the background. "Aiden, you're an industrial design major—start on some plans for a one-bedroom cardboard box."

Marcus laughed along, reveling in the close relationship he had with Aiden. When Aiden came out as gay in middle school, Marcus had a tough time accepting it. But Pete had shown him the way back to his son after his ex married a reborn Christian and threw Aiden out of her house. Now they were close, as was Aiden's boyfriend Malcolm, and they saw each other often.

"So, what's up, dad?"

"I know you and Mal planned on visiting sometime this summer. Could you move that visit up to this coming weekend? If not, it's no problem, but it would be great if you can make it work."

"Is it about Pete?"

"Yeah. He's doing well and he's coming out of the hospital on Monday. He wants to see you and Malcolm. Since his heart attack, he wants to see everyone he cares about, without delay."

"Faced his mortality?"

"Yeah, it's hit him hard. But there's another reason."

"What is it?"

The words stuck in his throat. He'd never introduced Aiden to a woman, or even mentioned that he was going out with one. He'd kept his booty calls a dirty secret. But after Aiden met Malcolm when they were freshman, and moved in together, Aiden mentioned to Marcus more than once that it was time for him to settle down.

What a shit father I was.

"What's going on, Dad?"

Man up. "I want you and Malcolm to come to Riverbend next Friday night and meet the woman I'm dating."

"Huh?"

"You heard me."

Aiden took the phone away from his mouth, "Hey Mal, get this. My dad's dating."

"*Your* dad?" Marcus cringed at Malcolm's shock.

"What's her name?"

"Cassandra Bennett."

"Pretty. Mal," Aiden called out, "Her name's Cassandra. He wants us to meet her in Riverbend next Friday. You in?"

"There's no way I'm missing that," Malcolm shouted.

"How about we get there around noon? We'll have lunch and catch up."

"Yeah that would be great. And son? Thank you. I mean it."

"I've got time right now dad, tell me all about her."

****

"Dad are you sure you're up to this?"

"Joe, stop nagging at me. The doc cleared me for going out tonight."

"Cassie, he listens to you, talk some sense into him," Joe pleaded, worry etched on his face. Maddy

234

snorted and Annie snickered, then continued reading their menus while sipping their wine.

Cassie tilted her head at Joe who was sitting across the massive table from her next to Pete. "Seeing as ten of us are sitting in the back room of Tina's Pizzeria and Spaghetti House with menus in front of us, it's obvious I have no influence over your pig-headed father."

Pete's laughter filled the room, but Cassie was as worried as Joe was that Pete was doing too much too fast after only four days out of the hospital. Now it was Friday evening, and Pete's stone-wall insistence that this dinner take place had eventually worn them all down.

"I'm alive, Cassie, and I'm going to live every moment of it, so we're celebrating."

Pete's shy granddaughter, twelve-year-old Beth, who was sitting next to him said, "Pop-pop, I love Tina's but if you're not—"

Pete turned to her, "Bethie, don't worry that pretty head of yours, I'm fine. Tonight we're having a party, right?" She smiled sweetly and nodded.

"Lanie and Justin," Pete said to Joe's two other children who were sitting next to Beth, "you agree with your Pop-Pop?"

"I'm hungry," Justin said, with a seven-year-old's focus on his belly. Pete smiled at him, "Me too, son."

"Can I have spaghetti, mama?" ten-year-old Lanie asked?

"You and everybody can have anything you want, sweetie," Pete answered for Annie. "I'm picking up the check," he looked around the table at the adults, "and I don't want to hear any arguments about it."

"I'm down with that," Maddy teased, "Maybe Tina's famous lobster fra diavolo?"

She sat across from Pete next to Eva, and he gave her a serious look, "Anything you want Maddy, I mean it. Fra diavolo? Perfect. It's just like you, spicy with a nice kick."

Cassie saw Maddy mouth, "Love you, Pete," and heard his soft, "Back atcha."

Cassie's eyes burned and filled. How would they all go on without him? God, she couldn't bear thinking about it.

"What are we celebrating?" Maddy's son Danny asked, interrupting Cassie's worry.

Pete cleared his throat and continued, "We're celebrating that I'm out of the hospital and feel good." The table went quiet, all eyes on Pete. "We're celebrating that Cassie has moved back home, and that Eva and Abby are here this weekend to spend time with their mom and with this old codger." Her breath caught in her throat, and she felt the burn of tears as Pete's eyes strayed to her daughters. They smiled back at him and Eva blew him a kiss. "My two beautiful girls," and he blew two kisses at them at once, one with each hand, making everybody laugh.

"I'm the luckiest man in the world," he looked around the table. Cassie watched Annie take Joe's hand and entwined her fingers with his. She ached to have that from Marcus. But she'd ruined that for herself tonight, and for him, too, with her baseless fears. Marcus should be here—guilt hit her hard.

"I propose a toast." He waited until everyone had raised a glass. "You too, boys and girls, pick up your water or soda." This toast is perfect for tonight

236

because I'm appreciating the moments like this precious one with my family."

A tear rolled down Cassie's cheek. She felt Maddy watching her and saw that her eyes were glistening too. With just a glance they communicated all of their emotions and thoughts to each other in the way that only sisters could. *Thank god, I moved back home.*

"It's in Hebrew." Pete continued, "On my mom's side of the family, Sadie, my little Jewish grandmother, was a five-foot-nothing dynamo who ruled the roost and liked her plum schnapps from time to time. And when we were all gathered together to share a meal, she would say these words like a prayer, "L'Chaim. To life.""

Ten voices echoed Pete's words, then they drank. There was the slightest moment of silence, then Jackie, their waitress, who had just entered the room asked, "Ready for me to take your orders?"

The children's voices broke the heavy emotional stillness.

"I want spaghetti!" "Me too!" "Can I have french fries?"

Cassie watched Pete look around the table taking in the scene, and her breath hitched when his face screwed up as if he were trying not to cry.

"Yes, Jackie, we're all ready," his voice was strained.

He must have felt Cassie watching him because he turned to her and tried to bluster his way out of what he was obviously feeling, "Shouldn't you be reading the menu, Cassie?"

She reached across the table, gave his hand a

quick squeeze, "Even warriors get choked up sometimes."

Pete rubbed her knuckle, and ordered, "Let's get this party started with a large antipasto." He got nods from everyone, and Jackie moved down the table with her pad.

Cassie was deciding on her appetizer and was going to ask her girls if they wanted to share when Pete, who had closed his menu, said to her, "We're missing some family. Cassie, where's Marcus? I thought he and Liam were coming with you and the girls."

Uh, oh. Her stomach dropped as if she were on a plane in a nose dive. All talking stopped, and everyone was looking at her.

"Mom? Who's Marcus," Eva asked.

"Pretty sure he's busy tonight," she said to Pete quickly, ignoring Eva.

Abby turned to face Cassie, her brow furrowed, "You're blushing, mom. Who is he?"

"Ah..." thank god, Jackie was standing between her and Eva, pad and pen in hand waiting for their order. She placed her order, while her mind raced on how to divert this conversation to something else.

Jackie moved down the table and as soon as she did, Abby said, "What's going on, mom?"

"Marcus knows Pete really well, and—"

"He's a *friend* of your mom's," Joe said, his emphasis on *friend* clear, that had Abby and Eva closely staring at her.

Maddy's low mumbled, "some friend," and Annie's soft laugh had Eva asking, "Aunt Maddy, what do you mean?"

Before Maddy could answer, Cassie quickly stated, "Marcus is a close friend of Pete's. He lives in Riverbend, and we went out a few times. That's all." *Well, we did go out*, she told herself.

"What kind of *friend* is he, mom?" Eva, like Maddy, could never let things go.

"I told you. We went out a few times, had lunch and..."

"I remember that lunch, alright," Joe said, shaking his head, she was sure of the image of she and Marcus making out at the diner.

"*Mom*," Eva and Abby said in unison.

"Girls," Cassie looked back and forth between them. "I'll fill you in later. He and I are just friends, as I said. Why don't we change the subject and enjoy the meal."

"I saw him kiss you at the picnic, aunt Cassie," Jason called out.

Maddy giggled.

Oh boy.

"Oh, he's that kind of friend," Eva said looking at her sister.

"Okay everyone, enough," Pete put in. "Marcus isn't here, and I'm not sure why not. Your mom said she'd fill you in later, and she will," he said to Eva and Abby. "Jason, no tattling, you hear me?"

Deep breath, she had a momentary respite.

"And, here comes the antipasto," Joe said, as Jackie and another waitress brought in the appetizer and fresh bread.

"Eva and I are happy you're getting out, mom," Abby said into her ear.

"You're so sweet, honey."

Eva asked softly so only the three of them could hear, "Why are you hiding this from us? Are you worried because you're afraid that we'll think you're betraying dad?"

Eva was always blunt. *No, I think I'm head-over-heels in love like I've never been in my life, and I'm scared out of my mind.*

Cassie took each of their hands, and they leaned into her so they could see each other, "How did you both get so smart?"

"Like mother, like daughters," Abby whispered.

They waited while she struggled, "Maybe that's part of it. But... Marcus is the first man I've been involved with since your dad, and I'm unsure about it. When we get back to the cottage, I'll tell you about him. Okay?"

Abby said, "We want you to be happy, mom." Her heart felt like it would burst out of her chest at how sweet and caring her daughters were.

As they began to fill their plates, she heard a noise at the entrance to the room. Before Cassie could turn, Pete bellowed, "Marcus and Liam! And my god, is that Aiden and Malcolm?"

Cassie's head whipped around. There he was. Marcus looked devastatingly handsome in gray slacks, a black sweater, and his classic black leather jacket. He was standing at the door with Liam and two handsome young men, one of whom was obviously Aiden, who took after his father in looks, if not breadth.

Pete had gotten up to greet them as they walked toward the table asking, "Isn't Sean coming?" Joe had risen, too, and was heading over with Pete. Marcus brought up the rear, and his eyes were locked on hers, a sly smile saying more to her than any words could.

That sneak. Her lips twitched into a shy grin, and joy flooded her. He was here with his son, and he looked happy.

Marcus bypassed Pete and Joe, who were greeting the guys with bear hugs. He prowled toward her, totally focused on her. It was the night at the Horse all over again. She felt herself flush.

"Hey Marcus," Maddy called out.

"Maddy," he nodded but his eyes never left Cassie's.

"Oh my *god*, mom," Eva murmured, watching Marcus's approach.

"Total score," Abby said in her ear.

Marcus stopped at her chair, put a hand on the nape of her neck, bent and brushed his lips over hers with the sweetest kiss. Cassie swore she heard her daughters sigh. Or maybe it was her. He ended the kiss and with his lips to her ear, said, "Sorry we're a little late."

She looked up at the man who she'd fallen in love with almost from the moment she'd met him, and laughed out loud.

The corners of his eyes crinkled with his grin, that really looked more like a smirk. He must have had a blast beating her at her own game. Marcus rubbed his thumb on her nape, then kissed the tip of her nose and said, "How about you introduce me to these two beautiful girls of yours?"

"Only if you introduce me to the two handsome men you brought tonight. And I want my girls to meet Liam."

241

"Deal."

"Hey dad," a vibrant voice just like his father's said, "Stop hogging Cassie. I want to meet the woman who stole your heart." Cassie froze and stared at Marcus. She heard her girls snicker, and what sounded like a guffaw from someone.

Marcus's eyes glowed with affection. But then that blue darkened with heavy emotion, and it wasn't sexual. He leaned in, and in a husky whisper recited, "i carry your heart with me (i carry it in my heart) i am never without it (anywhere i go you go, my dear..."

She felt giddy, lightheaded. Marcus rubbed his nose on the side of hers and said, "e.e. cummings."

Cassie had only had a sip of her wine tonight, but she felt joyously drunk. If Marcus's actions and words weren't a declaration of love, then she was a complete fool.

Chapter Twenty-One

Cassie stirred. She opened her eyes. It was early Monday morning, at the cottage. The nightstand clock read five-fifteen, confirming it. She lay on her side, naked, her legs pulled up almost into a fetal position. Marcus was spooned around her, fast asleep. His face was nestled in her hair, and little puffs of his breath tickled her ear.

One of her hands was tucked under her pillow, the other held on to Marcus's arm that was draped across her chest, holding her tightly to him. It was pretty much the way they'd fallen asleep, because anytime she'd tried to turn over, he would bring her back to this position, mumbling what sounded like, "Stay here."

She was a little sleep deprived, but Marcus wanting to hold her all night was a price worth paying. The room still smelled of sex, but she wanted more. Slowly she turned her head to catch his scent, and the stubble on his jaw scraped her cheek. Just a whiff of the hint of his woodsy aftershave and his distinctive male essence was a turn on. Of course, his sizable morning erection that was poking into her ass was cranking up her need, too.

She'd originally planned to wake him with a blow

job, but she wanted him to sleep in, knowing he had a busy day ahead of him.

A raspy mew from Grey was another signal that it was time to get up, or else that big boy would be sitting on her chest, demanding breakfast. Carefully, Cassie pulled Marcus's arm away. She squeezed out of his hold, pulled the light cover off of herself, and quietly got out of bed. He didn't wake, but muttered and groped for her, so she put her pillow into his arms, he held on to it, and quieted.

She pulled on a long-sleeve tee and pajama bottoms found in the basket of clean laundry, rubbed Grey's ears, and watched those lime-green eyes close with pleasure. "Let's go, buddy," she whispered. Her cell was on the dresser, so she grabbed it, exiting the room with Grey following, and quietly closed the bedroom door behind her.

Grey was fed and, like most cats, had already settled on his bed for a solid five hour morning nap. *What a life.*

She'd brewed coffee and was sitting at the kitchen table, sipping it from a mug. Her stomach rumbled with hunger, but she'd wait for Marcus to wake and have breakfast with him. He'd mentioned that French toast was his favorite breakfast food, and she had everything ready to surprise him with it when he woke. A sense of peace and stability stole over her. *I missed sharing my life. I missed giving happiness to someone, even if it's no more than French toast.*

Cassie sipped coffee and reflected back on one of the best weekends she'd had in a long time.

Once Marcus had shown at Tina's, and he wasn't angry with her, the weekend was incredible. Aiden and

Malcolm were lovely young men, handsome and charming. They brought a liveliness to the party that had been missing, with their funny and irreverent stories about Marcus, Pete, and even Joe that had the adults roaring with laughter. Abby and Eva joined in with their own stories about Cassie, making her cringe and blush a few times.

Marcus had charmed her daughters and they had done the same to him. And he had no problem with PDA, even with her daughters present. He'd sat close to her, his arm draped around the back of her chair. He'd held her hand, had played with a curl of her hair, even given her a light kiss. At the same time, he'd expertly divided his attention among everyone, including the children.

And seeing Marcus in the father role, witnessing the love between him and his son—that had blown her away. It was a side of him she'd never seen, a depth of emotion that showed the man's substance.

At some point during the evening Eva had whispered to Cassie, "Mom, Marcus is amazing. Abby and I like him for you. And Aiden and Mal are gorgeous and amazing. If they weren't gay, Abby and I would be fighting over them."

Cassie had smiled and whispered back, "I'm glad you like Marcus. He likes you, too. And his son and Mal are handsome, but please pay some attention to Liam, too. He's taken a different road in life, and I know that he tends to sit in the background and sometimes feels left out of things."

Liam had greeted Cassie cordially, and she'd welcomed him, but there was still that tension between them from his anger at the picnic about Marcus spending time with her. She hadn't seen him since, and it bothered her terribly that she hadn't gotten to know him better. She had to make sure that Liam felt included in the life she was creating with Marcus. Her daughters' attention was a good start, she believed.

Eva immediately got up and went over to Liam, saying, "Liam, I've heard so much about you, but can you fill in the details?" His laugh held a surprise, but he pulled up a chair for her next to his.

Then Abby had wandered over to them and Cassie had heard Liam telling them about the construction business and the fancy woodworking he did on the side, including creating birdhouses. *Ah.* She made a note to ask him for a commission to help break the ice between them.

Right after dessert, Pete looked tired, so Joe and Annie took him home. She, Eva, and Abby went back to the cottage. But instead of staying until Sunday as planned, Eva and Abby had hit it off with Aiden and Malcolm, and when they'd offered to drive the girls back to New York Saturday afternoon, they'd jumped at the chance.

She'd taken the girls to Marcus's house Saturday morning. Aiden and Malcolm, had shown them around the farm, then right after lunch they'd left for New York. After her girls and his boys had driven off, Cassie had cheered. "I miss them already, but we can have a date night!"

"How about this for a date." Then he'd flung her over his shoulder and hauled her into his bedroom, for what he told her would be, "A good, long fucking." And he'd delivered.

After, they'd taken his dogs on a long run around

the farm. They'd come back to the cottage to take care of Grey, and decided to spend the night there, had grilled hot dogs and watched a Phillies game—and later had torrid shower sex.

She turned when the bedroom door opened and her mouth lolled open. Tousled hair, sleepy, dark-blue eyes, bare feet, loose pajama bottoms, and naked chest—it was still hard to believe he was real. And all hers. Marcus ran a hand through his unruly hair as he shuffled toward her. He stopped behind her, gently pulled her head back, nibbled on her lips, then gazed into her eyes murmuring, "Mornin', gorgeous." He let her go, she turned in her chair, greeting him, "Mornin', gorgeous, yourself, but you look like you could use coffee."

"That would be great. I have to leave earlier this morning than I thought to meet Bret at his worksite."

"Fine, but not before breakfast. I'm making your favorite."

"French toast?"

"Yep, with a side of bacon."

He brushed his lips over hers, "I'll shower, dress and be ready in fifteen."

"And one more thing, Mr. Mackenzie, if you're in your office later today, I can stop at the Public Food Market in town and bring lunch to you."

He rested his forehead on hers, "Yes, I'd like that, very much. I'm already imagining you as my secretary, on your knees under my desk, blowing me, while I make a few phone calls."

Oh boy, just thinking about playing at his office was turning her on.

"I see it right on your face, you like the idea."

"No, I love the idea."

"I'm running late, so woman," he smacked her ass, "I need French toast," and he chuckled all the way into the bathroom.

Cassie hummed to herself as she prepared the dish. She loved that their sexual by-play was more than just a few hours in bed, but a large part of their daily life.

Weeks ago, Cassie had doubted her decision to move back to Riverbend. But now, she was in love, and her relationship with Marcus was stable—their feelings for each other were growing. She'd found more happiness than she'd ever imagined on her new life path in Riverbend. Life was wonderful.

****

Marcus reached the end of the drive from the cottage, checked for traffic, and turned onto River Road toward Bret's project. The weekend had turned out to be better than he'd expected. Cassie had laughed and was happy when he'd crashed the dinner, instead of being pissed off at him. And seeing Aiden happy with his studies and with Mal made Marcus a proud dad.

But the best was introducing Aiden to Cassie and her daughters, who were as lovely as their mother. He'd sat back and watched them talk and get to know each other, and Cassie had pulled Liam into the mix, too. She was caring, sensitive, and warm—he was crazy about her. The closest he'd ever had to this type of normal family interaction was with Pete and Shirl. It was phenomenal.

"This is what love must feel like," he said out

loud and listened to the words reverberate in the truck. He liked how it sounded. It wasn't just the combustible sexual heat between them. It was so much more. It was situations like this weekend that led to— *real contentment.*

That's it, I feel a sense of peace when I'm with Cassie no matter what we're doing. It was all new to Marcus, and even uncomfortable at times. But he believed that being with Cassie, connecting their families, their lives, was finally... right.

His cell rang, taking him out of his thoughts.

He pushed the button on his steering wheel, "Hey Li, what's up?"

"Mac," this wasn't his happy brother. "It's nothing to do with business."

Marcus's body tensed ready for a blow. He knew what that strain in his brother's voice meant. Something bad was coming. "Li. Spill it."

"Mom called."

Marcus's stomach dropped. "Hang on," he snapped, as he swiftly pulled off the road and parked on the shoulder, the engine running. Rage hit Marcus. It wasn't a deep burn, but a down-to-the-bone, white-hot fury, that was burning away the defenses he'd erected against the pain, anger, and trauma of his life. He'd buried it deep, like a fossil under thousands of layers of sedimentary rock. But now...?

Marcus gripped the steering wheel. His palms ached and his knuckles turned paper white. He had to stop the shit that was bubbling to the surface and would spill like a cesspool overflow. He wanted to lash out, to hurt, to smash, to destroy, to fuck his brains out, to somehow cope. He closed his eyes, put his head back, and took a deep breath. Then another, trying to calm the emotional storm that was battering him.

"Mom." What a fucking laugh. Beatrice Saxon Mackenzie was once a member of the wealthy, high-society Saxon family—until they'd disowned her decades ago for marrying his low-life, abusive, biker father, Nolan Mackenzie. Oh, and she wasn't a Mackenzie anymore... thank fuck for that. Was it husband number three or four she was working on? Maybe five. Who knew, since he and Liam hadn't seen or heard from her in eight years.

She'd finally disappeared from their lives after Marcus had threatened her to stay away from Liam for the last time. He'd made it absolutely clear to her, that there was no more money coming her way, ever again. There would be no more playing on Liam's guilt when she was in between men. Beatrice well knew that Liam was a partner in Mackenzie Construction, and that it was a goldmine. She was a succubus, a vile demon who would surface from time to time to bleed Liam dry with her sob story. *"My little man, I'm your mama and need your help."*

Marcus remembered that scene eight long years ago like it was yesterday.

He'd paid a surprise visit to Liam from New York City, where he'd been working for an engineering firm. And there the bitch was, a skanky bottle-blonde, wearing skin-tight clothing meant for a teen and smelling of stale cigarettes. She'd ensconced herself in Liam's house for weeks by then. And poor Liam, anytime she was around, he'd revert into that frightened, powerless little boy. So he'd stood helplessly by while she did whatever the hell she wanted: eating his food, trashing his house, making fun of him, taking his money.

When Marcus had looked at his brother's pale face when he'd walked into Liam's house and seen that cunt sitting in Liam's living room watching TV, as if she lived there... he'd lost his fucking mind. With his teeth clenched in rage, he'd told her off, and then had bodily thrown her out of Liam's house, tossing her clothes and shit out of the door after her.

Her parting shot at Marcus while she gathered her belongings was shouted at him in a voice made raspy from years of smoking and drinking. "I should have aborted you. You're no good Marcus. You're shit. You're just like him—your rotten, scumbag, son of a bitch father." Yeah, yeah, yeah—his DNA sucked. He was his father's son. She'd sung that song since he was a child.

"Marcus, are you there?" The pain was evident in Liam's voice. That bitch could still hurt him.

"When did she call?" he spit the words out like they were poison.

"A few minutes ago. She said she had to talk to both of us. It was important, but she wouldn't say why. I told her I'd call you, then hit your number right after she hung up."

"Did she call Uncle Brennan?"

"I don't think she has his number, she didn't say. I... I just wanted to get off the phone with her."

"Don't worry Li, we'll handle it. Do you hear me?"

"Yeah, Mac."

"I have a few things I've got to take care of, so

I'll meet you at your place in an hour. Text me her number."

"Okay. You gonna call her now?"

"I am."

"Okay, Mac. I'll make sure the crew knows what to do, ask Bret to swing by before he shuts work down for the day on his project. But bro, she sounded different. Not like she usually did. Something's wrong, but she said she needed to talk to both of us."

"Take it easy Li, I said we'll handle it and we will. I need her number." *No, I'll handle it and deal with that motherfucking cunt.*

"Will do. Later Mac," Liam ended the call.

Marcus waited for Liam's text. He took his cell out of its holder on the dash and held it, watching the screen. His heart pounded out of his chest, while nausea roiled his stomach. His jaw hurt. He was so tense, he could chew on a pane of glass and not feel it. Because Liam was right, something bad was coming. Every cell in his body was on high alert and had shifted into survival mode, as if he was facing enemy fire. He had to make the call, he had to take care of his brother. He had to clean up the pile of shit from their past—again.

The text came in. Marcus took a deep breath, exhaled slowly, hit call back, and put it on speaker.

And waited.

"Well, well, Marcus," her gruff voice grated against his brain. "I—"

"What do you want?" His words cut her off with the precision of a surgeon's scalpel.

The brutal meanness that he remembered well slid into her hoarse voice, "You're still the same asshole, I see."

"Shut the fuck up," he spat the words out. "Listen up. First, you better not be anywhere near Riverbend, or it won't go well with you. Secondly, you have five seconds to say why you're calling... your time starts now."

There was a moment's hesitation. Her next words shattered his world.

"You're bastard father is dying. He doesn't have much time. He wants to see you and Liam."

Marcus's body seized up as if he'd been sucker punched. He stopped breathing. His vision swam. Images of Nolan Mackenzie on a violent tear in their apartment, wrecking everything in his wake, slapping, punching, and kicking anyone in his way battered his mind.

The phone dropped out of his hand.

****

Later that morning, Cassie and Maddy walked out of their family home onto the back deck that overlooked the river. "It looks good, sis," Cassie leaned on the deck railing.

Silently, Maddy stared at the river.

"Those flood cleanup people really know what they're doing," Cassie added, wondering why her sister hadn't been her usual chatty self since they'd driven down to the house together. "It's amazing how fast they worked, don't you think?" Still no response from Maddy.

"Uh huh."

Cassie continued, "They vacuumed, removed mildew, washed everything down with disinfectant. Even the crawl space. It's cleaner than it's ever been.

The fans and dehumidifiers are doing their job. And the outside is ready for painting." *Can I ever move back here?* The thought roiled her stomach.

"Marcus told me last week as soon as cleanup is finished that he's going to give us an estimate." Cassie laughed softly, "Of course at cost, but he'll think of some way I can pay him back, I'm sure."

Maddy hadn't moved an inch.

Cassie quieted and they stood side by side looking at the beauty of Delaware on this lovely spring day as it moved calmly downstream. When she placed her hand gently on Maddy's shoulder, Maddy recoiled, and turned to her.

Aggressively moving until she stood toe to toe with Cassie, Maddy put her hands on her hips, and exploded. "You keep jabbering on about this fucking house as if it's something that's special to you. Or to me. But I don't give a flying fuck about it. But you, who knows what the hell you're thinking? You're going to fix it up and move in, that's your great idea? It's only been flooded out, what, a gazillion times? It's where dad drowned in a flash flood, remember that? One minute, he was pulling mom to safety, and the next the river took him," her voice cracked.

"Maddy..." Cassie's heart was pounding, "I know."

"You don't know shit Cass, because you weren't here," she barked. "You were in sunny California, already gone from our lives for a long time by then."

"I was, you're right. I'm... I'm sorry that I wasn't here for you."

Maddy's beautiful pixie face paled and a tear rolled down her cheek, but she pulled herself together, breathing hard.

Cassie stopped herself from going to her sister and taking her in her arms. She wasn't sure she'd be welcome there, and the pain of that realization stabbed at her heart. *How could I have abandoned her for so many years?*

Their house held many secrets, and right now on the deck of the house, the one that Cassie carried, that she'd run as far from Riverbend as she could, as soon as she could, was being dragged into the light.

"You weren't there." All the anger had gone from Maddy, leaving behind sorrow and misery. "You left for college the summer before you turned eighteen. I was turning fourteen. And you never really came back, did you?"

Cassie's eyes burned with unshed tears, but her heart wept at Maddy's words. "No, Mad, you're right. I didn't. I couldn't."

"I know that Cass. I should have done what you did, left Riverbend behind. But I was young and terrified of going out in the world. Instead I looked for a safe haven." Her laugh was bitter. "Yeah, I chose Ray Bristow, a small time criminal, eighteen years older than me. A safe haven, that quickly turned into hell. Think I have daddy issues, Cass?

"Maddy, please don't blame yourself."

"At least you left. Me? Though I love my boys, I trapped myself even more."

"Please, Mad, please, that's past. We both did the best we could to cope."

Maddy hung her head, "Yeah," she muttered. Then she looked up. "Cassie, I'm sorry that I went off on you. It's not your fault, it's our crappy parents who are to blame."

"Of course you're angry that I got away, but I'm guilty for leaving you with them. They were so terribly damaged."

"They were, Cass. But right now I have to know if you're going to move into this death trap?" Maddy took a step back and leaned on the railing, watching her sister.

"You know that was my plan. Our plan."

"It was, and I was so happy to have you back with me that I forgot."

"Forgot?"

"Yeah, Cass, I forgot that the river is a killer. Because this destruction," she pointed at the house, "was from another flash flood. Our neighbors, the Millers, barely escaped with their lives."

"I know, I know."

Her voice ragged with pain, Maddy pleaded, "You keep repeating, 'I know, I know,' but I want you to stop saying that. This is what I want Cassie: don't do it. Let's not fix it. Let's tear the fucking thing down."

"Maddy... what's in your head?" Cassie took a chance and put her hand on Maddy's arm. "Tell me, sis."

"It needs to come down. It's always been a broken house, because they were broken.

"Oh, honey," her heart was breaking for Maddy, for herself, for her parents. Cassie took her sister in her arms and tried to hold her. But Maddy gave Cassie a quick hug, then stepped away.

Cassie put her hands on the deck railing and looked at the river. "Yes, mom was gone for a long time, sis. She disappeared into depression, into her

256

bed, and he disappeared outside of it. By the time I turned ten and you were six, he was staying out of the house as much as possible."

She almost slipped that their father had another woman for years in another town, but she couldn't do that to Maddy. Not today, when they were both so raw.

"It was a sad, dark house Cass. They were sad, dark people. But at least we had Pete and Shirl, and Joe. I don't want to fight you about this, but I won't be able to sleep knowing you're here, and not just because the river's dangerous—I don't want this house to take you back to the past we've each fought so hard to leave behind." Maddy's voice became shrill, and she took Cassie by both hands and squeezed tight.

Maddy echoed what Pete said, he wouldn't sleep knowing I lived here.

"It's going to be okay. It will," Cassie's voice softened.

"Don't patronize me." Maddy yelled. "Don't do that. I just got you back after more than fifteen years. My kids are just getting to know you. I don't know my nieces real well, and I want to. Why are you being stubborn about this? Pete doesn't want you to move down here, he told me that, and that the cottage is yours forever. Rachel doesn't want you here. Marcus doesn't. Are you some kind of fucking martyr? Like Mom? Are you being like her? Or do you think if you can fix this house, it'll fix the things that happened there?"

Maddy's words lashed at her. *That's exactly what I'm thinking, isn't it?* The myth she'd struggled with for a long time: heal the house, heal herself.

Tears were streaming down Maddy's face, "I

257

can't lose you, too, please don't put yourself in danger."

Cassie took her sister in her arms, held her tight, and caressed her back as Maddy sobbed, and her own tears flowed. This was where the healing would take place, in each other's arms, right here in Riverbend, but not on the banks of the Delaware.

Maddy was right. Fuck the house.

"Maddy, I'm so sorry I ran away for all those years. And that I made you sad and afraid about the house. But... you're right. You and Pete and Marcus are right. I promise, I won't move in. I'm here with you forever. We'll decide what to do with the house another time. Okay sis?"

Maddy's head was buried under Cassie's chin, her sobs easing. Cassie held her tight to her chest and stroked Maddy's hair like she used to when they were growing up and Maddy needed comfort.

"Okay," Maddy murmured unintelligibly, "but you're squishing my face with your big tits."

"Maddy really." Cassie pulled away, but she was grinning. And Maddy wore her trademark smirk as she wiped her tears away with her hand.

"Love you baby sis." Cassie took tissues out of her pocket, gave one to Maddy.

"Back atcha," Maddy stood on tiptoe, put her hands on Cassie's shoulders and kissed her cheek.

"Hey, where are my girls?" they heard Pete holler from the front of the house.

"We're in the back, be down in a sec," Maddy yelled back. They walked through the house and came out onto the front porch and watched Joe help Pete cross the narrow bridge.

"How's the house?" Joe asked as he and Pete walked over to them.

"The house is shit. Cassie's not moving in." Maddy announced with a smile. "Our eyes are bloodshot from crying. Let's leave this dump and go to the diner. Joe, I need a brownie sundae to take the edge off, stat."

"So, Maddy girl, you convinced your sister to see reason and stay at the cottage?" Pete's eyes twinkled.

"Well, my tears helped, but her getting laid regularly probably didn't hurt."

"*Maddy!*" Cassie shrieked at Maddy's Cheshire grin, while Pete and Joe howled with laughter.

Chapter Twenty-Two

It was almost noon. Cassie had texted Marcus that she was planning to head into Eastbridge, pick up lunch for two, and come see her man. Her man. She got hot just thinking about him. But he hadn't texted her back, so she took a chance and called him but she got his voicemail. "Hey Marcus, I'm ready for lunch, are you? Wait until you hear what happened at the house today."

Minutes crept by, and it was getting close to one o'clock. Cassie was getting worried and a little pissed. No way was she going to wait around, clock watching. Only one way to find out what was what, so she sat down at the kitchen table and called his office.

"Mackenzie Construction and Engineering," Janice said.

"Hi Janice, it's Cassandra Bennett. Is Marcus there? We were supposed to meet for lunch but he's not answering."

"Hello Cassie. I'm sorry but Marcus had a family emergency, he and Liam left a few hours ago. I'm not sure when they'll be back in the office, at least a few days, but Bret is taking over. Do you want to talk to him?"

A family emergency? Maybe something had

happened to his uncle who lived in Arizona. But couldn't he have texted to say he'd be gone? She nibbled on a cuticle. Her stomach clenched. Is he pulling away? *Stop being selfish, she said it was an emergency. This is not about you.*

"Uh, no thanks Janice, just... when you hear from him, please let him know that I called."

"Will do, Cassie. You take care now," and she hung up.

It had been going so good between them, but Cassie had a sinking feeling that that was about to change.

****

Cassie washed her breakfast dishes, and stacked them on the drainboard to dry. From the screened kitchen window, she watched dark clouds roll across the sky. The pungent smell of approaching rain drifted into the room. The wind kicked up, swaying trees and bushes. In the distance, she caught a flash of lightning, and a low roll of thunder.

She squeezed out the sponge, placed it on the side of the sink, and checked on Grey. He was curled into his bed, but had picked up his head, eyes wide, body on alert. Storms frightened him. The shelter of her clothes closet made him feel safe, so she'd put a small bed in the back of it for him. She crouched down in front of him and gently stroked his head, "It's okay boy, whenever you're ready, the closet door is open just enough for you to squeeze through."

A clap of thunder startled her, and Grey streaked out of the kitchen.

It was getting close. Strong storms were predicted for most of the day, a perfect fit for Cassie's current mood because she hadn't heard a word from Marcus for two days.

Two days. Where was he? She'd gone from being concerned, to worried, to royally pissed. After calling his office on Monday and not getting any info, she'd gone to see Pete. He had no idea what was going on, but he'd emailed Brennan, getting a bounce back that he was away for the next week. His voicemail had gone unanswered too.

She was frustratingly stonewalled. She'd contemplated contacting Bret, but didn't want to seem intrusive or controlling. They were a couple, wasn't it her right to check on him? Wouldn't Marcus want to know what was going on, if the situation was reversed?

Pete had reassured her, "Marcus will get in touch when he can, all we can do is wait."

But the more she dwelled on it, the thinner her patience grew, and the worse it seemed as a continuation of past problems—push, pull. Tomorrow she would call Bret if she hadn't heard from Marcus. For the past few days, she'd forced herself to continue work on her articles, and even outlined an idea for a novel, but with Marcus constantly on her mind, concentrating had been difficult.

Maddy and the boys had met her at the diner for dinner on Monday night, and it had been good to be distracted. She'd told Maddy about not hearing from Marcus when Joe had taken Jay and Danny into the kitchen so they could pick out the ice cream they wanted. Big mistake. Maddy had reverted into her "All

Men Are Cocksuckers" rant. But when her sister had seen Cassie's sad expression, she'd hugged Cassie and said, "Hey, don't listen to me, it's projection, because of Derek. Sorry sis."

This wasn't Marcus dumping her, she knew that. It was that Marcus had trouble in some way, and she wanted to be there to help him, as a loving partner. But Maddy's visit had put her in a worse funk—maybe they weren't the loving partners she thought they were.

Cassie needed a distraction. She opened the front door wide, welcoming the smell of ozone from the lighting streaking across the sky. As the storm lashed the house, she grabbed a towel and cleaning spray from under the sink and attacked the kitchen's flat surfaces with a vengeance.

I've got to get my anger under control before I see Marcus. I have to listen to him, not jump down his throat. The storm moved on quickly, and as the rain stopped, it left behind the sweet, clean smell of washed earth, something she'd missed terribly living in the desert dry of southern California.

Maybe it was the electricity from the storm, but she felt even more frazzled and anxious then she'd been. *What if he doesn't contact me? What if something terrible has happened to him? What if this is the end of us?*

How was she going to calm herself down and get her emotions under control? Everyone had advised her to have patience. But after two days, her well of patience had dried up.

Now what? She shut the front door and returned to the kitchen.

She nibbled on a cuticle. At the sound of a

vehicle pulling up to the cottage, she swung her head around. "Marcus." She raced to the door.

Vibrating with happiness and excitement, Cassie stepped onto the porch. Her smile was so wide that her cheeks hurt. She was just about to race down the porch steps and run to him, as he climbed out of his truck, when the smile was wiped from her face by a terrible dread.

The loving, happy Marcus who'd walked out of her cottage whistling, two days ago was gone. In his place was a man whose body was as taut as a mooring rope tied to a tanker, ready to snap. His rigid, clenched jaw matched his expression—concrete hard and closed down.

Oh, no. With a lump in her throat she choked out "Marcus?" His eyes narrowed.

He cleared the first porch step. "Inside, Cassandra," his harsh voice lashed out.

Her heart pounded. Her face flushed. Her legs shook, all signs that there was danger lurking, that she had to flee. *You know he's an angry man, you've seen it before. Marcus would never hurt you physically. Hear him out.*

Cassie nodded, turned and walked into the cottage. Marcus followed her in, on her heels. She watched him close and lock the door. Before she could utter a word, he grabbed her roughly around her waist, and plastered her body to his. Instinctively, she held onto his shoulders for support. His other hand grasped a handful of her hair, and gave it a tug to angle her head where he wanted it. She whimpered, but he kept on.

No way. This wasn't a sexual tug with just a bite of pain that always ramped up her arousal. This was angry, not deliciously carnal.

264

She pulled her mouth away, "Marcus, st—" but he held her head prisoner and grated into her mouth with a bruising kiss, stopping her complaint.

This wasn't wild passion. Instead, his strong hold on her and punishing lips were something dark, ugly, brutal. It was lust, but lust born of demons. She pushed at his chest, hard, and he lost his hold on her.

She stepped back, fighting tears, but not anger. Crossing her arms over her chest, she glared at him.

A muscle in his jaw twitched. "What the—?" he snapped.

She flashed her palm at him. "Do not ever touch me like that."

His mouth set in a hard line, but a glimmer of remorse showed, then was gone.

Her chest squeezed with pain at how closed off he was.

"We'll talk about you man-handling me in a second."

"Man..."

"Yes, and you know it, because, for a moment your face changed from raw anger, to something that looked like, guilt."

The color drained from his face, but he only stood silently staring at her.

"And now the walls and the bars are back up. I can almost hear the clang of the jail cell door closing behind you, locking you back in. I want answers. Where have you been Marcus?"

"Away."

"Away? That's all I get from you? Something obviously happened. I've been worried. What was it?"

"It's not important. I'm back now."

Her pulse pounded, she trembled. Though he'd been rough with her, she saw that damaged little boy. She wanted to go to him. Soothe him. Take care of him. Love him. But they had to have it out right now, though she hated to do that to him. But she couldn't be with a man who could close off or be triggered and act out.

Still, he said nothing.

"On Monday, I called Janice looking for you. She said it was a family emergency. Care to sit down and share the details with me?"

"I said that it's not important." His frustration was showing.

Suddenly, he moved to her, put his hands on her arms, held her tight, and buried his face in her hair. Tension peeled off of his body, into his hands, that felt like steel clamps on her arms. His chest rose and fell with harsh rasps. He blatantly rocked his erection into her core.

"Baby, I'm so sorry that I scared you. But, please, I need to fuck you." He kissed her jaw and ran his lips down her neck. "I want to bend you over the couch, your legs spread wide, ass in the air and pound my cock, hard, into your tight, wet cunt." He licked and sucked hard on the spot behind her ear, marking her.

Her body responded to his, as it always did, she wanted him as badly as he wanted her. And she wanted to give him what he pleaded her to give, but not in this way. She was kind and loving, but she wasn't a doormat.

Cassie broke out of his arms and stepped back. "Stop."

He stilled, frustrated, but a look of wariness crept into his face.

"I've been worried sick about you for the past

two days. I don't even rate a few words in a text message?" She pushed again, but this time it was with words. "You left here on Monday a happy man. At least that's how you acted. Remember that?"

His eyes narrowed, his shields were up, but his expression was uneasy. All she wanted to do was love this man. *Keep going.* "I told you that I love you. You didn't say that directly back to me, but you've acted like you love me. Is that a lie?"

He shook his head in the negative and some emotion stirred in his eyes, but she couldn't tell what it was. His hands hanging at his sides tightened into fists.

She took a step toward him. "You came back today a different man. An angry, rigid, closed-down man who won't share something important with the woman who he professes to at least care about." She was destroying him, a haunted expression swept over his face. But she had to confront this.

"That order to get in the house was angry, not playful. That kiss and hold on my hair wasn't sexy, it was brutal. Those rough dirty words, 'I want to fuck you hard, pound into your cunt,' something you've said before that turned me on, today made me feel like one of the nameless women that you've fucked and tossed away like garbage."

He paled and shut his eyes.

"But, I know it's not that because that's not how you think of me. It's because something happened to you. What was it?" She whipped the words at him.

His eyes popped open, but he only shook his head.

"Tell me. What happened to the man I love?"

"Nothing, I..."

Cassie took two steps right to him, toe to toe, and

raised her voice, *"Who did this to you? Who? Tell me."*
She shouted the last two words.

"My father," he roared like a wounded animal.

His father. Cassie recoiled, as if Marcus had struck her.

His body trembled with fury as he came toward her, herded her until her back thumped against the front door. His hands slammed on the door above her head, caging her in.

"You want to know what happened, Cassandra?" His voice was rough and gravelly as if he'd been screaming and had ripped his vocal cords to shreds.

She nodded, swallowing hard.

"Right after I left on Monday, Liam called. My bitch mother called to say that my father was dying, and that he wanted to see me and Liam. So we went with my uncle Brennan. Do you want to hear that my uncle and I had to almost carry Liam out of that fucking prison, after our father, that motherfucking evil prick, did a number on him? Huh?"

She nodded, speechless.

"Right now, my little brother is at my house, lying on my couch, sleeping after we had to call Doc Taylor to give Liam a sedative because of the flashbacks from our lovely childhood." His voice cracked, and tears welled in his eyes, but somehow Marcus regained control. "Brennan is watching him."

"Marcus, I'm so, so sorry." She instinctively put a hand up to his face to touch him, to comfort him, but he jerked back.

That hurt. *He's been traumatized, too.* Just listen.

"You want the ugliness Cassie? The brutality?" He wasn't asking since his words spilled out as if a dam had broken. "Nolan Mackenzie was a biker and an abuser before he went to Vietnam. He came back a monster. He joined a biker gang—not a club, a gang—and was in and out of our lives. 'Booze, drugs, and gash' was his motto. But when he decided to come back to us for a few days or weeks, it was a living hell. He'd drink and then he'd go on a rampage, yelling and cursing. Smashing things. Smashing her. Smashing us. Hitting and slapping and kicking." He pointed to the scar on his face. "This isn't from the war. You've seen the scars on my chest, from the Gulf. This," he traced it with his finger, "is from Nolan, who was stoned on meth when he turned on me while I was protecting Liam."

Oh lord. The color drained from her face.

"Yeah," he whispered. "He liked knife play. Ugly enough for you?"

He took a breath and his voice got low and tight. Cassie couldn't move, she felt welded to the door, forced to hear the horror.

"And that wasn't the worst. No, it was when Nolan Mackenzie got quiet. He'd sit in a chair not saying a thing for a while, and we wouldn't move a muscle. We were like the kids from Jurassic Park who froze so the T-Rex won't see them. Anything not to stir the beast. Because we knew what was coming. There was no way to stop it. Sometimes my mother would be on the floor after he'd beaten her, and she'd be groaning."

He stopped talking for a moment, his chest rising and falling hard. His eyes were on her, but unfocused. He was in the past, remembering, the terror of it, etched across his face.

"But that fucker was only getting started. He'd sit

269

there looking down at his big, strong, hands, flexing them into fists. And before he used them, he'd call one of us over to him to stand in front of him. Then he'd look up and smile, a devil's smile that would freeze the blood in your veins. And then, POW," Marcus punched the door so hard that Cassie jumped.

"Marcus," she touched his back and stroked lightly as he bent over in pain holding his closed red fist with his other hand. But he shrugged her off, straightened, and leaned a shoulder against the door facing her.

"Nolan is pure evil, and will be until he takes his last cold-blooded, cruel breath. And that cunt of a mother, who never once in her sorry life tried to protect us. She told us that he was dying and wanted to see his boys. 'His boys,'" Marcus sneered.

"Did that fucker ask for forgiveness? Apologize for beating us? For traumatizing us? For killing a man? For attempting to kill our mother?" He laughed harshly. Marcus knifed away from the wall and began to pace in the small living room. He ran his hands through his hair and clenched them, making his hair stand up in spikes.

Cassie swallowed hard, and stayed by the door, watching Marcus's torment, wanting so badly to take him in her arms, to take some of his pain away.

He stopped in front of her. "My uncle cut off all contact from the moment Nolan was arrested. And you know what that bastard said to his two sons yesterday? Two sons who he hasn't seen in twenty-seven years?"

"No," she said quietly, sadness tearing at her chest.

Marcus looked at her, as if he'd just noticed she was there. He stared for a long moment.

She took a chance that he would continue talking when she walked to the couch and sat on the arm, hoping she could ease the tension in the room. "Please, tell me."

Marcus took in a deep breath and sat on the arm of the club chair across from her. She was disappointed that he hadn't touched her, but at least he'd stopped pacing, though he sat stiff and rigid, still holding his injured hand.

"That son of a bitch wanted to see if after all of the beatings, he'd beaten some sense into us. If he'd made us into men."

Her hand rose slowly to her lips.

"Yeah, it's hard to believe. But he wasn't finished with me because I looked a lot like my old man when he was young. And he hated me. Hated me more than anyone. He grinned at me and pointed to his face. 'Marcus, you little prick, we even look alike, except for that scar I gave you. You're just like me, a mean bastard with a black heart. A killer.'"

He looked right through Cassie. "Then he smiled at me with that devil's smile. I did kill men, Cassie. But instead of living in a six-by-eight cell, I had a medal pinned on my chest."

Oh, god. It was agony listening to him without being able to touch him.

"My uncle took the phone from me and held it up so we could all hear Nolan, though his voice was raspy and thin from disease. 'Nolan,' my uncle shouted, 'You're a piece of shit, and you hate that your sons became fine men, worthy men, despite being spawned by you and that bitch.'"

Marcus stopped for a long moment to catch his breath.

271

"My father's face twisted with rage, and he said with a sick glee, that he only had one son, because our cunt of a mother fucked everything in sight and that Liam wasn't his. Liam collapsed in his chair and started sobbing, while Brennan shouted into the phone, 'Brother, drop fucking dead,' then he slammed down the phone."

"Oh, Marcus," she put her hand out to touch him, but carefully pulled it back.

His voice was weary. His shoulders slumped, and his recitation was emotionless. "But I looked at his sick, dissipated face full of broken blood vessels, yellow skin hanging from his face from years of booze, drugs, hatred, and cancer. " He ran his hands through his hair, then looked up, his eyes glittering. "And I was *glad* that he'd lived the kind of life he deserved, living in a cage. And I was glad he was dying. And from stomach cancer, a painful cancer. So I smiled at him and started to laugh, and that pissed him off. Then we hauled Liam up from the chair, held him between us, and walked out of that hell hole."

"Marcus," she put her hand on her chest right over her heart. Would he allow her to comfort him, now?

He answered her question, by rising, taking her hands and pulling her up. Gently, he took her in his arms, one hand skimmed her back, the other held her jaw. She put her arms around his shoulders, holding him to her. His body trembled. He looked into her eyes, and gently ran a finger over her lips, watching the motion. Her heart broke again, because his shields were down, and she saw his devastation.

He buried his face in her hair and instead of the

272

harsh, cold words, and touch, now he pleaded, "Cassandra, I'm so sorry about how rough I was. I'll never do that again. Ever. But I need you. Right now. Please, let me have you. Let me be with you."

He didn't just want her. He needed her. He needed from her what she needed from him, closeness. Love. Healing. Sex was their real intimacy. She pulled back, so his head came up and they gazed at each other. She ran a hand up his back, and with the other, she carefully traced his scar with her index finger, and he allowed it, momentarily closing his eyes when she did.

She had never loved a man the way she loved him.

"Let me be here for you, Marcus." She took the risk and leaped, "Let me love you."

He gave her a hint of a smile, raised her hand to his lips, and kissed her knuckles, then turned her hand over, and did the same to her palm.

The storm is over. The moment was saved. Cassie took a deep breath and exhaled, easing the tension in her body. She gave him a sad smile, and led him into the bedroom.

Chapter Twenty-Three

Marcus lay on top of Cassie. His face snuggled into her neck, her long, soft copper waves covering his face. He took a deep breath, inhaled her coconut scent that was combined with the smell of their sex, so it would stay in his memory forever. Her arms and legs wrapped around him in a warm cocoon. His fading orgasm had been a punch to his gut and his heart—she'd done what she'd promised. "Let me love you, she'd pleaded." And she had.

Lovingly, she'd caressed and stroked him, her succulent lips following her needy fingers, worshiping every inch of his body, until he was thrumming with desire. She whispered sweet words to him, as if he were someone precious and loveable. She was so caring, so good at lifting him up and out of the ugliness of his life. And when she rose over him, stoking them both into a sexual fever, for those moments of intense passion, he'd been lost in her soft body, and her heart.

But now his heart was breaking, because he had to let her go. The harsh way he'd treated her just an hour ago in that raw moment, as if she was just another piece of ass, was the proof he needed. His father was right, he carried Nolan's sick, damaged,

DNA. He could never love her the way she loved him. *Can I love at all?* He ached even thinking about it.

He shouldn't have come back today. He'd fought with himself not to do it. That would have been easier. Easier? Who was he kidding? He had to come here today, to see her, to touch her, to have her... just one more time.

He hoped he'd become a different man with her, but what he'd buried inside of him for years was churning up to the surface since that phone call from his mother. He'd tried, but he couldn't fight the poison that was inside of him. Seeing his father, hearing that bastard's rough, hate-filled voice had punched through the veneer of hope and the lie that Marcus had told himself, that he'd become a better man. A man who could give Cassie a good life. That he'd changed his destiny.

He'd lied to himself all these months. He'd lied to her. He was still crap. Dirt.

He'd wanted to kill his father the other day. Wanted to wipe that nasty sneer off of his yellowed face. In that moment, Marcus had imagined himself beating Nolan Mackenzie until his face was nothing but dead, bloody pulp. But instead, the words that were racing through his mind every minute of the day since that damn phone call were pummeling him, beating him down.

You're just like me, you prick. A killer, his father's voice screamed in his head.

You're just like your father, I should have aborted you, his mother's words were etched into his heart.

You're a piece of shit, just like your father. You're a player, she's a good girl, Pete's words scored his soul.

275

And though Pete had apologized, Marcus believed the truth of what Pete really thought about him had been those words yelled out in anger when Pete's defenses were down.

His stomach clenched, and the weary heaviness of his grief kept him from getting up, getting dressed and leaving. Was he going to play the coward again? Was he going to leave Cassie as soon as he got up and dressed without telling her that this was the end of them? Would he just let it peter out, like he'd done with all of his fuck buddies?

No, she deserved at least a phone call. A phone call, yeah cowardly, because he would never be able to face her after today. He'd have to leave Riverbend, soon, move to Eastbridge or even better, out of state.

He should get up now and leave. But he couldn't make himself move. In fact, he gave her body a slight squeeze and nestled his face deeper against her neck. Big mistake.

"Mmmm," she purred into his ear, kissed his cheek and wrapped herself around him tighter. "I missed you, Marcus. I love you so much."

That was it, he was done, as her words stabbed him right through his very soul, as if she'd twisted a knife into his gut. He wanted to jump off of her and run, but he forced himself to roll off of her, without looking at her. No usual kiss before he did, no murmuring sexy things in her ear.

He threw out, "Gotta get going," sat at the edge of the bed looking for his clothes. *Please, please, don't touch me.*

"Oh, okay," he heard the disappointment in her voice and felt her sit up.

276

Tentatively, she put a hand on his back and ran it gently up and down, "Marcus, talk to me."

He had to grit his teeth. God, he didn't want to hurt her. But better now than stringing her along for the next few weeks. With a will of iron, he stopped from turning to her, taking her in his arms and pledging his love for her. *Get out. Get out.* The words screamed in his head.

"Gotta get to Liam." He quickly found his shirt, pulled it on, stood, found his briefs, pulled them on and stepped into his jeans.

Cassie got off of the bed and he turned his head to watch her grab a robe off of the chair in the corner and put it on.

"Do you want coffee or breakfast before you go?" He heard the wariness in her voice.

Of course she is, you're being distant and cold.

"Marcus," she pleaded.

He ignored her, grabbed his wallet and phone off of the dresser and said abruptly, "What Cassie?"

"Please, look at me."

He steeled his face and turned to her. Her mouth was a tense thin line, and her face had paled. Rich brown eyes shimmered with unshed tears.

Her pain crushed him, but he couldn't stop wrecking both of them.

"What's the matter, Marcus?"

"Nothing," the word came out hard and her face morphed into distress.

"Liam needs me," he said quickly to stop her questioning him, and he walked out of the bedroom.

"And what do you need, Marcus?" she called out.

The words hit him hard. He turned and she was

277

standing in the bedroom doorway, one hand was holding on to the door frame, the other hung at her side. Her hair was beautifully mussed, her lips bee stung from their deep, wet, kisses. The short, silky pink robe showed off every curve, and her long, satiny legs.

They stood only six feet away from each other, but they might as well have been on different continents.

How was he going to live without ever touching her? Without hearing her laugh? Without talking or arguing with her? Without being near her? Without holding her?

What do I need? You. I need you like I need oxygen to keep living. The pain of losing her would only cease when he died.

You piece of shit. You little prick. You're a player. She's good. She's good. She's good. Like father, like son. The words raced in his head, slicing through him.

The pain in his chest became excruciating. He couldn't catch his breath. He had to get out of the cottage. It was best to need nothing. To need no one.

"Gotta go." This was it. The last time he'd see Cassandra Bennett face to face, because she'd never want to see him again—not after he was devastating her so cruelly.

"Okay," she whispered and pressed her lips together. Sadness clouded every lovely feature of her face. She knew.

He opened the front door, turned back for a quick look at her, tossed out, "I'll call you."

"No you won't," her voice cracked, but it held firm.

He stopped moving, paralyzed by her words. They stared at each other for a moment. The anguish of heartache between them was a thick shroud.

Move, Marcus screamed at himself. He forced himself to turn and walk out the door. His legs shook and he stumbled down the porch steps. Somehow, with his limbs heavy as granite, Marcus climbed into his truck, turned it on and without looking back at the cottage, drove away.

His heart pounded through his tight chest. A reeling sensation distorted his vision. *Am I having a heart attack?* He deserved to die after ripping Cassie to pieces.

He forced himself to concentrate, his fingers white-knuckled on the steering wheel. When he came to the T in the road, Marcus stopped and waited for a slow-moving tractor to pass. But just as he was about to turn toward his house, he heard Pete's voice, loud and clear, *I saw not only good in you, but I saw greatness. I'm proud of you. You're the best man I know... take care of our girl... make each other happy.*

He'd stood in front of Pete and promised that he would love her, then he'd smashed that promise to pieces.

Panic hit him hard—his heart pounded, his mouth went bone dry. *You're the best man I know, you're good, you're good, make each other happy.* Shakily, Marcus pulled onto the shoulder of the road, and put the truck in park. Putting his head back on the seat, he closed his eyes, breathing deeply, trying to ease the panic. *Let go. Let the panic pass,* he repeated until it lessened a bit.

Unbidden, a startling image of himself as a young

child walking along the river bank with his mother came to him. He was four years old, because she was pregnant with Liam. Nolan had taken off weeks ago, so peace momentarily reigned in the house. She was holding his hand and had excitedly pointed out a mother mallard with ducklings trailing behind, swimming near the bank. "Soon, my baby boy, you'll have either a sister or a brother to love." She was gloriously happy that day, as was he.

A wave of grief slammed him so hard that if he wasn't sitting, he'd be on the ground. God, he'd loved her. But Beatrice Mackenzie was trapped in hell with the devil, Nolan, as they all were, and unable to protect them—after all, he'd killed her new boyfriend, and almost killed her.

She was also trapped in her own cold, damaged childhood, and had sadly turned into an ugly, verbally abusive, self-absorbed mother. That was on her. But for the first time, it became clear to Marcus that the loss of her love had turned his love for her into blinding anger.

Shame quickly followed grief, when he heard himself railing at her, calling her a "cunt." He had a right to his anger, but he'd treated her in the same way that his father had. No wonder he was poisonous to women.

In that moment, he knew in every cell of his body, that somehow he had to forgive her to heal himself. Tears were running down his face, and Marcus did something he hadn't done since he was seven years old: he put his head in his hands and let go, as sobs wracked his body.

****

As soon as Marcus left, Cassie walked stiffly to the front door and locked it. From a window, she numbly watched him until he drove away. *I'm never going to see him again. This is the end.* So how come she felt nothing? No rage or anger. No sense of loss or grief. No hate. No heartbreak. No tears. Nothing.

A mew made her turn from the window. "Hey, boy, you're hungry." Robotically, Cassie opened the pantry, took out a bag of cat food and filled Grey's bowl. She scratched the top of his head when he bent to eat, then put the bag on the counter. She slumped down on a kitchen chair. "I've been here before," she said out loud. She had. Losses had piled up over the years, and she was still standing. But she'd never loved a man like she loved Marcus.

In the past, she'd worked through her grief by hunkering down, taking care of her girls, and throwing herself into work. She'd learned how to let time pass, and found a kind of peace by not trying to control what was occurring... but to ride it out.

But today, she wanted to vent. To lay out what had occurred, and in return get comfort and understanding. And love.

Cassie rose, found her phone in the bedroom, and dialed.

"Cassie?" Pete's voice held a hint of concern.

"Hey, old man, if you're feeling okay, can I come over?"

"Sounds like you need me, honey. I just brewed a fresh pot of joe."

"I'll be there in five."

"I'll be here."

"You always are," her lips trembled, and she ended the call.

****

His sobs finally eased, Marcus pulled up the hem of his tee shirt, wiped his eyes and blew his nose. He took a deep breath. His emotions were like the tilt-a-whirl ride at the county fair—they raced, twisted, bounced, and spun out of control.

He couldn't stop his mind from obsessively replaying, the image of Cassie's pale, devastated face, right before he walked out of the cottage.

"No you won't," she'd said, her voice filled with heartbreak, when he'd promised to call. She knew it was their end.

She likely thought he didn't care, but he was as devastated about the break as she was, if not more. After all, he'd caused it. *Why am I destroying the best thing I've ever had in my life? Cassie loves me. I was close to believing that I could love her back.*

He closed his eyes, leaned back on the seat, and fell into deep thought.

The dirty backwash of the traumas he'd suffered had stayed behind the barriers he'd built over his lifetime. But then he'd seen his father, saw the evil sneer, heard the terrible words about himself. His walls had shattered in that prison, leaving him reeling and vulnerable. *Why, after twenty-seven years, does that prick still have power over me?*

He slowed his breathing, and allowed his thoughts to race without pushing them away... he observed them, but did not engage them. And after a time, he found an answer. Sitting up, he faced a terrible truth about himself... he was drowning in self-loathing.

Amazingly, it eased a little when he focused on the positive words that Pete, Shirl, Aiden, Liam, Sean, and friends had planted in his head and his heart. *You're a good father... a good brother... a good nephew and cousin... a good friend... you're good.*

And Cassie, god, she loved him, despite his flaws. She'd defended him against Pete. She'd helped him to break down those fucking walls. She'd taught him to begin to trust, and how to love a woman.

He'd learned how to take charge of his life, to bury the past, but now he was indecisive, and faltering badly. When he came to the cottage he was sure he had to break with her, for her sake. But now a new thought took hold. Maybe his tears had washed away some of the poison, because he wondered if something else compelled him to destroy the best thing that had ever happened to him.

Am I afraid of Cassie? Did I destroy us for my sake, not hers?

Damn it. He was too exhausted to think, or figure it all out. "I'm a shell of a man," he said the words out loud. "Why does she want me? What the hell is she doing with me?"

A frightening emptiness overwhelmed him. *I'm the scarecrow.* If someone banged on his chest it would ring hollow.

With an effort, Marcus put his truck into drive and drove home.

****

"Cassie, honey, take a cookie." Pete pushed the package of Ginger Snaps toward her.

She shook her head, "No thanks."

They were sitting across from each other at the table in Pete's cozy kitchen. Cassie held the coffee mug in both hands, and the warmth from it helped to ease the icy chill that had encased her body.

She sipped and looked up at an old framed photo of Shirl, her hair sticking up from the top of her head, and laughing while trying to lick off a mess of chocolate icing from her face. It had hung in between the windows facing the patio and fields for decades. Yep, that was Shirl, so full of fun and joy that she pulled everyone up with her. Cassie smiled, and the ice inside of her cracked a bit.

Pete's hand reached out, took the mug from her hands, put it on the table, and wrapped his hands around hers. She looked at him, her eyes burning with unshed tears.

"I imagine this is about Marcus, "What did he do now?"

She choked back a sob, "I'm easy to read," aren't I?"

He gave her hands an affectionate squeeze. "You look like someone did a number on you, shredded your insides. And there's only one person who would act up and do that to you. The jerk." Pete let go of her hands, sat back, took a cookie, dunked it into his coffee and ate it before it disintegrated into the mug.

She said nothing because she was numb with shock. She had to tell Pete what happened, maybe then she could cry, and grieve. And move on.

"I'm so lucky that I have you," she whispered the words to him.

"Not as lucky as me, my sweet girl. Tell me."

A single tear escaped and rolled down her cheek. Cassie took a tissue out of her pocket, wiped her eyes and blew her nose.

"Talk, my Cassie."

And she did. She told him every detail, even how rough Marcus had been when he first entered the cottage. And though she'd seen Pete's body tense and simmer with anger, he'd also had the same reaction when she told him about the phone call from Marcus's mother and what Marcus's father had spewed.

"I watched him stumble down the porch steps as if he was drunk. He was a mess, Pete. I almost texted to make sure he'd gotten home safely. But, I couldn't do that. I have to let him go."

After she finished, Pete sat there, shaking his head, lost in thought.

She let the silence be. Her mouth was as dry as a desert after venting the sad story. She picked up her mug and sipped the tepid coffee, wondering what Pete was going to say and do.

When she gazed at Pete, he was watching her.

"He was a brutal bastard today Cassie."

"I know, but..."

He put up his hand to stop her. "Just hear me out first."

She nodded.

"He comes from brutality, so yeah, that's in him. But I've known Marcus since he's sixteen years old. The first time I met Marcus was at the Overlook. I saw the desperate boy with rage simmering under the surface.

But I also saw the hurt, damaged boy who only wanted to be loved and cared for. And he was so damn smart by sixteen, better read than I was by that time. He wanted a good family and love, though he didn't trust it. Who could blame him for that? That's why Shirl and I took him in whenever we could, because we knew he wanted more out of life. We gave him what we could."

"You showed him love, Pete, but I don't think he believes that he's worthy of it."

"You're likely right. I never knew if he would take that hurt and murderous fury out on someone else or himself. In the end, he did both. Because of my service in Nam, and how he idolized me, he went into the army. It helped him channel the rage... to a degree. He took lives, but he was heroic, and he saved them, too. But he erected walls around himself that he thought would protect him from people's betrayal, especially a woman's. When he moved back to Riverbend, I hoped he would change, and he did, some. But those walls are years in the making, and he's never stopped reinforcing them. Neither Shirl nor I could break them down completely, no matter how much we loved him, or Liam, or Sean, or even Aiden."

Pete's studied her, "But you broke through, Cassie. You taught him to trust and to love, because I've never seen him happy like he's been since he met you. I've never seen him with joy written on his face, that only love can bestow on someone."

Pete took a deep breath. "Until you, Cassie. He loves you."

"Pete," her voice cracked as her heart broke, "I know he does. And I love him more than I've ever loved another man," she admitted to him.

"Then those bastards pulled him back into their sickness, their poison, and tried to break him." Pete rubbed his hands over his face with weariness. He settled back on the chair and asked, "Cassie, what are you going to do about this?"

She leaned over and took one of Pete's hands. "I know what you want for us Pete. You said it all in the hospital. But I'm finished, Pete."

He raised an eyebrow.

"I am. I can't heal Marcus. I can love him, but he has to want to heal. And Pete, I can't do this to myself anymore. I'm going to grieve the loss of him, I will," she sat back in her chair. "But I'm moving on. He has to be open to love. I'm not begging a man to want me. To love me."

Pete sighed in resignation. "You're right Cassie, but Marcus is running scared, now. And he's a fool. Maybe, he'll stop running, I think he will, and see what he's losing. I think he'll come back to you. And if he does? What then?"

"I doubt he will, Pete, and even if he does, I... can't. It's been a torturous push-pull with Marcus since day one. I deserve a man who isn't afraid to love. Pete, please, I'm begging you to not intervene. Just let it be. Okay?"

He nodded. "You're right, honey, and I'll mind my own business." He was pensive for a moment, then he said, "But what do you say we lighten the mood here and go down to the diner and get us some chicken croquettes? It was always one of your favorites."

Yes, let's, she thought. Life has to go on, and how it goes on is up to me. Cassie stood, took his hands in hers, and pulled Pete out of the chair.

Chapter Twenty-Four

A few hours later, Marcus, Liam, and Brennan were hunkered down on Marcus's long sectional in his media room. Beer bottles and the remains of chips and a dip were scattered on the coffee table. Trouble, Marcus's male pitbull, was lying on his back, on the floor snoring loudly. The rottie, Diesel, was camped out on a soft lounge chair, and female pittie, Honeybun, was lying alongside Liam who was stretched out in the middle of the couch.

The eighty-five-inch TV was playing a Yankees/Oakland game that Marcus had recorded, but the three fanatical New York fans weren't engaged in the game at all,

"Marcus," Brennan said, "shut off the game, we need to talk. And I can't hear a thing anyway, with that damn dog's snoring. It sounds like a freight train is running through the room."

"Yeah, Pits snore." Marcus who was on the other end of the sectional, grabbed the remote off the coffee table and powered off the TV. *What now*, he thought. All he wanted to do was numb out. Not be.

"Li, come on son, sit up," Brennan urged.

Without making eye contact with either man, Liam sat up, with his head down, and hands folded on his lap. Honeybunch practically crawled into Liam's lap, and he began to rub her head.

"Boys, you know I'm leaving tomorrow afternoon after I spend time with Sean, but if either of you want to come back to Arizona with me for as long as you want, you're both welcome. I talked to Sean last night and he said that he and Bret will take care of ongoing jobs, and cover for both of you, so not to worry."

"Brennan, thanks, you're the best, but I need to get back to regular programming, throw myself into work and move on. Li, do you want to fly back with Brennan for a while?"

"No," Liam mumbled, then looked at Brennan. "Thanks unc, but I'm with Marcus. We've got new jobs to begin, and I want to stay home."

"Listen to me." They turned their gazes on him,

"This crap has marked the both of you from the time you were born. If you need help, maybe talking to someone, please do it. Liam, you closed down at the prison, and I'm worried what memories Nolan brought back into your mind. Marcus, I can see the rage simmering in you right now."

Brennan, leaned toward them, "I'm not sure how or why my brother was a sick, abusive criminal. But he was like that from childhood. Luckily I was older, bigger, and stronger, so he learned early on that he couldn't best me. And your mother," he shook his head. "Those two are not worth either of you destroying your lives over them. Do not let them take away any chance of happiness in your lives. What I said to my brother, I meant. The two of you have grown into fine men. The best. I couldn't be more proud of both of you."

"We had you and Sean, and you were a tough son-of-a-bitch sometimes," Marcus said. Brennan laughed, and Marcus continued more solemnly, "But you took us in, took care of us and left us a legacy," Marcus said solemnly.

Brennan chuckled. "Yeah, I was tough and not affectionate, and after your Aunt Sarah and I split when you were boys, I never did find another woman who could give you that nurturing. Except for your mother, there were no women around."

Marcus felt like he was on another planet, listening to Brennan show he and Liam a softness that was unbelievable. He pointed a finger at Brennan, "Do not blame yourself. You did the best you could."

Brennan sighed, "I should have said this before, but I love the both of you."

Marcus stared in wonder. He knew his uncle loved him and Liam, but to say he wasn't touchy-feely was a radical understatement. He'd shown it in his actions, but, just as uncomfortable with emotional displays as any other Mackenzie man, he'd never said the words. To say it out loud to them... it was so powerful that the sheer emotion of it left him speechless.

"Are we going to exchange our dicks for vaginas and be kissing and hugging each other, too?" Liam joked, but Marcus saw that Liam was only covering up how overcome he was by their uncle's words.

"Maybe," Brennan laughed, but he was watching Liam closely. "How about instead of a group hug," Liam snickered, and Marcus smiled at him, "we get back to the game, and get a pizza delivered?"

"Make that two large, meat lovers," Liam piped

up, picked up his phone and called in their order, then he settled back on the couch, and turned to Marcus. "I figured you went to see Cassie, but you came back looking worse than you did at the prison. You screw up, or something?"

"Leave it be," Marcus growled, and his stomach clenched.

"Sean said she's a beautiful woman, that she suits you," Brennan raised his eyebrows questioningly.

She does suit me, I just don't suit her.

"Is Cassie mad at you?" Liam was pushing and Marcus was getting pissed. Time to end this conversation.

"We broke it off. And no Li, I don't want to talk about it."

"I bet you broke it off. You shouldn't have gone to her today. You were angry. You should have waited until you'd calmed down."

Marcus turned on his brother, "What did I say? I don't want to talk about it. And by the way, Li, you weren't really happy when I started seeing her. Remember that? You got jealous not having more time with me."

Liam sat up straight up and pointed his finger at Marcus, "I apologized for that. Yeah, I'd never seen you dating anyone, being with someone a lot, so I got jealous. It was always 'empty pussy,' as you used to brag, so I had more time with you. But I got to know her, and Marcus, I like her. She's good for you. Why are you fucking this up?"

"Are you in love, boy?" Brennan jumped into the fray.

He couldn't tell them that. "I'm no good for her." Fucking rotten DNA. PTSD not only from the war, but from his fucked up childhood, could spark the rage. "She's a good woman. I can't give her what she deserves. She's better off without me."

"You're stupid Marcus. You're letting our sperm donor control you. I'm not going to do that anymore. I fucking hate both of them, and I'm tired of living under the rock they crushed me with. Why aren't you?"

"I don't see you having any relationships either, Li. You talk about empty pussy, but you're not better than me."

"No, I'm not," Liam jumped up and towered over Marcus, who got up, too, and they were toe to toe. "But, brother, I've seen you with Cassie. And I've seen Sean in love with Shannon, and I want what Sean has and what you had. I'm thirty-five years old and I want... I want to be in love with someone and have her love me back." Liam's lower lips trembled and his eyes glistened with tears.

"Li," Marcus began, his voice low and soft.

"I'm going for a walk," Liam hurled at him and slammed out of the front door.

"Well, he got some of his anger out. Sorry it was aimed at you, Marcus."

"No, it's okay. I'd rather he was yelling at me than being catatonic." Marcus was reeling at Liam's confession, *I want to be in love... and have her love me back.*

All he could see in that moment was Cassie's pale face and hear her words, *No you won't.* He wanted to cry, himself.

"One more thing Marcus, listen and take this in, please," Brennan said. "There's a quote that I saw a while ago, that I think fits just where you are. It goes like this, 'Never be a prisoner of your past, it was just a lesson, not a life sentence.' Got it?"

He hadn't, but lied, "Got it."

****

Cassie leaned over her bathroom sink, peered into the vanity mirror, and put on another coat of lip gloss. When her cell chimed with an incoming text, she glanced at her phone, Rachel.

RachW: *On my way, be there in ten.*

"Ok" she texted back.

Her makeup was light tonight, just a dusting of face powder and one swipe of mascara was good enough. But she'd used more cover-up under her eyes than usual to hide the dark ugly circles. Crying and lack of sleep had made her resemble a pathetic racoon.

Rachel and Maddy had pushed her into going out with them tonight, just four days after the break with Marcus. She hadn't wanted to, but, they'd insisted that she get out of her funk.

She took a light black jacket out of her closet, and stepped in front of the full length mirror on the back of the bedroom door. The tight, slim, black pants she wore, topped with a cobalt-blue boatneck sweater and black flats, looked good. Her 'I'm okay' mask was in place. She'd pulled her hair back into a ponytail, and slipped her favorite silver hoops into her ears. But when she looked closely at her face, sorrow was written all over it.

"Oh well, it's only dinner," she mumbled, and with two people she dearly loved.

She dealt with loss by doing, and trying to move on. *What's the worst that can happen tonight? I'm miserable, but I'm that no matter where I am.* She pushed her thoughts away, and headed out the door.

"Since you won't tell me where we're going, I'm telling you right now that I'm not going near Twin Rivers Brew Pub that Marcus's friend owns," Cassie ordered, as Rachel drove around the circle in Eastbridge."

"Of course we're not going there," Maddy said from the tiny backseat. She leaned over and squeezed Cassie's shoulder. "And by the way, Rach, I'm all smushed back here. It's so small, I think my ovaries are stuck together. Can't you drive something new, something with room?"

"You're sitting in one of the coolest SUVs ever, a Toyota FJ40 Land Cruiser in Concours condition. My dad let us borrow it for tonight, and it's worth at least five times what your little Corolla is worth."

"Rachel, we're really impressed." Cassie pleaded, "Mad, please don't get her started on vintage cars."

Rachel snickered.

"Okay, Rach sorry about the put down, and it is cool, but as I was saying sis, you look both classy and smoking hot, so, if we did run into Marcus, he'll be one sorry asshole."

"Mad," Cassie twisted her head to look at her sister, "please stop with the putdowns, huh? Just for tonight at least. I'm trying to enjoy tonight, and the truth is, I am nervous that we'll run into him."

"Sorry, Cass, I'll cool it."

"There it is," Rachel said as she slowed down and pointed at the colorful neon sign on a large brick building, "The Billy Goat Bar and Grill, opened a few weeks ago, and I heard that they have a dozen craft beers on tap, and that their wings are phenomenal."

"Alcohol and fat, yeehaw," Maddy sang out.

"And since this is a converted factory, they have lots of off-street parking, though it's packed tonight," Rachel pulled into the parking lot and easily found a space.

They were walking through the parking lot to the entrance when Cassie stopped abruptly. "Oh god," she flushed red hot with an adrenaline spike so high it was like battery acid was running through her veins. "That's Marcus's truck," she croaked, pointing to a black Suburban. "It has the animal rescue decal on the left back window and the VA hospital parking permit on his bumper."

"Shit," Maddy said loudly. She took Cassie's arm, "Sorry, sis, this is a bust." Maddy looked at Rachel and shrugged, "Let's get out of here."

"No," the word came out of Cassie's mouth forcefully, surprising herself. "I want to go in. I have to face him sometime. I haven't done anything wrong, and damn if his presence is going to make me run away."

"Yeah, sis, fuck him, and if he tries to..."

"No, Maddy, not that way. I'm assuming he'll be at the bar, so we're going to go in and wait for a table. When we get inside, Maddy you do not look at the bar, look at everything else, if he's facing us. Understand?"

"Okay, sis, but I'm not sure where you're going with this."

"I don't want him to think we know he's there and think that I'm looking for him. Rachel, I want you to focus on the bar."

"Okay, Cass, what if he sees us?"

"Show no emotion, and whisper in my ear where he is. He'll see you doing it. Then I'm going to do my thing."

"What's your thing, sis?"

"You'll see it when I do it. And neither of you is to do anything but stand at my back no matter what happens? Maddy?" She arched an eyebrow at her sister.

"Not a peep or a snarl, I promise. This is going to be good."

No, Cassie thought, *this is going to be bad and will take every ounce of will power on my part to face him the way I want to.*

"And girls," they looked at her. "He may be with a woman, and if he is, the same goes. No emotion, no talking to him, nothing. This is my play."

Cassie straightened her shoulders, took a deep breath, "Okay, let's see what the Billy Goat Bar and Grill has to offer."

Her body language might say strong, but inside she quaked with fear, and her stomach clenched into a tight fist. *I can do this*, she told herself. *But if he's with a woman, it will kill me.*

They entered the vast front room to the buzz of conversation and laughter, utensils scraping on plates, and glasses clinking. Various size tables for two or more people were scattered throughout the room. A doorway on the right, Cassie saw, led to another dining room.

A large illustration, in vibrant colors, of two billy goats sitting at the bar and drinking beer hung on an exposed brick wall, dominating the room. Pipes and fittings on the high ceilings were painted black. Servers ran back and forth on gleaming yellow pine floors that lent warmth to the industrial feel of the place.

They stopped at the end of a short line of people waiting for a table at the host station. "Wow," Maddy gushed, "this place is fantastic. And that smell of beer and burgers is just delish, I'm hungry."

"This is awesome." Rachel echoed.

Her stomach in knots, Cassie couldn't help herself, she glanced over to her left at the stunning massive bar that was the centerpiece of the room. It was built of light wood and steel, and had at least 30 steel bar chairs lined up in front of it. The back wall was a gorgeous mix of wood and copper.

She spotted him immediately. She'd know those broad shoulders and muscled back anywhere. After all, she'd mapped every inch of them. Her mind and body cried out for his scent, his taste, his touch. She wanted to hear the sound of his voice, and to be the recipient of his handsome smile. She even missed his damn moodiness and temper. But with a will of iron she tamped down all of her wants and needs.

She was determined to face Marcus in order to move on and live her life, and by god that's what she was going to do tonight. But if they were seated in the other room, he would likely miss them.

"Cassie, you're staring over at the bar, isn't that my job?" Rachel asked.

"I know, but everyone at the bar has their back to us. Anyway, I've already spotted him. He's sitting in sixth place from the left."

"This place is huge," Maddy said, "What if he doesn't see us?"

"I know, I know, let me think about it for a sec." There was one couple in front of them, and it was likely they'd be seated in the second room, unless someone vacated a table in this room in the next sixty seconds.

"Maybe we should just go to the bar," Maddy offered.

"No. I want him to see me, then I have to be able to ignore him and get away."

The host came back to his station and motioned to the couple in front of them. He steered them into the second dining room.

"What now, Cass?" Rachel's forehead puckered.

Cassie hadn't taken her eyes off of Marcus. She willed him to turn around and, at the same time she wanted to hide in the back room. Too late. Her breath caught when he put his empty bottle on the bar, put dollar bills down next to it, and got up off of the stool. As if he sensed her watching him, their gazes collided like a car going one hundred miles an hour, hitting a brick wall.

Her legs shook and she clutched the handles of her purse to steady herself, but she never dropped her eyes. Even across the room, she watched him stagger to a stop. His eyes widened in shock and his face paled.

"Holy shit," Maddy whispered.

"Look away from him, both of you. Do it now." Cassie mumbled the order.

Just as she was about to turn away, a woman came out of the restroom, called, "Marcus," and trotted over to him. He hadn't moved a muscle, and paid no attention to her. When the woman stood in front of him and placed her hand on his chest, he frowned, said something, and stepped back. Then Marcus pinned his eyes on her.

"Uh, oh," Rachel whispered. "I'm watching him out of the corner of my eye."

Willing her face into a blank mask, because seeing that woman call his name and touch him brought back all of the ugliness of their earlier arguments about his past. She couldn't take this torture anymore, she was done, done, done. Cassie slowly shook her head from side to side at him, then turned away to huddle with Maddy and Rachel.

Without watching, she knew he was walking to her. "Get ready girls, here he comes," she whispered.

"We got you girl," Rachel said.

"Cassandra," his deep voice was shaky.

She steeled herself, and turned to him.

"Marcus, no, just no," she said it quietly and without wavering, turned back to Maddy and Rachel.

When he touched her arm, she jumped as if he'd tasered her. She jerked her arm away, looked at him, and said forcefully, "Do not touch me."

He recoiled at her words, guilt and shame racing over his face. Watching the man she deeply loved struggle with his emotions killed her. But wasn't this the usual Marcus M.O.? Push her away hard, then reel her in with his soft side?

"Please, Cassie, can I talk to you for a few minutes?"

Maddy and Rachel closed ranks at her back. He looked at them, "Would you step outside for a moment?"

Maddy growled under her breath, and Marcus must have heard her because he raised his eyebrows at her.

299

She had to end this now. "Marcus," she said as firmly as possible, when she really wanted to cry. "Please go, you're embarrassing your date," she said looking over at the woman at the bar who was watching them, her arms were crossed over her chest.

"She's not my date and you know it," he snapped out.

Just then the host walked up to them, "Ladies, your table is ready. Please follow me."

Maddy and Rachel took off after the host. Cassie looked directly at Marcus and said, "I've said it before, but this time I mean it Marcus. Do not contact me again. I..." she stopped talking because the burn of tears was right behind her eyes, and they'd be running down her face if she continued. What she did instead was to shake her head from side to side, and sadly say, "I'm so disappointed in you." Quickly turning, she followed Maddy and Rachel into the dining room.

Chapter Twenty-Five

Can a heart keep beating inside a chest turned into stone? When she'd said, "I mean it... don't contact me again," Marcus knew it was for real. There she'd stood, quiet and regal, tears shimmering in those warm brown eyes, and gave him that slow shake of her head. Then she'd delivered a killing blow, "I'm so disappointed in you."

She hadn't done what he'd expected, or what he deserved; yelled, cursed at him, slapped him, for what he'd done to her, to them. She wouldn't. She could get angry, really angry. *But remember*, he told himself, *Cassie is not like those other women who would text and call you incessantly when you dumped them, or shout at you when they saw you, until finally they faded away. Cassie has never begged you except the first night they met. It's you who's been chasing after her.* Yeah, he had. He'd chased her down and claimed her, then wrecked them. Again.

All he'd wanted to do in that moment was to get down on his knees, take her hands in his and beg her to forgive him, because he could finally openly admit that he couldn't live without her. He loved her deeply and maybe, just maybe, Marcus had real hope that he

301

could be what she deserved, a good man who would take care of her, and love her until the day he died.

That's what he'd been trying to work out for himself, for the past few days, and while sitting at the bar tonight.

You're the best man I know. You're good... you're good. Pete's words swirled in his head.

He caught his breath. What now? He'd made the biggest mistake of his life. He'd lost her.

But maybe not. She still loves you. She just can't take your bullshit. What did she call it, your push, pull? She doesn't trust you, asshole, and why should she? His inner voice was loud and more sarcastic than ever, today.

He saw a glimmer of hope crack open. *I'm the troubleshooter at work. I've been doing it for Liam since we were boys. I did it in the army. I find the problem, analyze it, and make things right.*

But not in his personal life, that was an ongoing shitstorm. The darkness of his past cast a heavy pall, and the poison from his childhood was right there waiting to strike him, to crush him.

"Shut it," Marcus said out loud, and a server who was passing him carrying a tray full of food, turned, startled, almost bumping into a busboy.

Moving out of the center of the room, Marcus noticed that Barb Robbins was still at the bar, watching him. She sent him what she must have thought of as a sultry look his way, but to Marcus it reeked of desperation. He couldn't remember a thing about her, that's how insignificant she was to him. Because there was only one woman who had taken up all the space in his head for most of the last year, and somehow, he had to win Cassie back. He had to plan carefully, think things through, before he'd screw up even more. And there was only one place on earth where he could do that. He shook his head at Barb and walked out of the bar.

The Overlook was deserted as he'd expected. He coasted into a parking space, turned off the engine, and exited. It was a perfectly clear night, and the heavens were putting on a breathtaking show. Stars and constellations were bright and shiny specks in the midnight blue sky. And though the moon wasn't full, it illuminated the Overlook, turning the surrounding woods into ghostly shadows.

Walking to the railing overlooking the mighty Delaware, he leaned on it, and looked at the reflection of the moon and stars sparkling like diamonds on the calm surface. The hoot of an owl, and the rustling of trees and bushes stirred by the breeze filled the silence.

His thoughts drifted, and he could clearly see himself, as if it was happening in this moment, as that sixteen year old boy who'd stood right where he was now, and had contemplated suicide because his life sucked and he couldn't find a way out of the pain. But somehow, as if someone up above was watching out for him, Pete found him that day and saved him.

Marcus had found the Overlook a few days after he'd gotten his license, and was finally able to drive the junker he'd fixed up. It was empty that day, when he felt the need to get away, to go, go, go, somewhere so he could stop himself from going fucking insane. It was the day that Nolan Mackenzie was found guilty of murder. He'd gotten life without parole.

Despair ripped at Marcus. He was trapped by

circumstances, by his tainted DNA. At that moment, he wondered what it would feel like to jump into the river. To let go without a struggle. To fall through the deceptive calm surface and let the swift currents suck him down to the bottom of the river, so he could find some fucking peace.

As he was about to climb the railing, a deep voice surprised him, "That river in the morning is a beautiful sight."

He whipped around ready to run or fight. They eyed each other. He was a large man, at least six feet tall, wearing faded khakis, and a black tee with white letters saying, "I'd Rather Be Fishing." He carried a travel mug, and wore a hat that had Marcus's attention—it read "Vietnam Veteran," and though the man's face was hard, his shining blue eyes were kind. Then he stuck out his hand and said, "I'm Pete Hoffman, mind if I share the view?"

That was the beginning of a new life for Marcus, because Pete pulled Marcus into his loving family and mentored him from day one. Now, twenty-seven years later, he'd built a life for himself, a good life in many ways. But beneath it all was still that damaged teen who wanted nothing more than to be loved. Maybe today he finally accepted that he had a family who loved him, both of blood and of the heart.

And for the first time in his life, not only did he want more, he believed he deserved it. He wanted that special love, that only the intimate love of a mate could give him. And there was only one woman in the world for him: Cassandra.

I'm free. He was, for the first time in his life.

But the stakes were higher than ever. He was

fighting for his new life. Cassie was his, and he was going to make sure she knew it. He took a seat on the bench that faced the river and pulled out his cell. She was a classic rock girl, and he knew just the words to text her tonight, and the song to reinforce those words. She wouldn't answer, but this was just the first bow shot in the first battle to win her, and he was an expert at war.

He thought for a moment then texted:

MMackenzie: *Cassandra, I'm so sorry for hurting you in the way I did. There's no excuse for how I behaved. But I'm asking again, begging, please let's talk. Here's a link that says it all, and no pun intended re the name of the group, but I cannot live without you.*

He pasted *Baby Come Back* by Player into his text, took a deep breath, and hit send.

Marcus was almost home when he heard a text come in. He slowed and pulled onto the shoulder, put his truck in park and opened his messages. His heart sank as he read:

CBennett: *Marcus, please stop contacting me. It's best for both of us to end this. If you contact me again, I will block your number.*

She'd said please. He shook his head, and smiled. She was ever the polite woman, though her reply was a firm fuck you. Okay. They lived within a ten minute walk from each other, so she'd better build a moat around the cottage if she thought asking politely and blocking his number would keep him away from her.

The part of him that wanted to claim her like a beast reared, but he had to step back and think things through, talk things through. He knew without a doubt that this was his last chance with her. There was only one person who he trusted to help him. It wasn't even seven o'clock. He scrolled to his contacts and hit the number.

"Are you finally ready to talk your shit out, Mac?"

A soft laugh escaped, "Pete, are you reading minds now?"

"Not quite, but I felt a disturbance in the force."

Marcus grinned, and his spirits lifted. Yeah, Pete was his Obi Wan, and Cassie's, too.

"I'll be there in ten."

"Two shots of good scotch will be waiting for you. Joe's pouring it right now."

"Old man, leave the bottle, it's going to be a long night."

"Son, I'll be here."

"You always are," Marcus's voice cracked, and he ended the call.

****

"Sis, are you doing okay?" Maddy asked from the jump seat of Rachel's Cruiser.

They were driving slowly down the lane to Pete's farmhouse, and in a few minutes, they'd be at the cottage.

Am I doing okay? She was and she wasn't. Seeing Marcus left another gaping wound in her body.

Turning him away had devastated her. But she'd had to do it. She had to protect herself no matter that she ached to forgive him, but she had to let him go.

Until, dammit, he sent her the link to *Baby Come Back*. When she'd pulled up his text during dinner, she couldn't help but laugh, and even Maddy joined in at his cleverness. But then her heart broke all over again.

They could never work because he had to love her, stay with her no matter what crap was playing in his head. He had to fight for her. For them. He had to get professional help, if he needed it. She knew he'd tried to stop his garbage from leaking onto them, but it had engulfed them both.

"Hey Cass, you've been quiet on the ride home." Rachel sounded concerned and brought Cassie back to the present.

"I'm sad, but I'm glad I came along tonight. I'm glad I saw Marcus, though it was hard seeing him. But I faced him, and it helped that I had both of you with me."

"We're always here for you, sis, you know that."

"Want to talk about it when we get to the cottage?"

"Thanks, Rach, but I'd like to be alone tonight."

"You're almost home," Maddy put her hand on Cassie's shoulder.

Yes, her beloved cottage was truly her home. She would heal and move on in it.

As they turned out of the long drive to pass by the farmhouse, Maddy said, "Oh, look."

There was Marcus's Suburban parked in front of his farmhouse.

Her heart started to pound. "He'll try and see me

tonight, but it's too soon. If he knocks on the door, I'm not letting him in."

"Good," Maddy said.

Rachel drove past Pete's slowly and Cassie grabbed her purse, ready to jump out and get inside as soon as Rachel stopped.

"Want us to come inside with you?" Maddy had leaned over almost into the front seat.

"No. I'll get inside and lock up, you two take off. I'll be fine," Rachel pulled up in front of the cottage, leaving the engine running.

The porch light lit the stairs and the front door. But as Cassie stepped out of the Toyota, and Maddy was climbing into the front seat, Marcus stood from a porch chair that was hidden in the shadows. He didn't say anything, just leaned against the porch railing, watching her.

Cassie startled, and Rachel said, "What the..."

"Oh boy. Want us with you, sis?"

She turned to Maddy, "No, I should have expected this. You go on, I'll call you both later."

As they pulled away, Maddy leaned out the window and called out, "Call us if you have to bury a body."

She heard Marcus's soft laugh, turned to him and on unsteady legs, and walked to the porch.

When she reached the steps, Marcus did something that surprised her. Instead of standing against the railing in his usual alpha-male pose, he sat down on the top step and made room for her to either pass him, or to sit down next to him. She wasn't sure what to do, sit, or go into the house, when he said, "I've been a dick. And I've been stupid about us. I know it. I own it."

At his words, Cassie stopped where she was and put her hand on the bannister to steady herself. She was going to listen to him, because it was the right thing to do. She tilted her head at him, he got the message and continued.

"I want to try again. No," he hesitated, "I'm begging you to give me another chance."

"You talked to Pete?"

He stood, "I did. He did most of the talking, though."

"Pete is a man who's full of opinions." Ironically, Pete wanted them together now, but sadly she couldn't keep her promise to him.

"He is, but he speaks the truth."

"Ah, the truth," she said and quoted, "This above all: to thine own self be true."

His eyes lit, "Hamlet. Polonius speaks those words to Laertes." She couldn't help being impressed with how smart Marcus was, and it was one of the sexiest things about him. She missed the intellectual connection with him, in the same way that she missed their sexual connection.

"That quote can have any number of meanings, but I'll assume the most obvious one: judge myself honestly, and do the right thing. I want to do that with you Cassie, with us."

"It's too late for *us* Marcus, and I have to be true to myself, don't I? To quote a cliche that fits Riverbend, 'There is too much water under the bridge.'"

He lowered his head. She felt herself weakening toward him, she hated that she was making him unhappy. *But what about you,* her head shouted. *Pull up your backbone.*

309

Their eyes met, "Please, can I have a minute? I'm not asking if I can come in."

"Good, because you can't," she said firmly and walked up the stairs and onto the porch, resting on the railing across from him.

A line etched between his brows. "Can we sit down," he pointed to the porch chairs, "and talk?"

"Marcus, I'm pretty beat, let's finish it right here."

"So no more chances, Cassie?"

"You know Marcus, you remind me of the river. Or I should say what we had reminds me of it."

He raised his eyebrows questioningly.

"The Delaware's lovely calm is sneakily deceptive when tiny ripples show on the surface as the river meanders downstream. But that's a fool's perception. Because we both know that unwary people believe that they can take a leisurely swim and paddle around without a care in the world. They wade in, start swimming, then, BAM, the bottom suddenly drops out and hidden currents that run deep pull them down. Down to the silty bottom, and they drown."

"Is that how it's been for you? With me?" He asked, his words were hushed, and his expression pained.

"Yes, Marcus. I never know when I'll be caught in a swift current and dashed against the rocks."

He ran his hand through his hair. "Of course it's been that. Why am I questioning it? To defend myself as usual. I'm messing this up, Cassie."

"Marcus," she softened her tone, "when you told me how horrible things were for you growing up, all I wanted to do was show you that I loved you. I tried, and I hoped that my love would help you believe that I'm here for you. That I would always be here for you when your demons surface, and wanted you to do the same for me. I believe that love can heal, I do, but for whatever reason, you can't let yourself have that."

She was exhausted, and wanted to go inside and crawl into bed to grieve and try to forget this night. But they had to finish it now.

"You're right, baby, I do that."

My god, his calling her *baby* scored right through her and she felt the bleed.

"I want—"

"I know what you want Marcus, but I cannot take another chance on you. And I can't because I'm not a martyr. I'm not going to keep hurting myself to try and get you to love me, then whining and complaining about it to you or anyone else. I need a man who's a true partner. Who will stand with me when the going gets tough, and you and I both know that eventually life gets tough. I'm not judging you, or I hope I'm not, but you cut and run, cut me out, and have done it multiple times. And what you did the other day... you crushed me."

His breath heaved. "Yeah, Cassie, that's the bald-faced truth about me. I've come to realize that I've tried to bury my past my entire life, instead of facing it and working through the... the trauma. I know that I'm damaged. But I'm trying to change that. And meeting you, well, I did change—but it's obvious I have more work to do."

He gazed at her, his expression tortured. "But Cassie, you had an easy childhood. Your parents were Riverbend royalty along with Pete and Shirl. You don't know what it's like to have to navigate a shitstorm of a childhood. I'm begging you to have patience and give me another chance."

In a second she stood up straight, and put her hands on her hips. "I had an easy childhood?"

He took in a sharp breath.

"My mother had severe depression, stayed in bed most of her life, was a martyr until the day she died, and was verbally abusive toward me and Maddy. My father suffered from PTSD and was emotionally unavailable. As Maddy and I grew up, he stayed away from the house a good deal of the time, so he wasn't around much."

His forehead puckered. "Cassie, I didn't know, I'm..." He put his hand out to her, but she shook her head and cut him off.

"The summer I turned sixteen—it seems that we have that age in common for experiencing a traumatic life-altering event—I was driving around the area with a group of friends, and we drove down into Harrow Hill. You know, it's about a thirty minute drive from Riverbend? They were having their summer carnival, so off we went. When we were pulling into the parking area, I saw my father walking to his truck with his arm around a woman who was not my mother."

"Cassandra," he whispered, and she could see the control he was exerting over himself not to take her in his arms.

"Only Rachel saw what I saw, and she played sick and made our friend Todd, who was driving, leave and take us home. We never talked about it after that. I put her off when she tried. I never told Maddy. After that, I began to follow my father. I found out who the woman was, where she lived. And in a way," she looked at Marcus whose eyes were piercing hers with such bold-faced love that she almost gave in to her sobs. But she steeled herself. "Who could blame him for wanting to be away from our house, with a whiny, bitchy wife, who complained about everything all the damn time, and two girls begging for his attention. I know that she suspected him, because I could hear them fighting about it."

"Did he ever catch on that you knew?"

"Not then. But six months before he drowned, I was visiting Riverbend and he was mad at me because I rarely visited. He accused me of turning my back on my family. That did it. The dam broke and we had it out. I told him I knew about his cheating for years, and that he betrayed us all. He'd turned his back on us, not the other way around. Easy childhood? Like hell it was." Tears burned like hot lava, but she wasn't going to cry, to give Marcus a way in.

Shock was written on his face. "Oh, baby," his words were just above a whisper.

No. No. Why did she spill her guts now? She had to get inside before he did something that she couldn't deny him. With one step, though she fought it, he took her in his arms, held her close, and gently rocked them back and forth.

Cassie wanted to stay in his arms forever, but she pushed back on his chest, and he let her go. She wiped her eyes with her fingers and looked out over the night blooming flowers. "Yes, Bill Harper was Riverbend royalty, a native son, war hero, master carpenter, church elder, family man." She huffed a painful laugh, "But he was also a cheater, a man who ignored his family, and betrayed his wife and daughters."

"Cassie, I'm sorry."

"It's in the past, and I deal with it, but it has scarred me, and I have trust issues, too."

"I see that, and if I only knew I could have—"

"Nothing would have changed between us, Marcus. You have your heavy baggage, and I have mine. But I will not take crumbs, Marcus. I want, no, I demand the full spectrum of love from a partner, not just glimpses of it from time to time. And I'm not settling for anything else."

He was watching her intently now.

"And I'm sorry to have to say this, but I don't think, from our interactions, that you're capable of giving that to me. I had unquestionable love from Ron, no matter what was going on in our lives. He would stand and support me, I would do the same for him."

"So, no man can compete, measure up to your husband. Is that it?" Marcus asked bitterly.

"I admitted to you in one of our intimate conversations that I wouldn't have gotten married if I hadn't gotten pregnant. Ron knew it, but that man loved me to the depths of his soul, no matter how sick he was for many years. And I grew to love him back. He tried to give me everything he could, that he was capable of." She stuttered the last few words, and tears fell.

Marcus made a move toward her again, but she put up her hand to stop him and shook her head.

"And I gave you things that he couldn't," Marcus said defiantly, surprising her.

"Yes, you did," her voice lowered. His eyes bored into hers. "Marcus, you opened me up sexually in a way that I could never have imagined." *Do not hold*

314

back, she decided. "I was freer with you as a woman than I was with Ron, than I've ever been in my entire life. And I don't mean only in bed. I was more playful, had more fun with you, and loved that sexual vibe that we always had going on no matter what we were doing. And more, I felt safe with you, you're protective. And you took over, like driving and helping me physically with things, and that was wonderful, too."

"And isn't that a lot, what I gave to you?"

"It is, but it isn't enough, because in an instant, you cut off and turn into ice."

He stepped toward her, his body rigid and tense, and his voice shook with emotion, "It was me," he pointed to himself, "who helped you live out your sexual fantasies. You told me that. Not just to dream about them, but to experience them. He couldn't give you that." Marcus stepped closer and she had to look up at him. "He couldn't fuck you, make you scream, like I could."

Her anger boiled over. "I am not comparing you to Ron or him to you in that way, that's on you, because you're so damn defensive. And you aren't getting what you want so you're angry. I told you those things about myself because I trusted you, and I wanted you to know how I felt about you, how special you made me feel." Her voice raised, "But do not throw what I said to you back at me in anger."

She moved to Marcus, so they were toe-to-toe and she had to tip her head back to meet his eyes. "Ron may not have had a dick that could fuck me the way you can, but he *never* turned into a dick and fucked me over."

Marcus backed away and rubbed his hands over his eyes. The tension was thick, crushing. Her chest hurt. Her head pounded. She couldn't bear her pain or his. She started for the front door, when he grabbed her hand.

"Cassie, I," he hesitated, "Goddamn, I keep screwing things up. I'm fighting for my life, and I'm ruining everything again. I don't know how to do this, I never have, but I have to try anyway because *I love you*, Cassandra. You hear that?" His voice cracked over the words as he shouted, "I fucking love you."

She recoiled, as if he'd punched her.

Suddenly, an eerie glow caught their eyes. It moved around the bend in the road leading from the farmhouse to the cottage toward them, and stopped.

A chill ran up her spine.

"What the fuck?" Marcus muttered.

"Pete?" She trembled.

Surrounded by the light, Pete wore his black *I'd Rather Be Fishing* tee, faded khakis, and his Vietnam Veteran cap. His lips curved into his big Pete smile, then he nodded, turned, and disappeared.

"Oh my god, Pete." Cassie tore off the porch toward the farmhouse, sobbing, with Marcus at her heels. "No, no, no." She stopped at the spot where they'd seen him, tears streaming down her face.

"Cassie, I got you," Marcus took her hand and together they raced to the farmhouse.

Chapter Twenty-Six

"Cassie," Marcus said softly, "I'm going to open the patio door so that Derek can wheel in." She nodded, and closed her eyes when Marcus brushed his lips over hers, before he left the room.

Maddy walked into the cottage, and took off her black jacket, "How about we gather in the kitchen?"

"Okay, Mad, I'll be there in a sec. Marcus is letting Derek in through the back."

Cassie watched Maddy's face turn down when she'd mentioned Derek. Poor Maddy.

"I'm going to check on the boys, Cass. They're upset, they wanted to come, but it's best they stayed at Wendy's."

"Good, sis, kiss them for me. Since the girls couldn't make it today, and they're coming this weekend with Aiden and Malcolm, they'll feel better when we all meet at the diner to honor Pete."

"Will do, they'll go nuts when they hear that, and I think it will help them handle Pete's death."

"I know, they loved him. The girls are terribly broken up."

"After your call, Maddy, let's find something to drink. We all need it." Rachel popped out of the kitchen. Maddy nodded, then went into the bedroom.

In a daze, Cassie stepped out of her heels and placed them near the front door. She was moving through a fog of grief since Pete died peacefully in his sleep, three days ago.

As he requested, instead of being buried in a veteran's cemetery, he was interred here in Riverbend, next to his beloved Shirl and their two-day-old daughter, Lainie June.

The outpouring of friends, townspeople, and members of Pete's American Legion post was beautiful—they all came to pay homage to a well-loved man.

He'd taken his last breath at the same time that Cassie and Marcus were thrashing out their differences on the cottage porch. She and Marcus hadn't talked about what they'd seen that night, what she'd thought it was—Pete's soul giving them his blessing, and his goodbye, one last time. Her eyes burned and hot tears ran down her cheeks at the memory. She wiped them away and took a deep breath.

It was after eight o'clock in the evening, and thankfully the gathering at the farmhouse was over. Marcus had asked if he, Derek, and Bret could join her, Maddy, and Rachel at the cottage after the dinner. Cassie was pleased that they were all here, they needed each other now.

Even Bret, who hadn't known Pete as long as all of them had, was shaken by his death in a way that had surprised Cassie. And though he'd broken with Rachel, who was still struggling with it, Bret had been attentive and caring toward her, and Rachel hadn't fought it.

Cassie sighed, life just kept on going, though the

world was a much poorer place without the likes of Pete Hoffman in it. She hung up her jacket in the hall closet as Bret came through the door carrying a six pack of beer, and raised her eyes at him.

"I brought it with me when Mac invited me. Sorry, Cassie, I didn't think about wine."

"No problem, Bret. Ah, Samuel Adams, Pete's favorite."

"Yeah, that old soldier wouldn't accept any other beer, so that's what we'll toast him with," Bret headed to the kitchen.

"That beer and good scotch." Marcus walked into the room. She smiled at him, but it hurt.

"Derek's at the table, we need another chair, babe."

She pointed to the coat closet, "There's one in there."

"Got it," his voice was soft. "Cassie, why don't you go to the kitchen and sit down before you fall down. Rachel fed Grey, who jumped into Derek's lap as soon as he wheeled to the table."

"Bet Maddy's jealous," Cassie said under her breath.

"What was that?" Marcus had the chair and was carrying it to the kitchen.

"Nothing, I'll tell you another time," and she followed Marcus out of the room.

"Here's to the best man I ever knew," Marcus raised his beer to "Ayes," and they all drank, sitting close to each other around the kitchen table.

"I can't imagine a world without him. He was so big in every way, tall, broad, strong as an ox, a booming voice..." Cassie began.

319

"A booming laugh," Maddy added.

"And a big heart that loved so well. He was the father we never had, Maddy."

"I wasn't as close to him, but I loved being around him and Shirl," Rachel added.

"Remember when you'd come over to hang out with me and Mad at the diner and he'd take us into the kitchen, sit us on stools in a corner," Cassie said.

"And he'd make us banana splits, and we would eat until we were bursting." Maddy chimed in. Her voice lowered and she choked, "God, I miss him hugging me and telling me that everything would be okay when I was down."

"I'll miss our trips with him to the VA hospital to talk to returning combat vets. The young guys all gravitated to Pete. He gave them hope that somehow they could have a life in spite of their injuries and memories. He did that for me when I moved here a few years ago, being lost. He understood recovery from war is a lifelong road," Bret said quietly.

"There's no other way to say it," Marcus said, rubbing a finger on the spout of the beer bottle. "Pete saved my life."

They all fell silent.

Then surprisingly, Derek, who was normally closed off, spoke in his deep, resonant voice that could move juries to tears or anger. His words sounded as if he were thinking out loud, as he stroked Grey who lay purring on his lap. "The first day I came back to Riverbend after my injury, Pete was waiting for me at the airport. I knew that my parents were sending a car for me, instead of meeting me themselves. My father was furious that I'd gone into the army instead of going to Harvard. And to come home broken... how embarrassing for the Prescotts. My mother was too upset to see her son in a chair. She told me later that it traumatized her."

His voice was monotone, simply reciting the experience as if he were reading a shopping list, but Cassie heard the sorrow and long-held anger in his tone.

Derek stopped for a second as if to calm himself, and Cassie gazed at Maddy who was watching Derek, her eyes wide and glistening.

Hesitatingly, he continued, "One of my father's drivers met me there. But when I wheeled toward the baggage area, there was Pete, standing, arms crossed over his chest. When I got to him, the driver moved to me and said, 'Derek, let me—' but Pete turned to him and ordered, "Go home, boy, I'm here for Derek."

"What happened?" Maddy asked.

Derek looked at her and his lips tipped up, "Pete got my bags, helped me into his truck, and took me to the farmhouse. He'd fixed up a small cabin on his property, and I lived there until my house was built."

"What about your parents?" Maddy whispered. She was sitting next to Derek and put her hand on his arm. When Derek lifted Maddy's hand off of his arm, and entwined hers with his, Cassie took him in fully, and understood Maddy's fascination with him. The man was breathtakingly handsome, with pitch black hair, except for an interesting streak of stark white right in the front. He was a big man—if he wasn't sitting in a chair, she'd bet he'd be about six and a half feet tall, to Maddy's five-foot three. Rare, silver eyes stared at Maddy, then he looked away. "That's for another day," he stopped talking but held Maddy's hand.

"Cassie, Maddy, Rachel," Marcus said, breaking into Cassie's thoughts. "It's after eight, and me, Derek, and Bret are going to go out, take a short ride, and do something that we have to do. We'll be back in a bit. Please wait for us here. Okay?" He looked at Cassie.

"Of course we will. It's for Pete, isn't it?"

"It is. We'll explain when we get back."

Derek released Maddy's hand and rolled away from the table. Bret got up to follow him out the back door. Marcus stood, took Cassie's hands in his, and said, "After we leave, go out to the front porch." He let go and walked out of the front door.

"What's going on?" Maddy turned to Cassie who shrugged her shoulders. The women followed after Marcus, stood on the porch, and watched as Derek, transferred into his van on the driver's side, while his chair was automatically pulled into the back seat by an incredible contraption. Bret walked back from his truck carrying a rifle, and Marcus did the same. Bret climbed into the front passenger seat, Marcus slid into the seat behind Bret. Derek started the van, pulled out, and they drove down the lane.

"Oh, my God," Cassie said in a low voice.

"What is it, sis?"

"They took their rifles. Though many of the veterans at the burial saluted when Pete's coffin was lowered, the burial wasn't military."

"They're going to give him a military send off, aren't they?" Rachel questioned.

"Yes, I think they're going to do just that," Cassie answered.

"Think they're going to the cemetery?" Maddy said.

"No," Cassie was openly crying, "I think that they're going to the Overlook."

The women stood silent on the porch and waited. Cassie's eyes burned with unshed tears. Not only from grief, but also for her love for Marcus. Pete was right, Marcus was the best of men.

Suddenly, off in the distance they heard the simultaneous shots ring out, one volley after another.

"Oh sis," Maddy collapsed sobbing in Cassie's arms. Rachel put her arms around Maddy and Cassie, and together they watched as a full moon rose in the sky.

****

The moon had set hours ago, and everyone was gone.

Cassie and Marcus sat on the top step of the porch. He put an arm around her waist and tugged her tightly to his side. She did the same with her arm and leaned her head on his shoulder. When she did, in a low voice, Marcus began to sing Paul Anka's *Put Your Head On My Shoulder*.

Cassie laughed softly, and Marcus kissed the top of her head.

She sighed. God, she'd missed being in Marcus's arms. She sat up. "What you did tonight for Pete, how you honored him, I'll never forget it."

"He deserved it, the best man I ever knew."

"You know, you remind me of him."

He squeezed her tight, but didn't reply.

Enough, she said to herself. *He's just learned to think well of himself,* and she snuggled closer to him.

"Cassandra?"

"I'm right here."

Marcus chuckled, "Know you are, but I want to know if it's okay if I talk about us. Can I?"

"Yes." She'd tensed up for a second, but this is what he needed from her, so she relaxed into him.

"From the time you decided to move back to Riverbend, Pete couldn't stop talking about it. Of course, I knew all about you and Maddy from the first time I met Pete. He took me to the diner the first day I met him, and he showed me pictures of Joe, you, and Maddy. And whenever I'd visit, he'd tell me what you and your sister were doing. I got to know you over the decades, and in a way you were always in my life, through Pete. That man loved you so damn much. 'She's the daughter I never had,' he'd repeat to me."

Cassie cuddled up to Marcus. "And he was the father that mine couldn't be."

"And I swear to you that once I learned that you were moving back, I never once hooked up with another woman. I fought it, I did, because I didn't know what was happening to me. You came here a widow, grieving, and I didn't care. I just wanted you, and nothing was going to sway me from having you. Then I played games with your heart and hurt you. You threw that at me, remember? That I push to be with you, then pull away. But I think I fell in love with you years ago, I just couldn't see it. I fought your pull up until the night that Pete died."

"Maddy and even Rachel told me that you never pursued women, but you did me. And, yes, you did hurt me. But I hurt you, too. Because of my cheating father, I couldn't trust you because of the other women, and came at you about it. I was so insecure. I'm sorry, too, Marcus. You know, we deserve the love we have for each other."

She sat up, and ran her fingers along his jaw, then lightly over his lips.

He gave her a hint of a smile, and kissed her nose. "The night after you told me off at the restaurant, and I went to see Pete, he made me promise to see a counselor at the VA hospital to 'Work out my crap,' as he put it. I'm going to call them next week."

"I'm glad Marcus, and I'm here for you in any way that you need me."

"Same here, Cassandra, I'm in all the way." He kissed her gently, then deepened it until they were both breathing hard.

Cassie pulled away and gazed into those mesmerizing, dark, deep-blue eyes that were lidded with desire, but now his love for her shone through, too. Marcus was as flawed as she was. But her true mate, as she was his. She needed their intimacy, and she needed it now.

Cassie rubbed his bottom lip with the tip of her finger and watched his eyes flash with heat. "Marcus, please take me inside and make me feel alive, and loved."

Chapter Twenty-Seven

A month later, on a clear, calm, June morning, Cassie and Marcus stood at the railing at the Overlook. He'd called her yesterday after he'd left for work, saying he had to check on a job, so he wouldn't see her that night, which was unusual since they'd spent every night together since Pete died. Then he'd gotten bossy and ordered, "Be ready at eight tomorrow morning. I'll pick you up." When she'd questioned him, he'd cut the call short.

Promptly at eight, he was at the cottage, and wouldn't tell her where they were going.

When she realized they were heading for the Overlook, she glanced at him, "What's going on Marcus?"

He'd sidestepped the question. "We're almost there, Cassandra, then I'll let you in on the secret." She'd frowned at him, and he'd laughed out loud then held her hand on his thigh until he had to turn off toward the river.

Now, here they stood, with his arm around her shoulders, and hers circled around his waist. Quietly, they watched the Delaware wind its way past Riverbend.

"Marcus, I can't thank you enough for helping Maddy and I have the house razed, and in its place build a lovely gazebo, that anyone in the area can use. Maddy was right, it was a dark, sad house, but now..."

"That's what happens when you put out to the owner of a construction company," he teased, keeping the heavy moment light.

She laughed and bumped his hip with hers. "Yesterday, Maddy and I went there. It was so peaceful, and we sat quietly watching the river, in all its beauty. Then a heron flew right down in front of us and waded on the banks, looking for food. Maddy took my hand, looked at me, and said the word that was in my heart, too... *free*."

"Cassandra, that's a beautiful story. I'm happy I could help."

"The cottage has always been the only home I really ever had. And when I'm there, I swear I can feel Pete with me. Shirl, too."

"I know," he leaned down and brushed her cheek with his lips.

"A few nights ago, when I was waiting for you, I sat out on the porch, and talked to Pete, hoping he'd make an appearance."

"You're not afraid that he might show up?"

"No. I would love to see him or have a sign that he's still close to me. Do you think we'll see him again, Marcus?"

He shook his head. "No, he's with Shirl and Lainie. That's where he belongs, now."

"I think you're right," she sniffled, and he turned her to face him.

He seemed pensive as he smoothed the hair back on her head and gently caressed the apple of her cheek with his thumb.

She waited. The air between them crackled with energy.

"Cassandra, I know that you love the cottage, but I'm hoping you'll make a move."

"Marcus," her words came out in a breathless rush, when he took her hand and dropped to a knee. He reached into his pants pocket, pulled out a small black velvet box, and presented it to her. "I love you, Cassandra Bennett. Please, marry me."

Trying to catch her breath, she held his hand, and surprised him when she knelt in front of him. Taking his handsome face in her hands, she kissed him deeply. Breaking the kiss, she looked into his dancing eyes, "Marcus Mackenzie, you're my true soulmate. Of course I'll marry you."

Marcus's smile was as wide as Pete's used to be, and she wished that he could witness this moment. Pulling her up to stand in front of him, he let go of her hand, opened the box, and she gasped. The platinum band was crafted into a fluid design resembling river water eddying around a stunning river stone, a large sparkling dark-blue sapphire.

A rush of joy overtook her, "It's dazzling."

He took her left hand, keeping her gaze on his, and slid the ring on her finger. "It's a custom design, that's why I had to wait an entire month to propose to you. Maddy got your ring size and, somehow, kept my secret."

"Maddy keeping a secret, a miracle." Cassie spread her fingers, admired the ring, and tipped her head back for a kiss. When their lips touched, they both felt a light breeze whirl around them, once, twice, and again.

Their eyes popped open. They broke the kiss, but held each other.

"Pete," her tone hushed.

Marcus's voice cracked, "It's okay, old soldier, I've got our girl. Go on home."

"No worries, Pete, I've got him, too." A loose curl on Cassie's face gently lifted next to the tears rolling down her cheek, and then all was still.

They wound their arms around one another tighter, and Marcus kissed Cassandra like only he could, as if he'd never let her go.

Epilogue

Three months later

"You're gonna kill me, babe!" Marcus murmured, his face buried in Cassie's hair as he floated back down from the crest of an orgasm.

"That was intense, like you were drilling me into the mattress," she giggled.

Their fantastic rehearsal dinner at the Horse had ended a few hours ago, and when they'd come back to the cottage—at Cassie's request, as it was the last night she'd be staying there—she'd attacked him as soon as the front door closed.

They'd spent hours reveling in each other's love.

Lying under him, her arms and legs wrapped around him, Cassie asked, "Now that we're getting married, do you think sex is going to become boring?"

Raising himself up on his forearms, he looked down at her gorgeous face, all the more so for the deeply satisfied look she was wearing. "You're kidding. Right?"

"It can happen, you know. Sex can become rote now that we'll be living together."

"Never," he leaned down and kissed her softly, then deepened the kiss until her hands were in his hair kneading his scalp. He loved when she did that.

Releasing her mouth, he kissed her nose and said, "Speaking of sex, I have another wedding gift for you, and for me, too. It should be here in a few days."

"Tell me please." Cassie begged. "I'll make it good for you, promise," her lashes fluttered.

He grinned.

"Please, tell me," she pouted. Rolling off of her, Marcus sat up and leaned against the headboard, then pulled her up and sat her on his lap. She put her arms around him and rested her head on his chest.

"Cassandra, you always make it good for me," he brushed her lips, and watched with awe as her love for him glowed in her eyes. How in the world had he gotten so lucky that this incredible woman who he'd been connected to through Pete for all those years, and whose photo he'd fallen in love with, should somehow, with all the shit he'd had clinging to him, have fallen for him?

"Love you," he said seriously, and he meant it deep into his soul. "And tomorrow, you're going to be Mrs. Cassandra Mackenzie." It was important to him that she take his name, and it had thrilled him when she'd agreed to do so. Cassie had talked to her daughters about it, and the girls had supported her. She was going to change her middle name to Bennett, so she'd still be connected to her daughters and their father, too. It was a perfect compromise.

"Yes, honey, I'll be taking your name, and I love you back," she kissed his nose. "But what is the gift? Toys? That bondage stuff you showed me?"

He smiled to himself—those things were going to be shipped a little later as a surprise, since she was interested in adding more kink to their sex life. After their honeymoon trip to Alaska, they'd be getting down and more dirty than usual.

"You're tenacious."

"Yep, I am. That's how I entangled you in my web."

"Yeah, you entangled me, and aren't I lucky."

"Spill, Mackenzie," she ordered.

"It's the updated modern version of the Kama Sutra, along with an additional booklet, the ten best blowjob positions."

"Huh?"

"Now, baby," he grinned, "you give great head, and we both like to mix it up, so I thought, I don't know, maybe me hanging from a chandelier and you on your tippy toes sucking me off can give us a new thrill."

"Maybe you're hanging upside down, while I stand on a ladder blowing you, and blood isn't rushing into your head but instead into that beast of a cock. Yeah, I can get into that."

"Beast of a cock?" he teased.

"You know it is. My jaw hurts for an hour after I suck you off." Then smacking him on the shoulder, Cassie started to laugh, and there it was again, the best gift that she'd ever given him: her head thrown back in joy and love, and it was all for him.

Suddenly she sat up. "I wish Pete was here. I wish he could see us taking our vows here at the cottage, and hear Joe marrying us, saying, 'I now pronounce you husband and wife.' God, I miss that man."

"I miss him, too, Cass," his voice broke, and she gently ran a hand up and down his arm. "But he'll be there, sweetheart, because he's all around us. He's everywhere. On his land. In the farmhouse. At the

332

diner. And in this cottage. He and Shirl are right here. And tomorrow, they'll both be right there, standing with us."

Sniffling, Cassie mumbled, "Marcus Mackenzie, sage," to his chuckle. When Grey walked into the room, she clucked to him, and he gracefully jumped on the bed and snuggled his big body onto her lap. Marcus reached out and scratched the cat's head, while Cassie leaned her head on Marcus's chest. She stroked Grey's body as his purring filled the room.

"You know, this little cottage was the only home I ever had. It wasn't the house on the river, or the house in Los Angeles. But now..." she looked up at him.

"Now Cassandra, my home is your home," he finished for her.

She put her hand on his cheek, "No, Marcus, no matter where we live, all I need is you."

He held his breath, took her hand from his face and brought it to his lips. "Cassandra," he murmured. But his breath caught in his throat when her eyes glistened with tears, "Marcus, you're my true home."

And it was the same for him. Somehow, he'd navigated his way out of the turbulent currents that had defined his life. Cassandra had become his haven. His homeport. He kissed her softly, then hauled her to him and kissed her deeply, until they ran out of air.

She leaned her head back on his chest. "I loved our party tonight, honey."

"I liked seeing our kids talking and getting to know each other, and that all the people we know and care about were having fun. Even Derek came out and gave a funny speech. Though he did his usual, got himself a whiskey, then hung out on the outside

333

looking in. Wish I could do something about that, but I can't. I didn't see him leave, but he disappeared outside for a while. I saw him come back in and go to the men's room before he came back to the party."

Cassie sat up. "Marcus, about Derek."

He saw it in her eyes, something was up.

"He was outside for a bit, but he wasn't alone."

"He wasn't? Who was he with?"

"Let me tell you what I saw and heard between Derek and my sister."

"Maddy and Derek? I know they'd flirted a few times at the picnic, and that night after the funeral he was attentive to her, but—"

"Shush, honey," she put a finger on his lips, "you're not going to believe this, so listen up."

And because tomorrow he was getting married to Cassandra, the love of his life, Marcus did what any man in love would do on his wedding night: he shut up and listened.

Coming Soon

Madeline and Derek's story, *Dark Waters*, coming 2021. To hear about release dates and more, please sign up for my newsletter!

Dark Waters

She longs for stability and devotion. He's determined to remain detached. Desire consumes them—intimacy and danger may rip them apart.

Single mother Madeline Harper works as a clerk at the county courthouse while she studies to become a paralegal. From the moment she sees the compelling assistant district attorney, Derek Prescott, she craves him with a burning hunger. She's determined to demolish his barriers, but will his fears—and an outside danger—break more than just her heart?

When Derek spies the delectable Madeline watching him during a trial, his need to claim her with raw urgency blindsides him. Certain that she cannot handle his damaged body and dark sexual needs, he struggles to fend her off. But when danger threatens, he must act. Will he conquer his demons to save the woman he loves?

Can Madeline and Derek destroy their adversary and finally find the happiness they crave?

****

But first: fall in love with Zoe Gifford and Zander Greybek in *Improbable Odds* a *Riverbend Romance* novella coming soon:

Improbable Odds

She strives for a new life. He seeks true love. Desire binds them, but clashing differences may tear them apart.

Divorcee Zoe Gifford hopes the move to Riverbend will lift her confidence after a shattered heart. When the college professor meets the compelling younger auto mechanic it's impossible to fight her fascination. Can she overcome her past when her insecurities emerge, or will she risk losing the one man she can truly love?

When Zander Greybek spots Zoe in yoga class the attraction is explosive. Blinded to their differences, he's in pursuit and intends to catch her at all costs. But he comes face-to-face with his own past when her doubts surface. Will he risk another heartbreak to try and claim her, or push her away to protect himself?

Can Zoe and Zander find a way to trust again and embrace the love they deserve?

Acknowledgements

Writing is a solitary endeavor, but finishing and publishing this book required the expertise, guidance, and support of many people. Without them, I'd still be spinning my wheels, or knocking my head against the wall, or... you get it.

Nicholas Mancuso, boy did I luck out when you agreed to edit my first novel, and how brave you were to tackle the first draft. You insisted that under the roughness, *yes,* I had a good story. Your editing skill and precision—mind-blowing. And you have my deepest gratitude for talking me off the ledge more than once throughout this process.

Victoria Oliveri, thank you for the countless hours that we spent brainstorming and for helping me work out everything from the plot to character names. More than that though, you've guided me as a new fiction writer, and you continue to help me in a myriad of ways. I cannot thank you enough for your friendship.

Emily Pennington and Marcy Sobolewski, you have my gratitude for agreeing to beta read, and reviewing my book with honest critiques. Your comments helped me immeasurably. Thank you!

Pocono Lehigh Writers, a wonderful group of

women who have supported and guided my journey as a writer in every way possible. Thank you, ladies!

My family includes my two amazing daughters and their wonderful guys who have helped with blurbs, book cover, marketing, and all that admin stuff that spikes my anxiety. But most of all, it's their continued love and support that has blessed my life.

About The Author

My love of romance began when I was nine years old, already a precocious reader, gobbling up everything from Dickens to Sherlock Holmes stories, but I'd never read a romance. Until my mom gave me Jane Eyre... I was hooked. Edward Fairfax Rochester was the first alpha male to permeate my consciousness, and shy, submissive Jane, who kicked butt when needed... and the feast continues.

Many years ago, I left Brooklyn, NY, and moved to eastern Pennsylvania and raised my children. Fast forward: My daughters are grown, and I have a scrumptious five year old grandson who fills me with joy. I live on a lovely bluff overlooking the Delaware river with two, sweet rescued cats... the perfect place to dream, and spin tales of love and passion.

Let's Keep in Touch

Thank you for reading book one of the Riverbend series! If you'd like to spread the love, thanks again, please leave a review. Much appreciated!

Follow me:

Izzy Matthews – Website:
https://www.izzymatthews.com/

Izzy Matthews Facebook Author Page:
https://www.facebook.com/Izzy-Matthews-Author-Page-111660193876432/?modal=admin_todo_tour

Izzy Matthews Newsletter: http://eepurl.com/g2-ncb

Bookbub: https://www.bookbub.com/profile/77418747